Advance praise for

MURDER WITH FRIED CHICKEN AND WAFFLES!

"I loved following the antics of soul food restauranteur Halia Watkins and her outrageously funny cousin Wavonne as they scramble to find the killer in this terrific debut mystery. Great characters. Clever story line. All this, and recipes, too. Can't wait for second helpings in this series!"
  —Laura Levine, author of *Killing Cupid*

"A.L. Herbert serves up some tasty recipes along with a delicious mystery in *Murder with Fried Chicken and Waffles* and I can't wait for second and third helpings of this scrumptious soul food mystery series featuring the irresistible, sassy, and completely enchanting Mahalia Watkins."
  —Leslie Meier, author of *French Pastry Murder*

"Murder with a side of soul food is a winning combination in this delicious cozy."
  —Lee Hollis, author of *Death of a Chocoholic*

"From my first taste of *Murder with Fried Chicken and Waffles,* I knew this was a book I'd want to overindulge in. The characters are real and unique, the plot will keep you guessing, and the foodie theme adds some delicious flavor. A.L. Herbert has cooked up a real winner!"
  —Diane Kelly, author of *Death, Taxes, and Green Tea Ice Cream*

Murder
with
Fried Chicken
and
Waffles

Murder with Fried Chicken and Waffles

A Mahalia Watkins Soul Food Mystery

A. L. HERBERT

KENSINGTON BOOKS
www.kensingtonbooks.com

KENSINGTON BOOKS are published by

Kensington Publishing Corp.
119 West 40th Street
New York, NY 10018

eISBN-13: 978-1-61773-175-4
eISBN-10: 1-61773-175-7
First Kensington Electronic Edition: March 2015

ISBN-13: 978-1-61773-174-7
ISBN-10: 1-61773-174-9
First Kensington Trade Paperback Printing: March 2015

10 9 8 7 6 5 4 3 2 1

Printed in the United States of America

Welcome to Mahalia's Sweet Tea!

When I launched Mahalia's Sweet Tea, I dreamed it would be a success, but I had no idea it would become *THE* restaurant of choice for delicious soul food. When I came up with the idea to open my own establishment that would allow me to prepare and serve my favorite foods, I couldn't have predicted that "my baby" (which is how I often refer to Sweet Tea) would make the Top 100 restaurant lists of local magazines and newspapers or that people traveling from as far away as California and Texas would make a point of stopping by for a glass of iced tea and a taste of my collard greens topped with homemade hot sauce.

Many of the mouthwatering items you see on the menu are based on my grandmother's recipes . . . if you can call my grandmother's way of adding "a dash of this" and "a sprinkling of that" a recipe. I prepare many of the dishes the same way I did thirty years ago when I learned how to cook by helping Grandmommy make Sunday dinner for crowds of up to thirty people every week. Entrées like my fried chicken and waffles and my cream of turkey over thick-cut Texas toast are made just as they were when I was a child. The complementary sour cream cornbread we bring to your table—that's Grandmommy's recipe through and through. And although I've updated a few recipes to make them a bit more contemporary and add a little flair (e.g., Grandmommy didn't include roasted red peppers in her macaroni and cheese), I mostly like to keep things simple here at Sweet Tea. You won't find any cilantro or curry in my kitchen, and a few menu items, like my creamy mashed potatoes for instance, are simply seasoned with only salt and pepper.

We make virtually everything here at Sweet Tea—from my chicken and dumplings to my fried catfish to my salad dressings . . . and even my croutons—from scratch. About the only thing not made in-house is that bottle of ketchup you see on the table (and don't think I haven't considered making that, as well).

I could go on for days about my food, but let me take a moment to talk about something even more important than that: **YOU.**

You, the customer, are what makes Sweet Tea great, and no matter how many best restaurant lists it graces or how long a wait we have for a table on a Saturday night, my staff and I strive to treat each and every one of you as if our very existence depends on you thoroughly enjoying your guest experience with us. Why? Because it does!

We make every effort to ensure we provide the best food and the best service at reasonable prices. If you ever find we are doing otherwise, I hope you'll let me know. I'm usually on the premises and easy to spot running around keeping this wheel of a restaurant in motion.

Sincerely,

Mahalia Watkins
Proprietor

CHAPTER 1

I still remember the first time I tasted my grandmother's corn-bread. I was maybe four or five. It was sometime in the seven-ties. If I close my eyes, I can still see the heavy cast-iron skillet being set on her wobbly table with a couple of pot rags under-neath to keep from burning the laminate.

"Now, don't you touch that pan, ya hear. It'll burn the skin right off your fingers, Halia," she said as she sliced into the pip-ing hot bread . . . all golden and steaming and smelling of sweetness. I watched her lift the first slice onto a plate and wished it was for me, but the first slice always went to Grand-daddy.

"When you work the night shift at the factory to pay the bills around here, you'll get the first slice," Grandmommy said to me as I watched the slice of cornbread pass on by me and land in front of my grandfather. I guess I really didn't mind, though. I loved Granddaddy. I didn't see him too often. He worked nights and slept during the day, but he always had a kind word for me, and, according to Grandmommy, "he was one of the 'good ones.' " She'd say it all the time: "I've got my-self a good man. He's one of the *good ones*."

When I did get my slice, I wasted no time cutting off a big

piece with my fork and plunging it in my mouth. It had a taste that danced on my tongue . . . a sweet yet salty flavor with a texture somewhere between bread and cake. Unlike a lot of cornbread, there was no need to spread any butter on my grandmother's recipe. It was so sweet and moist that more butter would have been overkill. She made it with cornmeal, flour, sugar, an entire stick of butter, and a full cup of sour cream. She'd add a can of cream corn and a can of regular corn, and then mix it all up before pouring it into a cast-iron skillet to bake to a golden brown in her prize possession, her 1964 Lady Kenmore oven.

From then on, whenever I ate that decadent cornbread, I thought that it should be served in restaurants. And now, more than thirty years after I first tried it, I serve it to all my customers—small two-top tables get a small pan, four-tops get a medium pan, and six-tops get a large pan. Eight-tops? Those get two medium pans. And don't ask me about ten-tops. If customers come in here with more than eight in their party, I tell them I can only accommodate them at two tables. As my cousin Wavonne, who has a way of telling it like it is, says, "Ain't nothin' worse than a large party. They'll run us ragged with special requests and complaints 'til our tongues be hangin' out our mouths and then leave a five percent tip."

The first pan of Grandmommy's cornbread is on the house, but we do charge for additional pans. I love and appreciate my customers, but we do get the occasional low-class fools in here who would have no problem filling up on my free cornbread and ordering virtually nothing else. I'm a cook (I've never felt comfortable with the term "chef," considering I don't have so much as a day of professional culinary training), and I love to see people enjoy my food, but I'm also a businesswoman, and a sister has to make some money.

When I opened Mahalia's Sweet Tea in the heart of Prince George's County, Maryland, I thought long and hard about whether or not my grandmother's cornbread was going to be free or available on the menu for a charge. I didn't like the idea of my customers filling up on heavy cornbread and later skipping appetizers or desserts . . . and affecting my bottom line, but I think restaurant patrons really like the idea of getting something "free" with a meal, so I decided to work it into my prices and make it complimentary—one of the many times I've followed the advice of Wavonne. "You know, Halia," she said to me when she was helping me launch the restaurant, which mostly amounted to her doing her nails or reading the latest issue of *Us Weekly* while I did all the work. "What would Red Lobster be without those free salty biscuits with all the cheese up in 'em? Hell, I wouldn't even go to the Olive Garden if I didn't get that big ol' free basket o' bread sticks . . . even if those greedy buggers do charge you for somethin' to dip 'em in."

I thought about what Wavonne said. I certainly wanted my restaurant held in higher regard than Red Lobster and Olive Garden (not that I don't like to help myself to one of those "salty biscuits with the cheese all up in 'em" every now and then myself), but she did have a point. Wavonne is not a girl of academic intelligence—I swear the only reason she graduated high school was because the teachers couldn't bear another year of her mouthing off. She's more concerned with Beyoncé's latest video than who was confirmed onto the Supreme Court, and, if she didn't work for me (and I use the term "work" loosely), I'm not sure she'd be able to hold a job at all. But the thing about Wavonne is that she has a sense about what makes people tick . . . what makes them behave the way they do. She warned me that the customers who kept their bluetooth earpieces on during dinner were most likely to be the ones to run my staff to death with complaints about everything from the location of their table to the prices on the menu . . . and then tip worse than a certain former Washington, D.C., mayor. She gave me some good advice about going with black linen napkins instead of white: "The white napkins'll get lint all over those tight black hoochie dresses your customers gonna be wearin'." And I even followed her advice about the dinner lighting in the restaurant: "Halia, you gotta lower the lights in here. A sistah wants to look good for her man over dinner and ain't all the Oil of Olay in the world gonna make some of the heifers who be comin' in here look presentable in this light."

So the cornbread, thanks to Wavonne and her vast insight, comes with my meals along with a small house salad. I'm looking at that very cornbread right now as I take it to table fourteen while thinking about my grandmother Mrs. Mahalia Hix. Everyone assumes my restaurant is named for myself, but it's really in honor of the grandmother after which I *and* my restaurant were named. Grandmommy's name on the marquee is much deserved—almost half the items on the menu are based on her recipes.

"Girl, he makes my wig go crooked!" Wavonne says as I head back toward the kitchen after making a cornbread delivery. I turn to see who her gaze is on and find Marcus Rand coming through the door of my restaurant. I suppose I should say *our* restaurant—Marcus is practically a co-owner. I didn't want his help or his money, but I got in a little over my head when I was opening the place and turned to him as a last resort. I don't like Marcus nor do I trust him . . . and I'm quite certain that the money he invested in Mahalia's Sweet Tea isn't exactly clean. Not that I think Marcus is involved in anything illegal. Unethical? Yes. But *illegal?* Marcus is too smart for that.

I think he makes some of his money as a financial planner, although financial *salesperson* is probably a more accurate description of what he does for a living, considering the mutual funds and other products he sells pay steep, some might say "predatory," commissions. I think he's also involved in some of those Ponzi-type schemes where you recruit members to sell all sorts of nonsense and everyone pretends that members, or "associates" as Marcus calls them, make lots of money selling quality items when the real money is made by finding other suckers to join the scheme as your underlings so you can take a percentage of their sales (think Amway, Avon, Mary Kay). Marcus is as smooth as butter and uses his charisma to recruit associates, most of them women, all over town. Despite his success in this area, I don't think you net a mansion on five acres in Mitchellville or a BMW 5-series by recruiting members for pyramid schemes. I'm not sure where his big bucks come from, but some of the people he brings in here for business meetings over my fried chicken and waffles look like they're into things far more serious than Tupperware or scented candles.

I met Marcus more than ten years ago when I was a line cook and occasional server at a restaurant a few miles outside D.C. in Virginia. Marcus was in his early thirties at the time but looked about the same as he does now. He has a shaved head, big brown eyes, and a smile for days. He's charismatic, charming, and confident. I guess he's about medium in height . . . maybe five feet nine or so and quite fit. He keeps his lean body firm and likes to wear tight shirts that show no hint of fat around his abs and highlight sculpted biceps so fine you just want to squeeze them. His skin is a rich dark color, and, to this day, his complexion reminds me of those Palmer hollow milk chocolate bunnies they sell at the drugstore before Easter, which is quite fitting—much like those hollow bunnies, as I'd learn shortly after I met him so many years ago, while pretty to look at, Marcus is made with cheap ingredients that leave a foul taste in your mouth.

"He makes me think of that song by that gawky white girl

with the long legs and the itty-bitty titties," Wavonne says as Marcus approaches. "Somethin' about 'I knew you were trouble when you walked in' or some shit."

"Hi, sugar, how's it going today?" Marcus, decked out in one of his Hugo Boss suits with coordinating French-cuffed shirt and silk tie, says to Wavonne as he reaches for her hand, giving it a quick kiss.

Wavonne smiles. "Just fine," she says, tilting her head and doing that thing she does with her eyes whenever an attractive man is around. "Don't you smell nice."

"Thank you, sugar," Marcus says. "It's my new custom scent. I had it made just for me."

Wavonne inhales deeply. "It smells good. Sort of like spiced rum." She takes another breath. "And maybe some dark chocolate."

Marcus, like so many brothers, wears too much cologne. I don't care if it smells like spiced rum, or dark chocolate . . . or Taye Diggs for that matter. I'm just not a fan of cologne and perfume. It gives me a headache and irritates my sinuses. Marcus's cologne is so strong, and he wears it so heavily, that it often lingers in the restaurant for hours after he's left. Sometimes, just from standing near him, the scent gets in my clothes and doesn't come out until I wash them. I ask my staff to refrain from wearing cologne or perfume even though Wavonne defies me here and there and sprays herself with all sorts of stinky nonsense. When customers come into Sweet Tea, I want them to smell my food, not Mary J. Blige's latest overpriced fragrance.

"And you, Halia?" he says to me, stopping himself in midreach. Not only does he know better than to call me sugar, he also knows I'll refuse to offer my hand for him to kiss. I ain't buying what he's selling, and he knows it.

"Busy. What do you want, Marcus?" I ask, knowing that the only reason Marcus would come by in the middle of the day is because he wants something.

"Can't I just stop by to say hi to my two favorite ladies?"

"Sure you can. It's just that you never do."

"Well, I *did* come to say hi, but I also want to talk to you about reserving a table tonight. I've got three associates to entertain this evening and Régine and Jacqueline will be joining, as well."

"You could have called, Marcus. You know I'll have the big table by the windows all ready for you."

"Great. I'm sure you'll be serving plenty of fried chicken and waffles, but one of my guests is a vegetarian. Any chance you'll be making that famous sweet corn casserole of yours?"

"No," I say flatly.

"Are you sure? I mentioned it to Heather, my guest who's a vegetarian, and she was very excited about it."

"Tell her to hold on to that excitement for a few more days. It will be a special on Monday night. And probably the last time I serve it until corn comes back in season in the spring." I often reserve some of my best specials for Monday and Wednesday nights when people tend to eat out less and need a little more motivation to come in here and spend their money.

"Can you move it up on the schedule? For me? Please." Being the snake charmer that he is, Marcus says this like he's asking. But we both know it's more of a demand than a request. If I refuse, he'll slyly remind me of the money he loaned me to get this place off the ground . . . how he helped me when I needed it, and now it's my turn.

"Marcus, that dish takes a lot of time. And I can't just make it for your guests. If other customers see it coming out of the kitchen, they'll want it, too."

"Great. Cha-ching Cha-ching. You'll rack up some serious sales."

"I don't have enough fresh corn in the kitchen today, and I can't get it wholesale at this late hour. We're into fall. Fresh corn is not as easy to come by as it was a few months ago. You get me the corn, and I'll do the best I can."

"Where should I get it from?"

"The Safeway for all I care. Wendy at Shadow's Catering always has a lot of fresh produce on hand, and she owes me a favor. Maybe you can work out a deal with her." I'm willing to cave to Marcus to an extent, but I'll be damned if I'm going to run around buying fresh corn on the cob at the last minute while I'm trying to run a restaurant. I'm sure he'll push the job off on his sister, Jacqueline, anyway.

"Okay. I'll get Jacqueline on it. Thanks, Halia. You're the best."

"Yeah, yeah . . ."

"If I can't get fresh corn, will frozen do?"

"You *did not* just ask me that? The only frozen thing I serve in this restaurant, Marcus, is ice."

He smiles. "My bad . . . my bad. That's why everything is so good."

And he's right. The best food starts with the best ingredients. Everything we serve at Sweet Tea is made from scratch. All of our meats and vegetables are fresh, many from local farms. We even cut and broil our own house-made sourdough croutons because no package variety comes close to my recipe. We make all our salad dressing in-house because the bottled brands don't have the creamy thickness I want, and we chop lettuce daily for all our salads—taste the lettuce that comes precut in a plastic bag, and you'll know why. And, of course, all of the tea at Sweet Tea is fresh brewed on the premises. Every day we offer unsweetened, sweetened, and a special flavored tea. Today's special tea is honey clove. And, okay, so we do use canned corn in my complimentary cornbread, but that's how Grandmommy made it, too, so I figure we get a pass on that one.

As Marcus leaves, I think of all the reorganizing I'll have to do to get a special on the menu that I hadn't planned for.

"I'm going to need your help husking corn," I say to Wavonne, who's watching Marcus's ass (and it is a fine one) while he walks out the door.

"I just got a manicure, Halia. I can't be huskin' no corn."

"Would you prefer bathroom cleaning duty?"

Wavonne groans. "Let me know when Marcus gets back with it."

"Oh, don't worry. I will."

CHAPTER 2

"God forgive me, but I just don't care for that man. Anyone that pours on that much sugar has got to be up to no good," Momma says. She's just stepped out of the kitchen and has her eyes on Marcus as he exits the restaurant.

"You won't get any arguments from me on that point," I say.

"Brotha is triflin', but I'd give him a lil' taste," Wavonne chimes in.

"I don't recall him asking," Momma says. "And you keep your *'lil' taste,'* whatever that means, in your pants, Wavonne. The last thing we need is a mini-Marcus to contend with around here."

Momma is wrapping up her morning baking. Aside from preparing Grandmommy's cornbread, baking is one thing I never had much interest in. I *love* to cook—I enjoy creating meals of meats and vegetables and savory sides, but *baking* cakes and pies and sweet treats for dessert has never really been my thing. Grandmommy was not a baker, either, which left Momma to fill the void back in the day. She's been baking since she was a girl. Every Sunday, Grandmommy would prepare Sunday dinner, and, usually the night prior, Momma would whip up dessert. She became known throughout our extended family for her sweet creations. My favorite has always been her red velvet cake—four layers of moist cocoa-infused cake with a fluffy cream cheese icing. It's a little piece of heaven on a fork.

Desserts are important for any restaurant and can really help boost profits, but for a soul food restaurant like Sweet Tea, the desserts need to be *killer*. Rich sweet treats are part of the soul food experience. Every day at Sweet Tea, I try to re-create the Sunday dinners I experienced when I was a kid, and I can't imagine those dinners without all the cakes, cobblers, and pies that were the grand finale of our Sunday get-togethers.

You'll never see any nouveau confections at Sweet Tea. My customers don't want some tiny little flourless chocolate disk-looking thing or a minuscule meringue shell with berries in it. If a dessert is going to a table at Sweet Tea, it had better have some butter in it, be big enough to share, and make customers go "Wow!" when you set it down in front of them.

When I was working on my business plan to launch Sweet Tea, I considered all my options for desserts. I wanted to keep it in-house (even though there are some good restaurant dessert wholesalers in the area), and a professionally trained pastry chef would have been very expensive. So, although I had some hesitation, when Momma volunteered to take responsibility for the desserts at Sweet Tea, I decided to give it a shot. Of course, I love Momma, but I already live with her, and our personalities tend to mix more like oil and water rather than peaches and cream. I thought having her in the restaurant with me might be too much.

Momma had recently retired when I opened Sweet Tea. She was a manager at Hecht's, a local department store that was bought out by Macy's shortly after Momma left. She worked at the big flagship store on G Street in D.C., so she was used to working hard and being on her feet all day, but she had never worked in a restaurant or baked on a large scale. Prior to opening, I tried to teach her the ins and outs of the restaurant business and the difference between baking one cake for family and baking a menu of desserts for a busy restaurant. She didn't like taking direction from me and, as I mentioned, baking is not my forte anyway. Luckily, I had already hired Laura, my assistant manager, when Momma came onboard. Laura took on the role of helping Momma adjust her recipes and teaching her about the workings of a commercial kitchen.

As luck would have it, there really isn't room in the kitchen for the baking and dessert preparation while we also prepare the main menu dishes, so Momma and I worked out a deal. She's an early riser and happily agreed to come in during the wee hours and prepare the cakes and pies for the day. She's usually done with the day's desserts and on her way out of the restaurant about the time I come in to start my day—a perfect arrangement. She doesn't have me nosing around her desserts while she's baking, and I don't have to hear about how I'm a childless spinster who had better focus less on Sweet Tea and more on finding a husband before what little chance of ever finding one is gone for good.

I have to admit, Momma has become a valuable asset to Sweet Tea. Eagar customers come in and ask what Celia has baked before they open their dinner menus. We don't have a set dessert menu—it changes depending on Momma's mood, so customers never know what to expect, other than that it will be delicious. One day Momma may make her sour cream coconut cake and banana cream pie. Other days she makes her famous red velvet cake and giant chocolate chunk cookies that we serve with ice cream and caramel sauce. And when fresh local berries are in season, people come in just for a slice of her strawberry pie.

"I wouldn't even want *you* taking up with him, Halia."

"What do you mean, Momma? Even *me*?"

"Even a woman of your years needs to be at least a little bit discerning."

"Don't be hatin' on Halia, Aunt Celia. She can get a man if she wanna."

"Thank you, Wavonne."

"There're plenty of desperate brothas out there. She just needs to offer them some free meals or somethin'."

"I retract my thank-you," I say to Wavonne with a laugh. "Glad to know you both think so highly of me."

"Of course we think highly of you, dear," Momma says. "But this restaurant is not going to keep you warm at night or take care of you when you get old. And it's certainly not going to give me any grandchildren."

"Grandchildren? Oh, Momma, that ship has sailed."

"Are you going through the change already?"

"No one calls it 'the change' anymore, Momma. And no, I'm not menopausal. I'm barely over forty"

Momma looks genuinely relieved. "Oh good. Then there's still hope. Remember Irene Beyer's daughter, Bernadette? You went to high school with her. Irene said she's getting married next month. And, God forgive me, but that girl is downright ugly . . . looks like a lizard. Some of the other girls at church call her Sheneneh, from that show we used to watch years ago. What was it called?"

"Martin."

"Irene's daughter does look like her. If Sheneneh can find a man, I'm holding out hope for you, Halia."

"That's your barometer for my hopes of relationship? Sheneneh!? Who, I think you'll remember, was played by a *man*."

"Oh, don't be so sensitive, Halia. An old woman has to grab hope where she can get it."

"You're not that old, Momma."

"Tell that to my bum hip and my sore back. I'm not sure

how much longer I'm going to be able to be the dessert goddess around here."

To hear Momma talk you'd think she was a stooped-over old woman, when she's still pretty spry at seventy-three. She's up at 5 a.m. every morning and into Sweet Tea shortly after six. She usually bakes until ten or so then keeps busy the rest of the day. She often goes to afternoon service at her church, plays cards with some friends, or does some volunteer work. But she threatens to quit on a daily basis due to her advanced age and whatever ailment she decides is the most pressing at the time—mostly so we all tell her how lost Sweet Tea would be without her and her creations.

I give Wavonne a look that says "it's your turn this time" and she begins to pour it on.

"Aunt Celia, you can't hang it up. There ain't nobody who can bake like you. What we gonna tell customers who come in here wantin' some of your cakes and pies? They might turn around and walk out if they hear you done put yourself out to pasture."

Momma is about to respond when we all take notice of Marcus coming back through the front door.

"What up, Marcus?" Wavonne asks.

"Hello, Mrs. Watkins," Marcus says to Momma. "You look particularly lovely this morning."

"Thank you, Marcus."

"May I ask what delicious desserts you've prepared today?"

"Red velvet cake, pineapple upside-down cake, and my spiced sweet potato pie. And we still have lemon berry bars and peanut butter pie from yesterday."

"No banana pudding?"

"Nope. Not today."

"Here it come," Wavonne says out of the corner of her mouth.

"Any chance you can whip up a batch for my guests tonight?"

"Did you not hear what she said, Marcus?" I ask. "We've got a host of lovely desserts."

"It's just that I raved about Mrs. Watkins's banana pudding to my guests."

"Marcus, assuming you can get the corn, you already have us preparing one unplanned special."

"I know. I just want tonight to go off without hitch. What do you say?" he asks, a bright smile that says he always gets what he wants never leaving his face.

"Don't ask me. Ask the dessert goddess."

Marcus turns his pearly whites toward Momma with a hopeful look.

"Wavonne, grab me my apron, would you? I guess I need to make some pudding for this gentleman."

"Thank you so much, Mrs Watkins. I'm sure my guests will love it."

Momma doesn't respond as she takes her apron from Wavonne, loops it over her head, and begins to tie it around her waist.

"Thanks again, ladies," Marcus says as he turns to leave.

"God forgive me," I ever so slightly hear Momma say as she turns toward the kitchen door. "But I just don't care for that man."

CHAPTER 3

I don't know where Marcus found so much fresh corn, but he did, and now he's thrown off my whole afternoon, and spun my kitchen into a frenzy. My sweet corn casserole is very labor-intensive to make; accordingly, I only occasionally serve it as a special instead of a regular item on the menu. The ingredients are simple: fresh corn, Muenster cheese, crushed red pepper, eggs, and salt. It's what you have to do with the ingredients that make it such a chore. One casserole dish requires the corn off ten cobs, so we'll be shucking two hundred ears of corn. Do you know how long it takes to shuck corn . . . especially when it's done to *my* standards—I won't allow so much as a sliver of corn silk left on the cob before we cut the nibblets off . . . which brings us to step two: hand-cutting the corn off two hundred ears, which then needs to be minced in the food processer. And, of course, my grandmother's recipe calls for Muenster cheese, one of the few cheeses I can't seem to find pre-shredded, so we lightly freeze twenty bricks of Muenster to give it some firmness before grating it through the food processor. Once we've drained a little moisture off of the minced corn, we mix it with the cheese and the other ingredients and pour the batter into oiled casserole dishes. If all of that wasn't enough, each casserole ties up my ovens for about two hours. We bake them on high until they brown a little bit on top and then cover them with foil and finish them off at a lower heat setting.

I'm cursing Marcus in my head as I work with Wavonne and Tacy, one of my prep cooks, to get the casseroles made. Tacy doesn't have much of an education, and he mostly worked at unskilled blue-collar jobs before I hired him three years ago, but he's reliable, has a good attitude, and follows instructions well. Unlike Tacy, Wavonne is not reliable, does not have a good attitude, and doesn't follow instructions well . . . mostly because she can't be bothered to listen to instructions when they are given to her, but the rest of my staff is busy catering to the lunch rush and getting ready for the dinner crowd. It's Saturday afternoon, and if history repeats itself as it does every weekend, we'll operate on at least an hour wait from 7 to 9 p.m. and remain steady until we close at eleven, so we need to do as much prep work during the day as we can.

"Wavonne, I'm seeing silks on these cobs," I say as I pull some of the corn from a large bowl between her and Tacy and put it back in front of her. "No silks!"

"Okay, okay. I know Marcus has you all stressed, but no need to go all Naomi Campbell on me," Wavonne says. "What do you say, one day next week we go to Red Lobster for some crab legs? That'll help you relax." According to Wavonne, there is no problem that a few crab legs from Red Lobster can't fix. Before I have a chance to respond she starts rolling again. "I'm not exactly thrilled with that damn Marcus myself. I just paid Kiki thirty dollars for this manicure, which I must say, Halia, was not intended to be used shuckin' no silly corn."

Kiki is the Korean lady who *used* to do both Wavonne's and my nails. She was replaced about two months ago by another Korean woman named Jai, but apparently Wavonne never noticed. "No. *I* paid Kiki . . . I mean, Jai thirty dollars for that manicure," I say, lifting her hand in mine. "And it seems to be holding up fine."

"Damn Marcus!" she says again, grudgingly removing the last of the silks from the corn I returned to her.

"What do you have against Mr. Rand?" Tacy asks. "He's a nice man. Always has a kind word."

"He's slick all right—could sell matches in hell. Don't you be fooled by Marcus Rand, Tacy. He looks out for one person and that's himself." Wavonne huffs, even though she was fawning over him like a crushing schoolgirl when he was in here earlier today. "Look what he did to my nails," she adds, showing her cherry-red painted tips to Tacy.

"They look right nice to me, Miss Hix."

Tacy calls every woman in the restaurant Miss This or Miss That. I've told him over and over again to call me Halia. Calling me Miss Watkins makes me feel old and reminds me that I have no husband, but he likes to be respectful and, somewhere along the way, I think he learned that being polite made people more comfortable around him. And, at six feet, five inches tall and weighing in somewhere in the neighborhood of two hundred and seventy-five pounds, he's a big man . . . a big black man, and that can intimidate people. I like having a big guy like him in my restaurant. It makes me feel safe, and I've sent Tacy out of the kitchen a time or two when the occasional obscenely drunk patron starts causing trouble and refuses to leave when asked politely. He's never had to raise his voice or manhandle anyone. A courteous word or two coming from a man his size is enough to shut up anyone and get them on their way.

"Would you stop worrying about your nails, Wavonne? I'll get you a new manicure on Monday if you just help me get these casseroles made."

While I generally don't take the whole day, I often take

much of Monday off as it's the slowest day of the week. I probably could take the whole day, but I'm just too much of a control freak to leave the restaurant in someone else's hands for very long. I leave Laura, my assistant manager, here alone for several hours at a time when I sneak out during the day to run errands or go to an appointment. Here and there, I'll even leave her alone for the dinner crowd if I really need a night off, but the rare occasion that I'm really sick (*really, really* sick) is the only time I go an entire day without stepping foot in Sweet Tea, which explains why I don't have a man . . . or at least partly explains why I don't have a man. Not only do I have very little time for a social life, it's also quite a challenge to find a man who can appreciate a woman who runs her own successful business. I try to keep in mind that if Oprah can find Stedman, there must be someone out there for me. But here I am on the less desirable side of forty, and I'm not sure I ever see a relationship happening. Not that I think there's anything wrong with the goods I'm out there peddling. I just haven't made finding a man a priority.

I'm holding up well for my age with a slightly round face and big brown eyes. I'm fortunate to have what, thanks to Chris Rock's documentary, even white people now know is called "good hair." I don't have to relax it to straighten it but keep it styled fairly short for convenience. And considering I'm surrounded by delicious food all day, every day, I figure I'm doing pretty well to still be getting into my size fourteen clothes. Besides, I like my curves—they're good for business. Who wants to eat in a restaurant owned by some waifish stick figure? That's like a beautician with bad hair or a fat personal trainer.

"Why do we have to make so many of these things anyway? Can't we just make enough casseroles for Marcus and his crew?"

"And what would you have me tell our customers when they see them coming out of the kitchen? 'Sorry, this is for some *special* guests. None for you.'"

"Sounds fine to me."

"Oh yeah. That will make them feel *really* valued."

I constantly remind myself and my staff to never take our customers for granted. Mahalia's Sweet Tea operates on a wait during peak lunch and dinner hours almost every day, and has been on *Washingtonian Magazine's* and the *Washington Post's* top restaurant lists since we opened. I've even had people from as far away as Hawaii say they've heard of my restaurant, but I still work to treat every customer as if they could make or break me. I tell all of my employees how important it is to be polite and welcoming to everyone who walks through the door or even calls for information. I emphasize that we treat customers who come during peak hours the same as the ones who slip in five minutes before we close. We try hard to please our customers, so we keep complaints to a minimum (and often, when we do get them, they are not valid . . . just someone trying to get something for nothing). When we do have the occasional unhappy customer, I try to give my staff the training and lee-way to fix the situation on their own. During their first six weeks of employment, they are required to take trainings on the Web about dealing with difficult people, defusing heated situations, and delivering top-notch customer service. Most of my employees come from working-class backgrounds and, sometimes, downright poor families. Before working here, they've never even been in a high-end restaurant. Hell, Wavonne still wants to know why I don't have any buffalo wings or cheese fries on the menu. I tell her that I didn't work my ass off to get my restaurant off the ground only to serve the same mundane fodder they offer at T.G.I. Friday's and Ruby Tuesday.

Wavonne continues to mumble to herself about Marcus, and I keep an eye on her while we prepare the casseroles. I almost want to tell her to watch what she says about Marcus. That I'm in debt to him for a hefty sum and neither one of us would be in this kitchen or this restaurant if it wasn't for him, but I keep my lips pursed. I don't need to remind anyone of Marcus's ownership in the restaurant. He agreed to be a silent partner, and I don't want anyone thinking that Marcus is the boss around here, not that he'd have time to be here any longer than it takes to entertain clients for dinner a few times a month.

Marcus has a lot going on and is always on the go. I'm not sure exactly what it is that keeps him so busy. Of course I overhear things when he's talking to clients at the restaurant, but I never get enough detail to piece everything together, and maybe that's for the best. As the saying goes, sometimes ignorance is bliss. But whatever Marcus is up to, it seems to be heating up lately. He's been bringing more people into the restaurant, and not just women who look all googly-eyed at him. He's been in here with couples and even entire families . . . two-point-five kids and all. Most of his meetings seem to go well, and everyone leaves happy, but last week he was entertaining a young couple, and, by the time we brought out Momma's pecan pie for dessert, no one at the table looked very chipper. Later, from the back of the restaurant, I heard raised voices. By the time I showed up to clear some plates, the couple had very cross looks on their faces and Marcus looked . . . well, Marcus looked *guilty*. I'm not sure of what, but I know guilt when I see it, and I saw guilt on Marcus's face.

CHAPTER 4

I'm already tired from a long day, and the Saturday night rush has barely gotten underway. I enjoy the bustle of busy nights, but between making casseroles that I hadn't planned for, and me and my kitchen staff having to sidestep Momma while she made Marcus's banana pudding, I'm beat.

I take a moment and stand outside the kitchen door. I do this a few times a night as I get the best view of the dining room from here and can see if anything needs my attention. I think about what a great team I have while I watch the servers tending to the tables. They are all wearing the Sweet Tea uniform: slip-resistant black shoes, black pants, a crisp long-sleeved white dress shirt, and a pastel-colored tie of their choosing.

Sometimes I'm not even looking for things that might need tending to—sometimes I'm just taking it all in and appreciating the people who have chosen to spend their hard-earned money in my restaurant. It was so much work to get this place opened and is equally hard work to keep it running on a daily basis, so I force myself to take some time every now and then to just soak it all in and enjoy it. I look around the room and recall the trials and tribulations of creating such a lovely space. I was encouraged by many to go with some of the more trendy looks you see in newer restaurants, but I didn't want to create a look that would be outdated in a few years and require an expensive remodel. I wanted a timeless design that would look as appealing ten years into the future as it does now. I opted for solid oak tabletops on double cross metal bases. The matching chairs are also made of solid oak. They have lattice backs and cushioned red upholstered seats. The booths along the wall are upholstered in the same red. I wanted Sweet Tea to sound lively and fun, but not so loud that my guests have to shout at each other over dinner, so I limited the hardwood flooring to the bar area and went with carpet in the main dining room to absorb noise. The front wall is windows. On the walls behind the bar and along the back is a mix of antique photos and paintings of women like my grandmother preparing meals, family gatherings around the dining room table, church ladies tending to the after-service buffets, and the like. Along the left wall is a mural I commissioned. It's based on a series of photos from a summer picnic in Grandmommy's backyard before I was even born—sometime in the sixties. Yes, I had the artist embellish a bit—Grandmommy's backyard was not on a lake, there was no white gazebo in the middle of the yard for the love-struck teenagers in the painting to be canoodling in, and Grandmommy's rosebushes never looked quite as good as they do in the artist's rendition. But I hope the mural does exude what I imagine to be the same feeling of that day so long ago—a feeling of family . . . of mothers and daughters, fathers and sons, aunts and uncles . . . all enjoying each other's company over good food on a beautiful spring day.

"We've got some cranberry drinkers at table twenty-two," Darius, one of my servers, says to me, prompting me out of my memories of summer picnics.

"Cranberry drinkers" is a term we use for patrons who sneak their own liquor into the restaurant. More often than not, these customers order plain cranberry juice. Occasionally, they mix their own rum into a Coke, and a few fools order tonic water to which they add their own gin, as if we are not immediately suspicious of someone ordering plain tonic water. I've seen customers sneak booze into Sweet Tea in all sorts of creative ways. I've had customers bring it in containers that look like binoculars. They've concealed flasks in phony Bibles. I've even seen a flask made to look like a smartphone. The topper was probably when we caught a customer who had rigged some sort of fake beer belly under his shirt that had tubing attached to disperse the alcohol. But, most of the time, people just have the women in their party bring in a few of those mini-bottles of liquor in their purse and pour it into their drinks when they think no one is looking.

"Really? It's been a while." I look over at table twenty-two and see four young women. They are all sporting heavy makeup and short skirts with heels I couldn't make it to the front door in. All four of them are wearing black. They look like four witches. Sweet Tea must be their first stop before a night on the town. I get being young and short on cash, but if that's the case, have a few cocktails before you leave the house or be happy having a Diet Coke with your meal, but do *not* come in my restaurant trying to pull a fast one.

"Did I hear him right?" Wavonne asks on her way to the kitchen.

I don't answer her. Instead, I turn my head to Darius. "Are you sure?"

"Yes. I could smell the vodka when I cleared one of the glasses."

"Oh. I got this!" Wavonne says.

I'm not usually one for unleashing Wavonne and her lack of discretion on my customers, but when it comes to trashy people trying to get one by me and threatening my liquor license, I make exceptions. "Have at it."

There is sheer joy on Wavonne's face as she approaches the table with Darius following.

"Hey, hey, hey. How is everyone doin' tonight?" I hear her ask.

The girls at the table nod and smile and a few say they are doing just fine.

"Good. Good. You know what? There seems to be a problem with your drink order. The bartender thinks he mighta added some liquor to them by mistake." Wavonne starts lifting the glasses from the table and setting them on a tray Darius is holding. "But don't you worry, we're gonna replace all of 'em for you. And we're so sorry for the mistake."

Everyone at the table silently stares at her with a "busted" look on their faces.

"I'm sure it was our bartender's mistake but, you know, every once in a while, we get some ghetto-assed street trash in here who be bringin' their own liquor up in here and try to sneak it in their drinks when we ain't lookin'. Can you believe that?"

Wavonne gets a few nervous laughs from the group of ladies.

"We'll be back shortly with some fresh drinks. You ladies enjoy the rest of your evenin'."

Darius takes the glasses to the bar and Wavonne approaches me. "I set 'em straight . . . thirsty heifers."

"I see that," I say to Wavonne, and I almost feel sorry for the girls at the table, but there's no time for that. I've got bigger fish to fry—I've just caught sight of Marcus coming through the front door.

CHAPTER 5

"Welcome to Sweet Tea," I say to Marcus and the entourage he's just come in with. Sonya, my hostess, seated them at Marcus's favorite table by the windows and has already taken a drink order. "If you need anything at all this evening, please let me know."

"Thank you," says the gentleman seated next to Marcus. Unlike Marcus, he's dressed casually in a pair of expensive-looking jeans and a Tommy Hilfiger knit shirt, which makes me think me he's probably more important than Marcus and feels no need to dress to impress. Marcus probably wants something from him.

I smile at the man. "At Marcus's request, one of our specials tonight is my hot pepper corn casserole made with fresh corn, cheese, and crushed red pepper. It's simply divine if I do say so myself."

I see smiles and looks of "damn, that sounds good" from everyone at the table . . . everyone at the table except for Jacqueline, Marcus's sister and assistant. She's seated to the right of Marcus trying to look as if she's above it all . . . or maybe she's not *trying* . . . maybe that's just how she looks. It's not that I dislike Jacqueline (do NOT call her Jackie . . . you *will* be corrected), and I'm not sure she means to come off as such an elitist, but the girl puts the tight in uptight. I've known her for years, and I've never seen her without her hair coiffed and her makeup perfect. She's always dressed in some expensive pantsuit accessorized with tasteful jewelry and gorgeous shoes. If I had to use one word to describe her, it would be pointy—if a balloon brushed up against her, it would pop on contact. Her eyes are pointy, her nose is pointy, and her elbows are pointy . . . mostly because she's so damn skinny. She's about five feet seven or so, and I bet she barely clears a hundred ten pounds soaking wet. She really is pleasant enough, I guess, but there's always been a coldness about her. She works for her brother, and he must pay her quite handsomely considering the clothes she wears and the car she drives, but she seems to have a smidgen of disdain for him that comes through in her tone and her facial expressions when she talks to or about him. I guess the thing that really bothers me about her is that she turns her nose up at my menu items and always asks the kitchen to make her a salad.

And then there's Marcus's date for the evening, Régine. My sense is that she's a gold digger on the hunt for fine jewelry, dinner at expensive restaurants, and the occasional shopping spree at Saks—all courtesy of Marcus. She's very tall and quite striking with a dark complexion and long jet-black hair that goes past her shoulders. She's all glitter and flash and makes no apologies for it. She wears too much makeup, fake fingernails, gaudy jewelry, and I'm not sure if her hair is her own or on loan from someone in India.

Across the table from Marcus is the couple that was in here with him last week. They appear to be in their early twenties. They have wedding bands on, so it seems safe to assume they are married. And oddly, they are white. Not that I don't get plenty of white folks in my restaurant, but Marcus's clients are almost always other African Americans.

"This is Darius," I say to the table as he approaches with the drink order Sonya passed on to him. Darius always takes care of Marcus and his guests. He's my best waiter. He's one of those people who are perpetually "on." He always has a smile, exudes positive energy, and is highly competent to boot. "He'll be taking care of you this evening."

Darius places the drinks on the table without having to ask who gets what. Like a lot of restaurants, every chair at the table has an invisible number, and we input all orders accordingly. There's nothing worse than showing up with a tray full of drinks or entrées and starting a bidding auction with waiters asking, "Who ordered the shrimp cocktail?" or "Who has the cheeseburger?"

"Darius, can you go over the rest of the specials with our guests? I've already told them about our corn casserole." I excuse myself and head toward the kitchen, where I find Laura supervising what is probably the restaurant's most important function—the preparation of our fried chicken and waffles. When I first opened Sweet Tea, I only served fried chicken and waffles during Sunday brunch, but I got so many requests for them during the week, I added it as a regular menu item. Since then, it's been our most popular entrée.

The secret to my grandmother's waffles is the addition of whipped egg whites to the batter. They make them extra fluffy. We serve each waffle with four fried chicken wings laid on top—one on each quarter. I had planned to serve a fried chicken breast with the waffle, but Wavonne made me rethink that: "Halia, ain't you ever seen the after-church crowd at a Sunday buffet? There may be a tray fulla fried chicken breasts, but when two sistahs reach for that last wing at the same time, you best stand clear . . . the earrings are comin' off and anything the preacher said that mornin' about being good to your neighbor is forgotten."

Wavonne did have a point, and I decided to go with her

advice. People really do seem to favor wings—I think because you get as much batter as you do meat with a wing. And with my chicken in particular, the batter may be the best part. We marinate the wings in a mix of seasonings. Then, right before we fry them, we coat them in my breading mixture, which includes my grandmother's special ingredient: instant mashed potatoes. Instant mashed potatoes mixed in with the flour and herbs makes Sweet Tea's fried chicken extra-crispy. Grandmommy found this out by accident when she was running low on flour one Sunday afternoon and made a quick substitute with Betty Crocker potato flakes.

I'm about to give Laura a hand when I see Wavonne on the other side of the kitchen. She's sitting on a stool, chatting with Tacy like she's at a cocktail party.

"Wavonne, you have three tables out there. What are you doing back here like you're waiting for your massage at the spa?"

"The first casseroles are about to come out the oven. I'm gettin' my slice while the gettin's still good."

"The casseroles are for customers, Wavonne. If there any left after the last table orders, you can have all you want. Now get out there and get to work." I want to add that it wouldn't be a bad idea for Wavonne to lay off the casseroles altogether. I'm a thick girl myself, and Wavonne is a size or two larger than me, which would be fine if she didn't insist on wearing a size or two smaller than me. Day after day she tries to shove that size sixteen frame into size fourteen clothes, and, if she puts on any more weight, I swear they are going to burst at the seams. Everything she owns is tight . . . tight and loud. All my servers wear the Sweet Tea uniform while on duty, but the moment Wavonne's shift is over you're more likely than not to find her in something made of animal print . . . quite possibly with a few sequins on it.

"I shucked all that corn this afternoon, Halia. I'm gettin' my slice of corn pie come hell or high water."

"Oh for goodness' sakes, Wavonne! Just be quick about it."

I'd never stand for another one of my employees talking to me that way, but Wavonne is family, and Momma and I promised her mother we'd take of her.

Wavonne is fifteen years younger than me and came to live with Momma and me several years ago when she was only thirteen. Her mother, my aunt Jolisa, is Momma's sister. Aunt Jolisa was one of those people who could never get her life together. As Momma tells it, "she came out of the womb looking for trouble." She dropped out of high school in her sophomore year, and, shortly thereafter, got messed up with some loser who knocked her up and disappeared before Wavonne was even born. Somewhere along the way Aunt Jolisa developed a drinking problem. Neighbors heard her yelling at Wavonne in drunken stupors, and when Wavonne didn't show up for school for more than a week with no phone calls, child services was alerted. For a while, Aunt Jolisa would manage to clean herself up enough to get the social workers off her back, but eventually she was declared an unfit parent, and Momma was asked to take in Wavonne. It was either that or a foster home. Momma was well into her fifties, had already raised me, and had buried my father about two years earlier. She was on her own and, quite frankly, I think she was enjoying herself. Of course, she loved me and Daddy, but I could be a handful at times, and Daddy was as needy as they come. The man couldn't fry an egg for himself, fold a pair of socks, or even work the dishwasher. I think Momma felt free in a lot of ways after my father passed, and she had even planned to put the house up for sale and get herself a low-maintenance condo before Wavonne ended up on her doorstep.

Momma agreed to become Wavonne's guardian, but only after consulting with me. I was in my twenties and no longer living at home, but Momma insisted that she could only take Wavonne if I'd help her out. "I'm too damn old to do this by myself, Halia," Momma said to me. I didn't hesitate. Wavonne was family, and she needed us, so I agreed to move back in with Momma and help raise Wavonne. She'd come to us after thirteen years of almost no parental supervision. She balked at anything you asked her to do, didn't understand the concept of going to school every day, and used some words that I had never heard before in my life . . . at least until one day when Momma lost it after Wavonne's repeated use of the f-bomb and took an S.O.S. pad to her mouth.

Momma and I took turns going into school when she was caught smoking in the bathroom or selling cosmetics she'd lifted from CVS. Essentially, Wavonne had three mothers: the alcoholic one who gave her up, my momma, and me. And believe me, we could have used three more to keep her straight. I really do believe that Wavonne is a good person and has a big heart, but it's like something in her brain doesn't always understand that there are consequences to her actions. Like now for instance, she's standing here in the kitchen waiting to scarf down some corn casserole when we've got a restaurant full of customers who need to be served. This explains why she only handles a maximum of three tables at one time when the rest of my wait staff carries five. Of course, she makes less in tips than the rest of the servers, but considering she doesn't pay any rent to share a house with Momma and me, she mostly just needs money for her hair (and by "hair," I could be referring to a weave, a wig, or the occasional synthetic ponytail she's picked up for twenty dollars from a kiosk at the mall), nails, clothes, and such.

Frustrated with Wavonne, but knowing full well that Jesus Christ himself would have to wait in line behind her for a slice of my corn casserole, I exit the kitchen to make a run-through of the restaurant. I like to walk by the tables, say hi to customers, and keep my eye out for any customers with unhappy looks on their faces. Tonight those unhappy looks are coming from the couple dining with Marcus. They were only seated a few minutes ago, and they all have their drinks, so I doubt the gloomy looks have anything to do with the restaurant.

Both the young man and the young woman look cross, but it's the woman who seems to be doing most of the talking. She's small . . . maybe five feet three with a twenty-something-inch waist. She has blond hair and her light eyes look as if they're sending daggers in Marcus's direction. She's moving her hands as she talks while her husband sits quietly next to her with an uncomfortable expression on his face. I see that he has a conspicuous scar on his left cheek. He looks like the family cat might have given him a good swat when he tried to take its catnip away.

"Things okay at Marcus's table?" I ask Darius as he walks by.

"Hmm. I suspect not. The little blonde with the split ends and fake Burberry scarf has quite the temper. Ms. Thang is all up in Marcus's face. She keeps saying, 'You promised!' and, 'But you said.' I'm still trying to get the deets, but I could only linger by the table for so long. She's doing that thing white girls do . . . you know, how they yell without raising their voices . . . like a strong, mean whisper."

"Don't you worry about getting any details, Darius. Marcus not keeping a promise of some sort is hardly news. Just concentrate on giving them good service. The further we stay out of Marcus's business the better."

CHAPTER 6

"Two slices of red velvet cake. One pineapple upside-down cake, and two big helpings of banana pudding," I say, eyeing the tray before handing it off to Darius. The tray is headed toward Marcus's table. It's nearly midnight and Marcus and his guests are the only patrons left in the restaurant. I wish they'd finish up and get out of here, so we could go home. The last of my kitchen staff is washing up and will leave any minute, and I sent most of the wait staff home already. Darius is still here, but I'll let him go after he serves dessert. And of course, Wavonne would have been gone hours ago, too, if I wasn't her ride.

It doesn't surprise me that there are six people at the table but only five desserts on the tray. I'm sure Marcus's sister, Jacqueline, abstained. She always eats like a bird when she comes to Sweet Tea. Like tonight for instance, we sent their table two fried chicken and waffle platters, two corn casseroles, a plate of fried catfish . . . and *some mixed greens, topped with grilled chicken, and vinegar and oil* (on the side, of course). Can you believe that? Coming into my restaurant, a regular fiesta of fine food, and she makes us prepare a plain salad with grilled chicken, which, mind you, isn't even on the menu. I'm not sure if it's all for real or not—if she eats that way all the time, or if she just pecks at salads in front of people and then makes a beeline for Bojangle's and scarfs down a bag of biscuits in her car while no one is around. It wouldn't surprise me if she did. Lord knows, she exercises enough to melt away any calories she eats. I hear she's at the gym every day (sometimes twice a day) and goes for regular runs in the mornings. She runs her own fitness business on the side in addition to working for Marcus. From what I know she does some personal training and teaches some sort of jumping-up-and-down-type classes at one of the local health clubs. I think she might be one of those people with a lot of nervous energy, and exercise is a good outlet for her. I, fortunately, don't have that problem—I don't have a lot of nervous energy, and exercise isn't a good anything for me. She's always asking me to come to one of her classes, but even if I had any interest, I simply don't have the time.

I let go of any annoyance I might have with Jacqueline and walk out with Darius to serve the desserts. I often make dessert runs with my servers. It gives me a chance to check in with guests and see how everything was for them. And it's always fun to see the looks on their faces when I place Momma's sweet creations in front of them.

I place the banana pudding in front of the young woman with blond hair ("Ms. Thang," as Darius called her earlier) and the red velvet cake in front of her husband while Darius serves the remaining desserts. Their eyes go wide as we set the plates down, and they look decidedly more relaxed than they did earlier in the evening. Even Ms. Thang lets a huge smile come across her face when the pudding lands in front of her.

"Wow. That looks really good."

"Made today with fresh bananas and Momma's own vanilla wafer cake recipe. I've loved that recipe since I was a girl," I say to her before turning my gaze to Jacqueline, who, for just a nanosecond, I swear was eyeing the young lady's pudding like a lion circling a gazelle.

"No dessert for you tonight, Jacqueline?" I ask.

"It looks divine, Halia, but I try to stay away from sweets. I'm teaching a spin class early tomorrow, so I don't want to eat anything too heavy tonight. You should come and try it out."

I laugh. Yes, because the idea of me at a spin class does, indeed, make me laugh. "Thank you, but I've got the brunch crowd to prepare for."

"Another time."

"Sure," I lie and turn my attention to the entire table. "How was everything this evening?"

"It was fantastic," says the gentlemen to Marcus's right. "I'm going to need someone to push me in a wheelbarrow to get out of here I'm so full." He lightly pats his belly. "But don't think that's going to stop me from eating this pineapple upside-down cake."

"So glad to hear it. We aim to please. Enjoy the desserts."

"Thanks, Halia," Marcus says. "You mind if we hang around a bit longer? We have some business to wrap up."

"How much longer?" I'm trying to make it sound like a friendly question, but it's late, and I want to go home. I've already bent over backward for Marcus today. I don't feel like staying up until the wee hours of the morning waiting on him and his clients.

"I'm not sure," he responds, and that's when I notice a few legal-size manila folders on the table. I'm guessing they are filled with some sort of paperwork related to whatever Marcus has going on with these people . . . maybe some contracts for them to sign. "Why don't you go on home? I'll lock up when we leave."

I'm so tired that I agree to leave Marcus and his guests at the restaurant. Marcus is practically a partner in the business and has a key. He can come and go anytime he wants, so it's really not a big deal.

"Okay. Let me go fetch Wavonne. I'll lock the back door before we leave. Don't forget to lock the front door."

"I won't."

"Oh, and there's a tray of fried chicken in the walk-in. Feel free to wrap up a few pieces and take them home."

I go back into the kitchen and see Wavonne watching something on her cell phone.

"Halia. Look at this. This dog's ridin' a skateboard! Let's get a dog like that. We'll name him Flo Rida."

"Let's go. Marcus will lock up," I say, ignoring her dog comment, giving the kitchen a good once-over to make sure all the ovens and burners are off, and head toward the break room to grab my coat and purse.

"You're leaving Marcus here alone?" Wavonne asks as she follows.

"Yes. It's not a big deal, Wavonne. He's an investor and has been a good customer for years."

I watch as Wavonne pulls some sort of faux fur nonsense from one of the hooks in the back room and puts it on. We pop back into the kitchen to make sure the door to the alley is locked. Then Wavonne and I head toward the front door through the dining room.

"You all have a good evening. Please come back again," I say as we pass Marcus's table.

CHAPTER 7

"Damn, it's cold out here," Wavonne says as we approach my van.

"It's only October, Wavonne. It's not *that* cold . . . just a little chilly."

"I just hate the cold! One of these days I'm going to move to Palm Springs and just lie on the beach all day."

"Oh, you are, are you?" I say, not bothering to tell her that Palm Springs is in the California desert and the closest beach is miles away.

"Wait until winter really gets here. If we never get snow again, it will be too soon," I say. "I can't wait to get home, crawl in bed under my comforter, and get some sleep. I am beat."

"Didn't Aunt Celia say something about pickin' up some groceries for her tonight?"

"Damn. I'd forgotten about that."

Momma has some sort of church potluck tomorrow. She'd given me a whole list of ingredients to pick up, so she could make her smothered pork chops in the morning. She claimed she didn't have time to do it herself after getting sidetracked with Marcus's request for pudding. If I don't get her items tonight, she'll have to go out in the morning and get them herself, and I'll never hear the end of it. We only serve pork chops as an occasional special at the restaurant. If I'd had any on hand I would have grabbed them from the walk-in fridge. And of course, I offered to bring Momma a whole platter of whatever she wanted from the restaurant to take to her potluck, but Momma values her independence and likes to keep busy, which is half the reason I think she goes to that church of hers. She used to go to an everyday Methodist church in Temple Hills, but after Daddy died, some friend of hers took her to the Church of the Holy Bible, one of those black megachurches that take up so many collections you get tired of reaching for your purse. I went with her a time or two but decided it wasn't for me . . . especially when the pastor's wife introduced herself to me as the "First Lady." *First Lady?* I initially thought she was joking, but when I realized she was serious, I knew I had no business at the Church of the Holy Bible. I'm not calling anyone, no matter how overblown her ego, First Lady unless her last name is Obama. And it was really over for me when I saw the pastor drive off in an eighty-thousand-dollar Mercedes SUV. He can drive whatever he wants, but I'll be damned if I'm going to pay for it. Wavonne goes to services with Momma now and then, but I suspect it's either to manhunt or get out of coming to the restaurant to help me set up for Sunday brunch.

"Makes you long for the days when the grocery stores actually closed for the night, doesn't it?"

"Huh," is Wavonne's response. Sometimes I forget she's so much younger than me. Grocery stores have probably been open twenty-four hours since she can remember.

"Nothing. We'll stop at the Giant over by the house."

It's well after midnight when Wavonne and I walk through the door of the grocery store, which is surprisingly busy. I figure I might as well do some grocery shopping for the house while I'm here. One less thing I'll have to do when I take a few hours off on Monday. I start in the produce section and before I bag a few apples, I notice Wavonne is nowhere to be seen. I'm sure she's run off to the cosmetics section.

I go up and down the aisles trying to ignore how sleepy I am. If I wasn't so tired from a long day, I wouldn't mind being here so much. Much of the time, I almost like grocery shopping. The same way I sometimes like doing laundry and cooking at home. When you own your own business and spend so much of your time there, little domestic activities can sometimes be stress-relieving. It's actually nice to shop for food for a family of three instead of a restaurant that seats nearly two hundred people at peak capacity. And I can't tell you the joy I take in cooking for small groups. Some Mondays, the only day of the week I'm not at the restaurant most of the day, I make a full dinner for Wavonne, Momma, and me. It's nice to make things in small quantities and just tend to one roast chicken or three salmon filets instead of seven pot roasts at a time or a tub of mashed potatoes so big you could almost dive in and go for a swim. It also gives me a chance to try out new recipes. It doesn't happen a lot, but here and there I do make something new at home that I end up putting on the menu or serving as a special at Sweet Tea. Just last month, I was experimenting with a sausage, apple, and cranberry stuffing recipe. It turned out to be so tasty, I put in the orders for the bulk ingredients the next day, and began offering it as a side to our roast turkey special.

"Hey," Wavonne says, as she nonchalantly slips some eye shadow, a barrette, and a tube of mascara into the cart.

"What's all that?" I ask, as if I don't know her game plan. She wouldn't be so bold as to put something really expensive in the cart, but she figures I'll let a few cheap sundries go unnoticed and just pay for them when we check out, which, I admit, I have done on occasion.

"Just some makeup and a barrette."

"And who's paying for 'just some makeup and a barrette'?"

"I've got money," Wavonne says and starts patting her side and looking around. "Damn. I think I left my purse at the restaurant. Can you spot me the cash, and I'll pay you back later?"

I give her a look. "Fine," I say and decide right then and there that we're going to go back to the restaurant and get her purse tonight just in case she left it there on purpose, knowing that I was supposed to stop by the grocery store. I wouldn't put it past Wavonne. If she spent half as much time doing something constructive as she did coming up with schemes to get out of paying for stuff (or getting out of work), she could probably run her own company.

"Can't ya open another register?" Wavonne yells toward the cashier after we wrap up our shopping and approach the checkout line.

For whatever reason, the Giant is quite busy tonight and there are four or five people in line ahead of us. The cashier glares at Wavonne and doesn't reply. She's got an "it's after midnight, and I'm schlepping groceries across a conveyor belt. Don't antagonize me or I might just *cut* you" look on her face.

"Lord. I'm gonna be old as you, Halia, by the time this chick gets us through the line."

I laugh.

"Man, those celebrities look rough without any makeup," Wavonne says, staring at one of those "Stars Without Makeup" tabloids on display when we finally get close enough to start unloading the groceries on the counter. "Some of them look like that haggard woman behind the counter at the KFC across from Sweet Tea."

I want to say that if Wavonne doesn't shape up at Sweet Tea, she might find her own self behind the counter at KFC. And what is she doing going to KFC anyway when we serve the best fried chicken in town?

"Yes. Makeup . . . well, *money,* really, can make anyone look better."

"Girl, they got to get you some help. This line is *crazy,*" Wavonne says to the cashier when we finally reach her.

"Yeah. We're not usually this busy so late at night."

"My cousin here is so tired. She can't be waiting in line all night after working at her restaurant. She ain't no spring chicken no more, ya know."

I glare at Wavonne.

"I hear ya. I'm tired as all get-out, as well. And I've got six more hours to go on my shift," the cashier says to Wavonne and then turns to me. "You have a restaurant?"

"Yeah. Mahalia's Sweet Tea over at the King Town Center."

"Oh. I've heard such good things about that place. But I think it's out of my price range. I'm not exactly making the big bucks working the night shift here."

I want to say that I'm not exactly making the big bucks, either. People think that when you own your own successful restaurant you must be raking in the dough, but let me tell you, I'm not making any millions. I earn a nice living, but rich I'm not. By the time I pay my staff, rent, insurance, utilities, random repairs, and make the payments on my loans, I'm almost bled dry, but I love it nonetheless. Life is about enjoying what you do in the moment, not about being rich . . . or so I keep telling myself.

"Oh, come on over, girl. We'll hook you up. We got good prices at lunchtime, and I'll sneak you a free dessert if you sit in my section."

I chuckle, hoping that Wavonne is joking and isn't really passing out free desserts to her tables. "We really do have some good values on our lunch menu. Give us a try."

Once we've wrapped up with the cashier, Wavonne and I load the bags into the cart and make our way to the exit.

"You know. I think I'd sleep better if we make a quick run

back to the restaurant and make sure Marcus locked up. He'd had a few drinks and may have forgotten," I say to Wavonne once we pushed the cart into the parking lot and loaded the van.

And that is part of the reason I want to go back. But I also want to make Wavonne get her purse and see the look on her face when I ask her to pay me back for the makeup.

RECIPE FROM HALIA'S KITCHEN

Halia's Sour Cream Cornbread

Ingredients

1 cup all-purpose flour
1 cup yellow cornmeal
¾ cup white sugar
1 teaspoon salt
3½ teaspoons baking powder
2 eggs
1 stick softened butter
1 can cream of corn (8.75 oz.)
1 can drained whole kernel corn (8.75 oz.)
1 container sour cream (8 oz.)

- Preheat oven to 375 degrees Fahrenheit. Generously grease a 12-inch cast-iron frying pan.

- In a large bowl, combine flour, cornmeal, sugar, salt, and baking powder. Stir in eggs, butter, cream of corn, corn, and sour cream. Mix using an electric mixer at medium speed until well blended. Pour batter into prepared pan.

- Bake in preheated oven for 25 to 30 minutes, until lightly browned, or until a toothpick inserted into the center comes out clean.

Eight Servings

CHAPTER 8

"Honestly, Wavonne, you'd lose your weave if it wasn't attached. How'd you manage to leave your purse behind?" I ask
after we've settled into the van and fastened our seat belts.

"First of all, this is a wig, not a weave, thank you very
much . . . and I don't know how I forgot my purse. I think I
left it in my locker. It was late, and I was ready to go home. . . ."

"You and me both. Marcus really had us scrambling today,
trying to get all those casseroles ready for the dinner rush."

"You shoulda just told him no, Halia."

"Marcus is not the easiest man in the world to say no to,
Wavonne. You know that."

"Yeah. He'd just keep laying on the sugar 'til you said yes
anyway."

"He's a regular sweet-talking shyster. At least *I* know who
I'm dealing with. I'm afraid his guests tonight might think he's
actually genuine. God knows what sort of business he's gotten
them mixed up in."

"What do think he's up to?"

"Your guess is as good as mine, but from the day I first met
Marcus, that man has been scheming."

"Where'd you meet him, again?"

"He came into the restaurant I worked at more than ten years ago. And if you think he's handsome now, you should have seen him then. He wasn't as polished . . . his suits weren't as expensive and his ties were not necessarily silk, but he was hot with youth and a real head turner. He was barely over thirty."

"Thirty ain't hot with no youth, Halia."

"It's all relative, Wavonne," I say. "He was entertaining some clients. I don't remember what sort of business he was in back then. That might have been when he started selling life insurance or mutual funds. I could tell he was putting on airs from the moment he sat down at one of my tables. He studied the wine list like he had a clue about wine and ordered an expensive bottle to share. Then he treated his guests to the works: appetizers, entrées, desserts, and cappuccino. Only problem was, when the bill came, Marcus's credit card was declined."

"Reject!" Wavonne yells like she always does when a credit card swipe is declined by the approval machine at the restaurant.

"I didn't want to embarrass him, so rather than tell him that his card was declined in front of his guests, I slipped a note in the leather bill folder before I handed it to him that said for him to see me at the bar. You should have seen him approaching me, like a dog with his tail between his legs."

"So what happened?"

"We tried another card, and it was declined, as well. We finally maxed each card with some of the total bill, but he was still thirty dollars short, and that was before my tip."

"He stiffed you?"

"Not only that. I loaned him the thirty dollars."

"You did *what?*"

"I felt sorry for him. He was so desperate to impress. He promised me that he was about to close a deal, and he'd pay me back as soon as he could. And you know what?"

"What?"

"That little scoundrel never did pay me back . . . and he still had the nerve to keep bringing his clients back to the restaurant and always asked for me to be his server."

"You're shittin' me?!"

"I kid you not. He left me decent tips from then on, but he never did pay back the money I loaned him or give me that tip he skipped out on."

"You let him off the hook?"

"I did . . . until a few years ago when I needed some investors to get Sweet Tea up and running. After he'd reviewed my business plan and listened to my pitch about the restaurant, he seemed to be on the fence about whether or not he wanted to invest. That's when I reached back several years and reminded him of the time I bailed him out, and how he'd never paid me back. I honestly think that is what sealed the deal and brought him on board as an investor," I say to Wavonne as we pull into a parking space in front of Sweet Tea.

"Girl, I'da had his balls in a vise grip if he'd tried to stiff my ass."

We walk toward the restaurant. When we reach the entrance, I put the key in the door. "That's funny," I add, when I notice my key won't turn properly. "The door's unlocked. Marcus had better still be here. If he left without locking up, I'll beat his ass."

"Marcus?" I call out, wondering why he'd have all the lights off in the dining room if he was still here.

"Anyone here?" Wavonne yells from behind me as we both stride toward the back of the dining room. "It's stuck," she says when we reach the kitchen door. She tries to push it open. I watch her push the door, and push it again . . . and push it again, while each time, it hits against something on the other side. Finally I say, "You *do* know that the door opens both ways?"

I reach in front of her and *pull* the door toward us.

"What the . . . ?" is all that comes out of my mouth when I catch sight of what was blocking the door—it was Marcus, lying facedown on my shiny ceramic tile.

"It's Marcus! Is he okay?"

"Is he okay?!" I say back to Wavonne, my heart starting to race. "Does he *look* okay to you? Call nine-one-one."

Wavonne pulls out her phone, and I crouch down and take Marcus's hand. I'm about to call his name to see if he answers . . . to see if he's conscious, but I can tell from the feel of his hand that he's not conscious—I can tell from the feel of his hand that he's not alive.

CHAPTER 9

"Oh my God!" I drop his hand and quickly stand up. "He's dead."

"Dead?"

"Yes, Wavonne. Dead. D-E-A-D!"

"Oh, *hail* to the no! I ain't stayin' in here with no dead body! I'll call nine-one-one from outside."

"You're not leaving me here alone." I grab her hand and take a quick look around.

"I don't like this, Halia. I'm no good with dead people." She starts dialing her phone. I see her press the nine key, and she's about to press the one when I see *it*.

"Wait! Don't call anyone." I've just caught sight of one of my cast-iron frying pans. It's lying next to Marcus, whom I now see has a big welt on the back of his head. At first I thought he had fallen over drunk or something like that, but now I'm pretty certain that's not the case.

"Huh?"

"Don't call anyone!" I repeat, my breath quickening. "This wasn't an accident." I point to the frying pan. "Someone hit him over the head with it."

"Who?"

"How the *hell* should I know?!"

"We gotta call the police, Halia."

"Just hush for a minute. Let me think." I start pacing back and forth, my hands shaking.

"Think about what? What's there to think about? You find a dead body, you call the police."

"Not when that dead body is in your restaurant, you don't. Who's going to want to eat here once word gets out that someone was murdered in my kitchen?"

"Not me, that's for damn—"

I cut Wavonne off. "Would you just shut it for a minute? I told you, I need to think." I keep pacing the floor, looking at Marcus, then looking away, then looking at him again. I can't believe the man who was so alive and well and full of charisma such a short time ago is now lying lifeless on the floor at my feet. I was never a fan of Marcus, and sometimes he annoyed the crap out of me, but I never would have wished this on him.

I can't get a grasp on what this all means. Too many thoughts are rushing through my head. I think of Marcus, and the effect his death will have on the people close to him—people like Jacqueline and Régine. But, honestly, thoughts of my livelihood are coming to mind, as well. I have put years of blood, sweat, and tears into this restaurant, and I'm not about to let it go under. I've poured everything I have into Sweet Tea. Even with a bank loan and help from investors like Marcus, Momma and I had to take out a second mortgage on the house and tap Daddy's life insurance money to get this place off the ground. Not to mention I employ an entire staff who depend on me for wages. There is just too much at stake for me to let word get out that a prominent businessman was killed in my restaurant.

I try to calm myself while Wavonne looks on from the

other side of the room. I stare down at the lifeless body and take a deep breath . . . and another. "You've got to help me get him out of here," I finally say.

"Get him outta here? Lord Jesus! Have you done lost your mind, Halia? Where you gonna take him?"

"I don't know." I'm still walking back and forth across the kitchen, more quickly now. "We'll drag him out back into the alley behind the bookstore or the coffee shop. *Anywhere* but here."

"*We?* I ain't touchin' no dead body, Halia. For Christ's sake, shuckin' all that corn this afternoon did enough damage to my manicure."

"Wavonne," I say, steadying myself and looking directly at her. "If my restaurant goes out of business because no one wants to eat at a murder scene, who do you think is going to pay you what *I* pay you to sit around and run your mouth and paint your lips all day?"

She looks at me for a second or two . . . then at Marcus . . . then back at me. "I'll get the feet," she says. "You get the head."

CHAPTER 10

"I just thought of something," Wavonne says. "What if the killer is still here?"

"I'm sure he . . . or *she* is gone. He probably hightailed it out of here the moment Marcus hit the ground. He would have shown himself by now if he were still here. What would he want with us anyway? Marcus was involved with all sorts of questionable businesses. I'm sure this has nothing to do with us. Now help me. I think we both need to get him from up here. You get under his right shoulder, and I'll get under his left."

Wavonne does as she's instructed. "I don't like this, Halia. I got a police record. I don't need to be movin' no dead bodies around."

"If anything happens, I'll take the heat, Wavonne. Now help me flip him over."

We manage to get him turned on his back. We both pull from under his shoulders and slide him over to the door that leads to the back alley. I release one hand, open the door, and poke my head out. All is clear, so Wavonne and I keep pulling. He's not a real big man . . . and he kept himself nice and lean, but he feels like a lead weight. I hear a *thump* as his butt hits the ground when we get him past the one step from the door to the asphalt.

I almost feel like I'm out of my body . . . like I'm looking down at Wavonne and me from the roof and wondering what the hell those two women are doing dragging a limp corpse down the alley. He seems to be getting heavier and heavier, but neither one of us dares to take a break. We want to get this done as soon as possible. By the time we get him several yards past the restaurant and drop him next to a Dumpster behind the bookstore, we're both huffing and puffing like two fat girls in gym class.

"Now what?"

"I don't know," I say back to Wavonne. "We'll leave him here, and someone from the bookstore will find him when they take out the trash. They'll call the cops. We'll just say the last time we saw him was when we left the restaurant at midnight."

I give Marcus's body one last look. I still can't believe he was just entertaining clients in Sweet Tea. Only hours earlier he was eating my fried chicken in between forcing that phony smile of his and trying to sell his clients whatever bag of goods he was hocking tonight. He may not have been the most principled person in the world, but he always seemed to have so much energy and life in him. To see him lying cold and stiff on the ground next to a Dumpster almost brings a tear to my eye. Even Marcus didn't deserve to go like this. But I don't have time for tears or any further reflection. At the moment, what Wavonne and I need to do is get the hell out of there.

"We have a receipt from the grocery store showing what time we were there, and we chatted with the clerk about the restaurant. She'd probably remember us and could serve as an alibi," I say to Wavonne as I begin to walk away. "We'll say we went home from the store. Momma's been asleep for hours, so she won't have to lie about what time we got home if she's asked. Like I said, Marcus kept company with all sorts of people. The more the police investigate, the less interest they'll have in us. Besides, we didn't do anything but try to keep my business from going under. All we have to do is . . ." I let my voice trail off when I realize Wavonne is not behind me.

"Wavonne! What were you doing?" I ask, relieved to see her come from the other side of the Dumpster.

"Nothing. I was just giving him one last look. He was one handsome brotha, Halia."

"Now is not the time, Wavonne. Let's get inside, straighten up, and get on home."

"I just helped you move a dead body, Halia. Do I have to help you clean, too?"

I don't respond, but the streetlamps provide enough light for her to see the glare from my eyes, and she doesn't say another word while she follows me back into the restaurant.

Despite the fact that someone was killed, and there's a frying pan lying on the floor, there's very little to indicate that anything out of the ordinary happened in the kitchen. Everything else seems to be in order.

Aside from the pan, there's really nothing out of place. I reach down and pick the frying pan up off the floor. Without thinking, I walk over to one of the oversized sinks filled with a few soaking pots. It's not until I let go of the frying pan, and it sinks into the soapy water, that it occurs to me that fingerprints . . . *murderer-identifying* fingerprints . . . might have been on the handle.

"Damn it!" I quickly reach my hand into the water and grab for the pan handle even though I know it's too late.

"What?"

"The pan. It might have had fingerprints on it."

Wavonne looks at the dripping frying pan in my hand. "*Had* bein' the key word."

I drop the pan back into the water, livid with myself for being so thoughtless. I'm not sure how I could have turned it over to the police without being implicated for moving Marcus's body, but now I've ruined what might well be the most helpful piece of evidence to lead the police to Marcus's killer.

CHAPTER 11

I usually don't get to the restaurant until nine on Sunday mornings. Laura gets in at seven and starts the prep work with the line staff, and I usually work very late on Saturday nights, so I allow myself to sleep in until seven-thirty on Sundays. But I could barely sleep a wink last night, and after hours of tossing and turning, I finally decide to say "to hell with it," trudge out of bed at six, and head toward the shower.

I'm about to leave my bedroom when I stop cold. I get a whiff of something . . . something sweet and spicy . . . sweet and spicy and *disturbing*. It takes only a second for the scent to register. What did Wavonne say Marcus's cologne smelled like? Spiced rum and dark chocolate? Yes. That's what I smell. My shoulders quickly lift with tension, and I feel a flush of heat to my face. *Oh my God! Marcus, or the ghost of Marcus, is haunting me! He's right here in my bedroom to exact revenge on me for moving his body and not calling the police.* I'm about to go into full-fledged panic mode when I see my clothes from last night lying on the dresser. I grab my blouse and put it to my nose. It smells pungently of Marcus's cologne. I sigh with relief as I realize that his obnoxious fragrance must have seeped into my clothes when Wavonne and I were manhandling him out of the restaurant.

I pick up the shirt and pair of slacks from the dresser and toss them into the washer on my way to the bathroom, where I step into the shower to wash off as much of last night as possible. As the water cascades across my body, I have to keep reminding myself that last night was not a dream. *Did I really find Marcus dead . . . murdered in the kitchen of my restaurant? Did Wavonne and I really drag his stiff corpse down the back alley? Did we really tamper with a murder scene? Was it really Wavonne, and not me, being the voice of reason and telling me to call the police?* I know the answer to all my questions is a solid yes, and as I rinse the soap off my body, I still think I made the right decision. If we had called the police, who knows what would have happened. They might have shut me down for days. And when word got out about a murder at Sweet Tea, who knows how many customers I'd lose. I don't care how good my greens and macaroni and cheese are—people don't want to eat at a murder scene. I just need to play it cool . . . keep a low profile and not mention a word about anything to anyone.

If the police start asking questions, Wavonne and I will just say everything appeared fine when we left the restaurant. From there we went by the grocery store and then straight home. I put the fear of God in Wavonne before I let her go to bed last night and made her promise me that she wouldn't breathe a word of this mess to anyone. Wavonne is no fool. She might not have a lot of education or much of a work ethic, but she knows we'd both be in big trouble if anyone found out we moved a dead body from a crime scene. Hopefully, that will be enough to motivate her to keep it zipped.

After I get dressed, I head toward the kitchen and am surprised for the second time by the smell hitting my nose. I wonder why the kitchen smells of roasting meat so early. Then I remember that Wavonne and I picked up pork chops for

Momma last night. She's already been up and has them smothered and simmering in a pan on the stove. I'd normally sneak a
quick taste of the sauce, but I have no appetite this morning,
and after last night, the last thing I want to look at is a frying
pan.

I consider getting the cereal out of the cabinet and pouring myself a bowl with some milk, but I'm too much of a basket case to down any food. Instead I decide to just go into the
restaurant early, start for the front door, and walk out to my
van. I'm about to get inside my vehicle when I stop myself. I
don't want to do anything out of the ordinary today. The last
thing I need is someone telling the cops that "Halia usually
doesn't come in until nine, but the day a dead body was found
in the alley she came in early for some reason," so rather than
leaving, I pick up the Sunday *Washington Post* from the
doorstep and sit down at the kitchen table.

I'm about to start reading the paper to take my mind off
things when Momma emerges from her bedroom. She doesn't
work on Sundays. She doubles up on her baking on Saturday
mornings to cover the Sunday crowd. Sundays are all about
church for Momma, so there is no time for baking at Sweet
Tea.

"You're up early for a Sunday. What time did you and
Wavonne get in last night?"

"It was almost . . ." I'm about to say "it was almost two
a.m.," but I stop and reset. "I guess it was about one.
You didn't hear us come in?"

"You know I'm out cold by ten o'clock. You work me to
the bone at that restaurant. It makes an old lady tired. I don't
think an earthquake would wake me up."

I'm glad she went to bed early and didn't hear us coming in
so late. Now, if the need arises, she won't have to lie if the police
ask her what time Wavonne and I came home last night.

"I was beat last night, as well . . . went straight to bed."

"Did Marcus and his guests enjoy my banana pudding?"

"They did. They enjoyed all your desserts. We served them some pineapple upside-down cake and red velvet cake, as well. Raves all around."

"Any single men in the bunch?"

I sigh. "I didn't ask, Momma."

"Have you noticed the new UPS man who comes to the restaurant almost every day?"

"Stan?" I ask, recalling the portly white guy who delivers our packages.

"Yes. I didn't see a wedding band on his finger."

"Really? Then I guess you can ask him out on a date."

"Now, be serious, Halia. What's wrong with him? He's seems very nice . . . has a steady job. Of course, it would be better if he was black, but beggars can't be choosers, you know. And besides, Georgia Wallings, my friend who volunteers with me over at the hospital gift shop, has a daughter who married a white fellow, and let me tell you, Georgia now has the most beautiful grandchildren—not too light, not too dark."

"Good for Georgia," I say. "Shouldn't you be checking on your pork chops?"

While Momma turns from me toward the stove, I grab the paper and make a run for the living room before she has a chance to start in on me again. I sit down on the sofa, and as I look at the front page, I can't help but think that tomorrow there will be a headline reading "Local Entrepreneur Found Dead behind King Town Center." Then I remember that the murder happened in Prince George's County, Maryland. In a county that has, at times, averaged one murder a day, I guess it's not incredibly likely that Marcus's death will make the front page. It may end up buried somewhere in the *Metro* section.

How is that possible? A man is murdered, and it's not even news. If it happened in one of the white upper northwest sections of D.C., it would be news. If it happened in neighboring

Montgomery County or over the bridge in Alexandria, Virginia, it would be news. But in Prince George's County? Not so much.

Things didn't used to be like that here. When I was a kid, growing up in the seventies, we lived in Clinton, only a few miles outside the Beltway and maybe ten miles or so outside D.C. Back then, Prince George's County wasn't much different from any of the other D.C. suburbs. It was a county of mostly middle-class white families, with good schools, nice shopping, and well-maintained homes. In fact, Momma, Daddy, and I were the first African American family on our block back in 1976, and while we were never called the n-word or had our house vandalized or anything extreme like that, there was definitely an unwelcome feeling from many of the neighbors. We weren't invited to many of the parties or barbecues, some parents scooted their kids past our house on Halloween, and whenever I'd start playing with this one little white girl across the street, her mother would see us through the window and always suddenly need her daughter in the house for something. But slowly things began to change— more and more black folks were making their way out of the city, and Prince George's County became the suburb of choice for African American families in the D.C. metro area. One year after we moved in, another black family bought a house a few doors down, and, a few months later, another black family moved in farther up the street. By the late eighties, there were more black families on my street than white families, and Prince George's County remained a great place to live with good schools, nice shopping, and well-maintained homes . . . only by this time it was a mix of white *and* black families. It wasn't until later that things really started to take a turn toward decline. I hate to say it, but I think white people were plain uncomfortable sharing their neighborhoods . . . their schools, their stores, their shopping centers, with so many black people, and as white people moved out, more black people moved in. By 1990 it was uncommon for white people to move to Prince George's County. If you were white and living in Prince George's County, you had most likely purchased your house a long time ago and hadn't yet partaken in the white flight to neighboring Montgomery or Charles County or across the Potomac River to some Virginia suburb.

It's sad to say, but somewhere along the way, people decided that houses in majority black neighborhoods were worth less than houses in white areas, and, as real estate prices fell, lower-class people moved in, which made prices drop further, which led to even lower-class people moving in, and things went from bad to worse. Crime was on the rise. Everything from shoplifting to robbery to carjacking was happening more often in Prince George's County (which, by this time, was often referred to as PG County in what felt like a derogatory manner) than any other suburban county in the D.C. area. And, from 1985 to 2006, my home county accounted for 20 percent of all murders in the state of Maryland.

The high crime levels, and, if we're being honest, blatant racism led to a decline in the retail services offered here. In the seventies, Prince George's County was home to Landover Mall, a true regional shopping destination with a Woodward & Lothrop and a Garfinckel's, two now defunct high-end department stores. I was so sad when I heard that the entire mall (except for the Sears . . . something about Sears owning the land underneath its store) was being bulldozed a few years ago. Iverson Mall in Hillcrest Heights, the first enclosed climate-controlled mall in the D.C. area, is still hanging in there, but the Woodward & Lothrop and a Montgomery Ward that used to anchor the mall are long gone. The Ethan Allen furniture store on Branch Avenue closed years ago. One of the main shopping centers that used to house a Zayre and a Chesapeake Bay Seafood House in Camp Springs is now a self-storage facility.

Hell, even the Chi-Chi's by the bowling alley closed. A real sore point with us Prince George's County residents is that Whole Foods, that overpriced, hoity-toity organic market, has a warehouse in Prince George's County, but no stores.

The county had been in decline for a long time, but over the past few years, a revival of sorts has been taking place. Crime rates have been going down, and retailers seem to have finally realized that while we may be black, and our county may have a higher crime rate than other areas, we are mostly a county of hardworking people who make good livings. In fact, we are the wealthiest and most highly educated majority African American jurisdiction in the country and would be happy to spend our money close to home if only there were somewhere to spend it.

New town centers in Largo and Bowie opened a few years ago; FedExField, home of the Washington Redskins, was built near the old Landover mall site; trendy shops and restaurants have opened in Arts District Hyattsville; and Wegmans, a specialty high-end grocery store chain, opened in Lanham. But the crown jewel in Prince George's County's rebirth was the opening of National Harbor on the Potomac River in Oxon Hill. It was a project that was in development for years, and I, like so many jaded residents, never thought it would actually happen. But in 2008, the three-hundred-acre positively elegant waterfront development opened. It's now home to the Gaylord National Resort & Convention Center and several other hotels, waterfront condos, offices, retail stores, restaurants, and a marina. And thanks to a successful gambling ballot measure (that I have mixed feelings about) a full Las Vegas–style resort and casino is in the works. It's the biggest thing to hit Prince George's County in decades.

Well, no one can accuse me of being a "Moesha Come Lately." I opened my restaurant long before Wegmans came to town, or National Harbor opened for business. I helped ease the shortage of high-end restaurants that had existed in the county for years. In many parts, if you wanted something more than a burger or some fried chicken from Popeye's, you had to drive for miles.

I got the idea to open my own restaurant years ago when I worked nights as line cook at a nice all-American restaurant in Arlington, Virginia. My day job was at the Census Bureau in Suitland, Maryland. Four days a week I'd make the hike from Suitland to Arlington, which usually took more than an hour in heavy traffic. The part-time line cook job did bring in a little extra money, but I mostly did it because I loved to cook, and I enjoyed the hustle and bustle of a busy kitchen. And to be honest, my day job at the Census Bureau didn't exactly leave me exhausted. Often I could get most of my duties for the entire week done in a day or two, so being a little fatigued from a late night broiling crab cakes and sautéing pecan-crusted trout didn't really get in the way of my day job.

My official title was line cook, but I was sort of a jack-of-all-trades at the restaurant. If they were short on servers, I'd step in. I functioned as the hostess here and there, and sometimes I even ended up supervising the kitchen. But mostly I cooked. I sautéed shrimp, and grilled steaks, and fried fish, and roasted chicken. I had a knack for it, and it was me who developed a shrimp scampi recipe on the fly when we ran out of grit cakes for the shrimp and grits entrée on the menu one busy Saturday night. That recipe became a regular menu item and is still served there today. I may not have gotten straight As in school, and I may not be the most beautiful or thinnest girl on the block, but the thing about Mahalia Watkins—girl can *throw down* in the kitchen.

I grew up cooking with my grandmother. Truth be known, and for better or for worse, my adventure into the culinary arts began as a way for me to get out of going to church. Every Sunday, Grandmommy would host a big family get-together after service. Anywhere from fifteen to thirty people would show up on Grandmommy's doorstep after services, and there was no way Grandmommy could go to church *and* prepare a meal for that kind of crowd unless people wanted to eat at midnight. Grandmommy always said feeding the churchgoers was her way of worshiping God. It wasn't long before I realized that, if I stayed back and helped her, it could be *my* way of worshiping God, too, which was a hell of a lot better than trying to sit still for three hours while some old windbag preached, and a bunch of fools got to hootin' and hollerin' in the aisles as if they were overcome by the Holy Spirit . . . when the only thing those damn drama queens were overcome with was the desire to be the center of attention.

Grandmommy and I would start cooking at nine in the morning. The menu varied from week to week, but one thing that was always a staple was fried chicken and waffles. Often it was my job to batter the chicken, which Grandmommy always marinated in seasonings the night before. Sometimes I'd mix up the waffles using the whipped egg whites we always added to make them extra fluffy. Other days I was busy rinsing greens or mashing sweet potatoes. I don't remember if pre-shredded cheese was as available in the seventies as it is now, but regardless, I often spent a good deal of the morning grating cheese by hand for the macaroni.

I learned so much on those Sunday mornings, and I loved that time with Grandmommy. I was one of thirteen grandchildren, so I considered myself lucky to get a whole morning of alone time with her once a week. I helped her almost every Sunday from the time I was twelve until after I was eighteen and left for college. It was after I'd gone away to school that she had a heart attack and just didn't have the strength to host Sunday dinner anymore. But I never forgot her recipes, and after six years of apprenticeship, I could make a soul food meal that would knock your socks off. Before I opened the restaurant I would even have family over once every six weeks or so for Sunday supper. Of course, it didn't have the same feel as when we all gathered at Grandmommy's house, but the food was just as good, and it helped to keep the family connected.

Sweet Tea has been such a great way to keep my grandmother's memory alive, and despite the hours I have to put in there and the headaches it gives me every day, I love that restaurant, and I can't bear the thought of anything happening to it. Maybe calling the police and letting them find Marcus's dead body on the floor of my kitchen wouldn't kill my business. I honestly don't know how my customers would react to the news, but I just can't take the chance. I have bills of my own to pay, and I'm mostly supporting Momma and Wavonne, as well. *No, I just can't take that chance.* The police will be notified of his body soon enough, and they can investigate from there.

I try to put the whole thing out of my mind, but the memory of Marcus's stiff hand is hard to ignore. Marcus was smarmy and always up to no good, but one thing I will say about him: the world is now a much less interesting place without him in it.

CHAPTER 12

I pull into the King Town Center with the expectation that I might see a spectacle of red and blue flashing lights and yellow police tape. Surely someone has stepped into the alley behind the shopping center and seen Marcus's body. But everything seems to be "business as usual" as I maneuver my van into a parking space and turn off the ignition. And that's when I see it: Marcus's car, a sleek black BMW. I was so frazzled as we left Sweet Tea last night that I didn't even notice it in the parking lot.

When I step into the restaurant, it's bustling like a busy beehive. My servers are straightening up the dining room and filling condiment containers. I hear Laura's voice in the back supervising the kitchen, and Tacy is rolling silverware at one of the back tables. Everyone is scurrying around getting ready for the Sunday brunch crowd. Nothing seems out of the ordinary—nothing except for the huge knot in my stomach and the eggshells I'm walking on waiting for someone to rush in the restaurant screaming about a dead body.

Clearly the body has not been found. Wavonne and I left it *next* to the Dumpster—not *behind* it or *in* it . . . just next to it. You'd think someone would have taken out the trash or made a delivery and seen the body by now. But it is a Sunday, which isn't a big day for deliveries, and most of the businesses in the shopping center don't open until ten. It's only nine now.

I say hi to my staff and make my way to kitchen. As usual, Laura has everything under control. I see eggs being prepped for omelets, fruit being sliced for garnish, potatoes being chopped for home fries, and Laura is in the far corner standing next to one of my industrial mixers, which is whipping up the batter for our salty/sweet cheese nips. Sunday brunch is the one and only seating at which we don't serve my grand-mother's cornbread. Instead, we offer a complimentary basket of salty/sweet cheese nips, a concoction I developed on my own using Grandmommy's drop biscuit recipe as a base. We mix up flour, shortening, and other dry ingredients with a healthy helping of Monterey Jack and Cheddar cheese. Then we drop the slightly larger-than-bite-size biscuits by spoon onto a cookie sheet. After we bake them to a golden brown, we brush them with salted butter, let them cool a bit before sprinkling them with course sugar crystals, and get them to the tables while they're still warm. They are a challenge to exe-cute. If we put the sugar on too early, the crystals will melt, and, if we wait too long, the crystals won't stick, and we end up serving cold biscuits to my patrons. But the customers rave about them and always ask for the recipe (which I'd give them over my dead body), so they are worth all the trouble.

"How's it going?" I ask Laura.

"Good. The temperature is off in oven number two. I called the repair shop, but they can't get anyone out here today, so we're down to two ovens until then."

"Okay. I'll give Harry a call at the repair shop, and see if I can sweet-talk him into getting someone out here today. Any-thing else going on?"

"No. Everything is pretty well under control."

I want to ask her if she's sure . . . if she's *sure* there's nothing else going on. Or if she saw anything suspicious when she came in this morning, but I decide it's best to keep my mouth shut.

"Great. I'm going to go look at the reservations on the computer and see what kind of crowds we can expect this morning."

When I first opened Sweet Tea, I didn't take reservations. As anyone in the restaurant business can tell you, taking reservations creates a host of problems. You have the no-shows whom you've held a table for, the folks who show up late and get an attitude when you've given their table away, and the diners who linger at their table well beyond the allotted time for which we plan for them to be there (we call them "campers"), which makes us run behind with other reservations. It's much easier and more profitable to take customers on a first-come, first-serve basis, but as my restaurant became more popular and waits of up to two hours were not unheard of on Friday and Saturday nights, I started getting more and more requests from patrons for me to start taking reservations, so I eventually decided to reach for some middle ground and began offering a limited number of reservations, but still make most tables available on a first-come, first-serve basis. This way, as long as customers call far enough in advance, they can usually get a reservation for their preferred seating time and avoid a long wait.

As I make my way out to the host stand, I see a Prince George's County police car pull into a parking spot outside the front door. My heart starts to sputter as I watch Jack Spruce get out of the car. I know Jack well, and Wavonne teases that he has a crush on me. I don't think anyone would call him handsome, and much like myself, it wouldn't kill him to drop a few pounds, but he has a kind face and is always very nice. He is one of many officers who patrol the parking lot on a regular basis. On some Friday and Saturday nights we have a cop in the lot for the entire evening, which is more to keep an eye on Fast Freddie's (a sports bar and pool hall, several doors down from Sweet Tea that often has a pretty rambunctious crowd) than my restaurant, but their presence is still appreciated. We always welcome the police into the restaurant and offer them free sodas or cups of coffee.

My hands are trembling as I mess around with the keys on the computer to look like I'm keeping busy as he makes his way to the door. I pretend to take a moment or two to notice him standing outside. When his eyes catch mine, he smiles and offers a quick wave. I force a return smile and remind myself to walk slowly toward the door.

You don't know anything about any dead body behind the town center. Nothing. Absolutely nothing, I say to myself in my head, thinking that these thoughts might help my face project innocence.

"Morning, Halia," Jack says, when I unlock the door and let him in. "How's it going?"

"Just fine, Jack. How are you?"

"I'm good. You got any coffee on?"

"Sure. I believe we've started brewing it already," I say, and turn toward Tacy, who's a few yards away at one of the tables. "Tacy, can you get Officer Spruce a cup of coffee?"

"You bet," he says, nods at Jack, and heads toward the coffee station.

"What's new? Good crowd at dinner last night?"

"Yeah . . . yeah. It was good," I say awkwardly, waiting for him to bring up a dead body.

"Good. Best food in the area. No wonder you keep so busy."

I nod to acknowledge his compliment and then just look at him, waiting for him to break the news . . . to start asking questions, but he just stares back at me.

Oh, for Pete's sake, I think to myself. *He doesn't know about the body. He's just here on a social call.*

Conversation usually flows freely between Jack and me, so I need to break this uncomfortable quiet before he gets suspicious.

"I'm sorry," I say, breaking the silence. "I'm a little distracted. One of my ovens is down just in time for the brunch rush."

"Really? Sorry to hear that. If I were handy, I'd offer to take a look at it for you, but I struggle with changing light bulbs."

"You and me both." I begin to relax a little bit. "So what are you up to this morning? Making your regular rounds?"

"Yeah. There was break-in at a house in the neighborhood across the street. The owners had let their newspapers pile up on the front porch. Burglars figured they were out of town and starting trying to break in the door. But, of course, they weren't out of town . . . just lazy about picking up their papers. They called us and screamed that the police were on the way, so by the time I got there, the perpetrators were long gone . . . never a dull moment around here."

"That's for sure," I respond, thinking about just how much less dull it was going to get around here very soon.

Before I have to force any more conversation, Tacy approaches with Jack's coffee.

"I put it in a Styrofoam cup in case you want to take it with you," Tacy says as he hands over the coffee.

"Thanks," Jack replies. "Well, it sounds like you have a lot to deal with this morning, so let me get out of your way."

"Thanks for stopping by, Jack. Hope you have a good one."

As he walks out the door, I think about what he said . . . about me having a lot to deal with this morning.

"You have no idea, Jack," I say softly as I watch him get in his patrol car. "Boy, do you ever have *no* idea . . ."

CHAPTER 13

"What are those?!" I say with a cross expression to Linda, one of my servers, as she passes by me, and I catch a glimpse of the two baskets of salty/sweet cheese nips she's carrying—two baskets of salty/sweet cheese nips that are burned on the bottom. "I *know* you are not about to take those burned biscuits out to one of our customers."

Linda looks at the biscuits, looks back at me, and hesitates a moment before responding. "I'm sorry. I grabbed them quickly. I didn't realize they were burned."

"Throw them in the trash and wait for the next batch to come out of the oven," I say quickly and walk past her to do a quick check around the restaurant to see if any more of the burned nips have made it out to my tables. Brunch is in full gear . . . not an empty seat in the place, and I've got a crowd in front of the host stand and outside waiting for tables. I'm thankful for the distraction of being busy, but I'm about to blow a gasket waiting for the news to break. It's noon, and as far as I know, no one has found Marcus in the alley. I keep waiting for sirens and police cars to show up, but so far, nothing out of the ordinary has happened.

This is one of the few times that I wished I had a television in the restaurant, so I could keep an eye on the TV and see if any news breaks about a dead body being found behind King Town Center. Customers always ask if I'm going to install some flat screens, so they can catch CNN or watch the football games. I even get sales reps in here from time to time trying to offer me a deal on a few Sony or Samsung TVs (and don't get me started on the guy who came in trying to sell me newspaper frames to hang over the urinals in the men's bathroom . . . can we not at least be alone with our thoughts when we pee?). But I refuse to allow TVs in my restaurant. We're surrounded by televisions everywhere we go these days—at restaurants, bars, health clubs . . . even my dry cleaner has a flat screen going behind the counter from open to close. Hell, you can't even get a burger at McDonald's without watching turmoil in the Middle East or the latest politician caught with his pants down. I want my restaurant to be a respite from all of that constant peripheral stimulation. I want people to come here to focus on their family and friends, and most important, my food.

"Hello," I say to the one and only table that seems to have gotten a basket of the burned nips. "I'm Halia, the owner. How are you folks doing this afternoon?"

The pleasant-looking couple smiles, and they both say they are doing well.

"These biscuits are a little charred on the bottom and not up to my standards." I take the basket from the table even though they've clearly already downed two of them with no complaints. "Let me get you a fresh basket."

The woman at the table laughs. "They tasted fine to us."

"You'll like the new ones even better then. Please, pardon the inconvenience."

I head back to the kitchen, and once I'm behind the line I raise my voice. "Who's on biscuit duty?"

"I was," Roger, one my youngest kitchen helpers, says with a meek expression.

"Well, number one, Roger. Why are you burning my biscuits? And, number two, why on earth didn't you throw them out once they came out of the oven burned?" I then turn to everyone in the kitchen. "And why did anyone take these burned biscuits off the sheets, put them in baskets, and serve them to our customers?"

"You know how customers get when we're running behind on the cheese nips," Linda says. "It's like mutiny out there if they don't get them right away. They weren't really burned . . . just a little dark on the bottom."

A hush falls over the kitchen. Linda's new, and although I went over my expectations with her as I do every server, she clearly has not yet grasped the passion I have for the food we serve here.

I look at Linda and then cast my attention to the entire kitchen. "Listen up, everyone. Nothing, and I mean *nothing* leaves this kitchen that isn't perfect." My eyes linger on Linda as I scan the room. "That means no slightly-browned-on-the-bottom cheese nips, that means no salads with croutons missing, that means no French fries that aren't hot and crisp. Have we got that?"

I see several nods.

"You guys do a great job, but let's not have any more mishaps."

Honestly, I'm a little thankful to Linda for the brief distraction she's given me. I've been on edge since last night, and at this point, I just want the cops to arrive, so I can pretend that I don't know anything about *anything*, get them out of here, and let them move on with finding out who did Marcus in . . . and hopefully that will be the end of it from my perspective.

As the day wears on, and I seat diners, pop in and out of

the kitchen, and check in with customers, I start to think I might lose it. By three o'clock the restaurant quiets down, and there are still no police, no news . . . no *nothing*. I decide that I just can't take it anymore. I need to make some excuse to be in the alley and be the one to find the body my damn self. I think on it for a while and come up with a reasonable excuse. I decide to ask Tacy to break down a few boxes for me in the store room, so I can take them home to use for collecting stuff to take to Goodwill. I tell him I'll drive around back and load the boxes into my van in the alley rather than traipsing through the restaurant with them and out the front door.

I'm nervous as I walk out of the restaurant toward my van, but I can't take the waiting anymore. I hate the idea of me being the one to "find" the body, as that will tie me that much closer to the murder, but the sooner the police know about the body, the sooner they can start investigating, the sooner I can tell them whatever version of the truth I come up with, and the sooner I can have this lead weight lifted from my shoulders.

I start the van and back out of the parking space, giving the area one last look to see if any police cars are making their way in the parking lot, but no such luck. I drive along the front of the shopping center, turn the corner to whip around to the alley, and slowly maneuver the van toward the Dumpster behind the bookstore. As I get closer to my destination, I slow down and take a look. My eyes widen and the hairs on the back of my neck stand at attention, but I don't stop. There's nothing to stop for. The body's gone.

CHAPTER 14

"Where's Wavonne?" I ask Tacy, who's standing in the kitchen next to the broken-down cardboard boxes I asked him to get for me.

"I think she's out front. Do you want me to put the boxes in your van?"

I ignore the question and slam through the kitchen door into the dining area.

"I personally think she wears padded underwear. What white girl has an ass like that?" is all I hear Wavonne say to Linda, who's putting an order into the computer. I don't know who she's talking about, and I don't care.

"Linda, can you cover Wavonne's tables? I need to talk to her."

I don't wait for Linda to reply. I grab Wavonne by the elbow, haul her through the kitchen, and out the back door just as Tacy is shutting the door on my van.

"I put the boxes in the back."

"Thanks, Tacy. Wavonne and I need to run a quick errand. We'll be back soon."

Wavonne follows my lead and gets in the van. I start it up and just drive with no particular destination in mind.

"He's gone!" I call out.

"Who?"

"What do you mean, *who?* Marcus. He's gone!"

"Gone? Where'd he go?"

"How the *hell* should I know!? I drove around back, and there's no body by the Dumpster."

"What!?" Wavonne responds and turns around to look behind us out the window. "You sure he was dead, Halia? Maybe he got up and walked away."

"He wasn't breathing, and he didn't have a pulse. He was *dead!*" I take a quick look at Wavonne before turning my eyes back toward the road. "Shit! Shit! Shit!"

Wavonne looks at me, and I think, for the first time, the gravity of the situation is hitting her.

"What are we going to do now?" I'm more asking myself than Wavonne.

"Just play it cool, Halia," Wavonne says, making some calming motions with her hands. "We need to just play it cool. His body's bound to turn up eventually."

"Maybe. Maybe not." I take a breath as we come to a stoplight. "But until then there is a murderer on the loose, and no one except for the two of us even knows that a crime has been committed."

"You said yourself, Halia, that whoever killed Marcus doesn't want anything to do with us. It had to've been related to some funky monkey business deal gone bad."

"I don't know what else it could have been about, but it happening in my restaurant scares me. Whoever killed him must have come back or seen us moving the body. Who else would have taken him?"

"You *sure* he was dead?"

"He was *dead,* Wavonne!"

Wavonne and I are quiet for a moment as we both stare straight ahead before I let out a long sigh. "I really don't know what to do. I thought the cops would find the body, start an investigation from there, and find out who did him in. But now it could be days or weeks before he's even reported missing."

Wavonne turns her head in my direction and seems to be studying me as thoughts rush through my head. "Now, don't you go gettin' any big ideas about tellin' the police the truth, Halia. You dragged me into this, and I ain't goin' to the big house 'cause you made me help you drag his body around."

"*I'm* not going to call the police, but what if an *anonymous* caller did and said they saw a dead body behind the town center late last night?"

"Don't you be makin' any anonom . . . anono . . . whatever that word is—calls, either. They can trace numbers . . . analyze your voice. I watch *CSI*. Cops can do all sortsa crazy shit. You let it take its course. Someone'll figure out he's missin' soon enough."

I think about what Wavonne says. I'm quiet for a minute or two before responding, "Maybe you're right."

"Damn straight, I'm right. I ain't no dummy."

"Never said you were, Wavonne," I say and decide we might as well turn around and head back to the restaurant. Wavonne probably is right. The more we stay out of this business, the better.

CHAPTER 15

So it's day two since the night we found Marcus dead on my kitchen floor, and I'm still a nervous wreck. I always pay attention to who is coming in and out of my restaurant, but I now find myself looking up with a different kind of urgency every time someone comes through the door, wondering if it's the police, or someone looking for Marcus, or, God forbid, whoever killed him.

I've been thinking a lot about who that person might be. I was up half the night obsessing about it. Marcus knew a lot of people. I don't know much about murder, but I do know that people are usually murdered by someone they know. I doubt I'm even familiar with a fraction of his friends and acquaintances. There was the couple that was in here last week, who were clearly not happy with Marcus . . . and back here again the night he was killed. Could they have done him in? They didn't look like murderers, but what does a murderer look like? Then there were his other guests at Sweet Tea on that fateful night: the more casually dressed man whom I know nothing about; Marcus's sister, Jacqueline; and, of course, there's Régine. Sure, she's sort of trashy and dresses like a street walker, but I don't think Régine's a murderer, and why would she murder her meal ticket? I can't imagine she stood to gain anything if Marcus died. He was no fool and, assuming he had a will, I'd be highly surprised if he left Régine so much as a nickel or named her on any life insurance policies.

I'm mulling over possible suspects in my head when I see Stan, the UPS man, outside the front door. I go over and let him in. It's not quite eleven o'clock, so the doors are still locked.

"Morning, Stan. How are you?" I ask as he wheels our latest order through the door.

"I'm good. Sorry to come through the front, but I'm in a hurry, and it's only a few boxes."

"No problem. We're not even open yet."

I follow Stan as he wheels the boxes toward the kitchen just in time for Momma to hold the door open for him. She must be on her way out. She's got her jacket over her arm and her purse in her hand. I poke my head in the kitchen behind Stan and ask Laura to check the boxes and sign for the order.

"Why don't you go back in there and talk to him?" Momma says to me as we stride toward the front of the restaurant. "He's handsome enough. Seems so nice, and I hear those UPS drivers have good benefits."

I'm about to respond when I see Wavonne knocking on the front door, assuming it's locked. She'd run a few doors down to the coffee shop to get some sort of pumpkin latte something or other. I didn't relock it after letting in Stan, so I wave her in.

"Wavonne," I say. "Momma has a crush on Stan, the UPS driver. She thinks he's handsome . . . and likes that his job has good benefits."

"She got a thing for Stan?" Wavonne says before turning to Momma. "You go on, Aunt Celia. Get yourself a boo thang."

"Yeah, Momma likes the younger men," I say with a wicked smile on my face.

Momma rolls her eyes at us.

"Ooh. Aunt Celia a *cougar!*" Wavonne howls while making cat-claw gestures with her hands. "Rawr!!!"

We both laugh.

"Now, you girls stop that," Momma snaps.

"What? Did you not just say he's handsome or 'handsome enough'?"

"You know I meant for *you*. You girls are nuts." She begins to stomp away. "I'm leaving. I'm done with my baking, and you two are getting on my last nerve."

We can't help but keep laughing as we watch her head toward her car. I'm thinking about how maybe . . . just maybe, she'll back off for a little while now that I've turned the tables on her, when I see Jacqueline emerging from her BMW in the parking lot. As she gets closer to the door, she catches my eye and waves . . . not a hearty back-and-forth wave . . . more of a "Jacqueline" wave, a pretentious quick flick of the wrist. Everything about her is always "just so," and today is no exception. Her hair is pulled back in a ponytail, and she's wearing a beige suit with shiny nude patent leather pumps.

"Hello," I say when she enters the restaurant. "How are you?"

"I'm well. Thank you."

"Did you come for lunch?" I say. "I've got a great special today—chicken and dumplings." I know she'd sooner slice off a finger than eat chicken and dumplings . . . or at least eat chicken and dumplings in public, but I'm trying to keep the conversation light and appear relaxed.

I see a spark go off in her eyes at the mention of chicken and dumplings, and I swear she's about to say she'd love some before she stops herself and, instead, says, "That sounds really nice, but I just stopped by to see if anyone here has talked to Marcus."

"Marcus? I don't think so. I haven't seen him since he was here with you and his other guests on Saturday night."

"Really? Mother called me on Sunday morning and said that he never arrived to take her to church." Jacqueline has a way of talking that sounds slightly British (e.g., referring to her mom as "Mother"), even though she was born and raised right here in Prince George's County. "Then Régine called looking for him Sunday evening. Apparently they had had plans to meet for dinner." Jacqueline rolls her eyes when she says the word "dinner." We both know what Marcus was meeting Régine for, and it likely was not dinner. "I keep trying him on his cell phone, but it just rings and goes to voice mail. I'm starting to get a little worried, not to mention perturbed. I'm getting phone calls for him left and right." She sounds more concerned about Marcus's absence being a nuisance to her than his well-being.

"I wouldn't worry too much. Marcus is a big boy and can take care of himself."

"As far as I can tell, here was the last place anyone saw him."

"He didn't leave with Régine on Saturday night?"

"No. Régine drove herself home. Marcus spends Saturday nights at Mother's so he can take her to church in the morning."

"What about his other guests? Have you checked with them?"

"No. They all left before I did. I was the last one here with Marcus. He said he was going to wrap some fried chicken to take to Mother and then be on his way, as well."

I want to ask more about Charles . . . and Marcus's other guests, but it might seem suspicious if I start asking too many questions. I'm not supposed to know anything bad has happened.

"This isn't like him at all. He can be inconsiderate and self-involved, but he usually answers his phone and returns calls . . . and he never stands Mother up for church."

"I didn't know Marcus was so religious."

"Religious?" Jacqueline says with a laugh. "Marcus goes to

church for one reason and one reason only—it's a well-stocked pond of fish waiting to take his bait. He's landed more clients at the Church of Christ than anywhere else. It's hard not to trust a man who takes his mother to church every Sunday, and Marcus knows it."

I chuckle and try to remind myself to speak of Marcus in the present tense like Jacqueline is doing now. I'm not exactly sure what she means by clients. I know Marcus had a lot of clients, but it wasn't like he was a lawyer or a therapist. I'm curious as to what he was doing for all these "clients" and under what pretense he was finagling them out of their money, but I've always tried to stay out of Marcus's business affairs. Beyond accepting a loan from him and making my payments to him every month, I kept my nose out of his dealings.

"I'm sorry. I don't have any information for you. Are you sure you don't want to stay and have a bite? We're brewing some raspberry iced tea as we speak."

"Thank you, Halia, but I really have to go. I've already gotten one phone call from a client Marcus was supposed to meet this morning, and there may be more. On top of handling his dealings, I'm teaching a yoga class later this afternoon and have two personal training clients of my own after that. If Marcus doesn't get in touch with me soon, I'm not sure what to do."

"I wouldn't worry about it too much," I lie. "He's bound to turn up in a little while. He probably just lost track of time."

"Let's hope so," she says. "It was nice to see you. Can I take a rain check on that tea?"

"Of course."

"And you know you're always welcome at any of my classes." She looks me up and down. "I do a Pilates for beginners class two nights a week."

"I'll keep that in mind," I lie. I barely know what Pilates is, but I know enough to know I'm not interested.

As Jacqueline leaves the restaurant, I think about how, very soon, she's going to learn that she's lost her brother. I also think about how I'm not sure she'll be that upset to hear the news. I've never gotten the feeling that she's terribly fond of him. In fact, there were times, like today, when I've sensed animosity toward him—the way she rolled her eyes when she spoke of him and Régine or talked about the real reason her brother goes to church. Jacqueline may be snobbish and uptight, but she's got a good head on her shoulders. Much like me, she's one of the few people who are able to look past Marcus's charm and good looks to see the fiend underneath. For all I know, she hit him over the head with my frying pan and was just over here this morning trying to look innocent.

CHAPTER 16

Missing dead body or no missing dead body, I have a restaurant to run. While it would be nice to have time to stew about the implications of a murderer on the loose, there are water glasses to be filled, cornbread to bake, and sweet tea to brew. It's Tuesday afternoon, and the lunch rush is just getting started. As usual I'm running around like a chicken with its head cut off—seating patrons, checking in with tables, making sure the kitchen operations are running smoothly, etc., which takes my mind off Marcus. I just can't think about him anymore. I keep telling myself that his body will turn up soon enough. And, if it doesn't, Jacqueline will file a missing person's report. One way or another, an investigation will be started, and the police can get down to business. Maybe it's better that someone moved the body—the farther away from my restaurant Marcus is found, the less chance of anything about this situation being connected to me and Wavonne. The only thing that makes sense is that the murderer moved Marcus . . . maybe to buy some extra time before any police involvement. But how did he or she know that Marcus had already been carted out of the restaurant by Wavonne and me? It really scares me to think that someone may have been watching us as we dragged a corpse along the alley. Then again, maybe the murderer came back after we left just to make sure Marcus was dead, found the restaurant locked, and searched the area until he or she came upon Marcus out back.

I try to lay to rest thoughts of Marcus as I carry a pan of cornbread out to a four-top where three men in suits are seated on a lunch break from work.

"Good afternoon, gentlemen. I hope Darius is taking great care of you." I set the pan on the table. "Be careful. It's hot."

For a brief period I stopped serving my cornbread in the cast-iron pans. They're heavy and hard to clean, and occasionally I get customers who touch the searing pans and burn themselves. But when I started baking the bread in sheets, cutting it into slices, and serving it in baskets, I got so many questions about what happened to the cast-iron pans and comments about what a nice presentation they made, I decided to bring them back.

"Thank you," says one of the men while the others at the table nod.

"My pleasure."

I turn toward the kitchen, and I'm almost out of earshot when I barely overhear their conversation. I can't make out exactly what they're saying, but I hear the words "dead" and "body" and "pond."

My antennas go up, and I immediately grab a pitcher of water to have an excuse to go back to the table.

"I don't know. There were four police cars over there. When I stopped at the traffic light, I asked one of the by-standers what was going on, and she said they had pulled a body out of the pond," I hear one of the gentlemen say as I top off water glasses that are almost full to begin with.

"What's all this?" I ask as if I'm just generally curious. I figure if you hear people talking about pulling a body out of a pond, it doesn't sound suspicious to inquire further about their conversation.

"Apparently the cops found a dead body over in the pond at the entrance to Wellington Acres."

Wellington Acres is a newer housing development down the street from the restaurant. As you drive into the neighborhood, Wellington Lake sits to the left, but as my customer said, it's really more of a pond. It houses a small fountain that seems to be broken more than it's working, but it's pretty when it's in operation. There's a jogging trail around it and sometimes people picnic on the perimeter. I've never seen anyone swim in it. I'd be surprised if it's more than three or four feet deep.

"Really?"

"Yeah. The woman I talked to said it was a black man in a full suit and tie."

My breath quickens, and I notice a slight tremor in my hands as I hold the water pitcher and hope the men at the table don't notice. The news rattles me, but I also experience a sense of relief that Marcus has been found . . . assuming it's him . . . it *has* to be him.

"A news crew arrived just as I drove off. I'm sure there'll be more details on TV later."

"I hope it was some kind of accident. You hate to hear of things like that so close to home." I can't think of anything else to say, so I tell them to enjoy their lunch and try to gracefully walk away.

TV. TV. I need to get to a TV. Once again I'm wishing I had one in the restaurant.

It's eleven forty-five. The local news will be on in fifteen minutes. I find Laura in the kitchen and tell her I need to run a quick errand.

"Is everything okay?" she asks, a genuine look of concern

on her face. It's not unusual for me to leave the restaurant now and then, but it is rare for me to do it during peak hours.

"Yes. Fine. I won't be gone long. You can hold down the fort?"

"Sure."

When I get out to the parking lot and inside my van, I'm not sure where to go. I can't run home to catch the news. Momma will be there, and me coming home in the middle of the day will take more explaining than I have the energy for. Fast Freddie's has like a hundred TVs, but they don't open until three and, besides, I can't very well go have a beer at Fast Freddie's, only three doors down from Sweet Tea, after leaving in the middle of the lunch rush saying I have to run an errand.

Think, Halia, think. Most restaurants have TVs these days, but they're likely to be broadcasting the national cable news channels, which won't be covering a local story like this. There's a Sears that's only about twenty minutes away. I think they have an electronics section. If I hurry, I can get there shortly after the twelve o'clock news starts.

I point the van toward the parking lot exit and head to Sears. Traffic is light this time of day, and I manage to get there in less than twenty minutes. When I get inside the store, I look up and scan for the electronics section. I see it in the far right corner and quickly walk in that direction.

Jackpot! I think to myself as I see the wall of flat screens. Two of them are broadcasting the local news on Channel 4. I pretend I'm shopping for a television and hear one of the anchors speaking of a water main break near Logan Circle in the city.

"Can I help you with anything?" a salesperson asks me from behind.

"No, thank you. I'm only looking at the moment."

"Okay. Let me know if you need anything."

He walks away, and I continue to act like I'm reading specs about the televisions while keeping my ears focused on the sound of the TV closest to me. There's talk of construction of a shopping center being delayed due to traffic concerns and something about a D.C. council member who may have granted favors to a friend in the form of government contracts. Finally, ten minutes into the broadcast I see a photo of Wellington Lake appear next to the anchorwoman's head.

"In other news today, the body of a deceased African American man was found in Wellington Lake, a small lake that sits at the entrance of Wellington Acres, a housing development in Prince George's County. Police say the man was in a suit and tie. He was five feet nine inches tall with a shaved head. According to police reports, he did not have a wallet or any identification on his person, which has led police to suspect robbery as a potential factor in his death. Authorities are urging anyone with information that may be helpful in identifying the man or the circumstances surrounding his death to contact the Prince George's County Police Department."

"That's it!?" I actually say out loud before I can stop myself. *A man is dead and that's all we get? A thirty-second blurb on the news.*

I storm out of the store, convinced that if it were a white man found in a lake in Montgomery County it would have been the lead story of the day. I get back in the van feeling like this little boondoggle had been a complete waste of time.

Now what? I wonder to myself. *More waiting.* I just hope that Régine or Jacqueline, or someone else who has noticed that Marcus is missing, managed to have the TV turned to the local news and caught the minuscule story so they can identify Marcus's body.

CHAPTER 17

It's been four days since Marcus was killed, and even though his body was found yesterday, it still seems that aside from the murderer, Wavonne, and me, no one knows he's dead. I keep waiting to get the news from someone and have been thinking about how I should react to hearing it. Should I try to have an emotional reaction or accept the news with subdued grief? Either way I need to pretend to be surprised, but not so surprised as to go overboard. Regardless of how I decide to feign that I'm just hearing about Marcus's death, I trust myself to act appropriately. Wavonne, on the other hand, is a different story.

"Have you thought about how you're going to react when you get the news that Marcus is dead?" I ask Wavonne. We're in my van, but she's driving. She asked to borrow it on her day off, so she could use it to make a few extra dollars delivering phone books. I decided to come along while she picks up the books, so I can chat with her and see where her head's at around all of this . . . and make sure she has, and will continue to keep her mouth shut about our activities the night of the murder. I also want to coach her on how to react when she gets the news of Marcus's death.

"What's wrong with you, Halia? I already know he's dead."

"No. No. I mean when someone tells you the news. You're going to have to act like it's a surprise."

"Don't you worry about me. I'll give a performance worthy of an Oscar."

That's what I'm afraid of. "I think it might be best to keep it low-key, Wavonne. If you act crazy with grief, it will look suspicious."

"I ain't gonna act all crazy. But don't you think I can't shed a fake tear or two if I wanna?"

"Just don't go overboard. I don't want you screaming and carrying on like Aunt Faye at a funeral." Our aunt Faye shows up to any and every funeral she can and puts on a show worthy of an admission fee. Between the weeping, the howling, and the occasional fainting spell, she always manages to make someone else's death all about herself. Everyone (well, everyone but me and Momma, who just roll our eyes from the sidelines) rushes to her side to comfort her. "There goes Faye . . . drama, drama, drama," Momma would say to me about her sister as we watched her antics. "She needed to be the center of attention when we were kids, and she needs to be the center of attention now."

"I ain't gonna act like that ol' fool."

"I hope not, Wavonne. The less attention we draw to ourselves, the better. Keep it quiet and dignified," I say, before adding, "You haven't told anyone about us moving the body, have you?"

"Oh *yes,* Halia. I just went and told everyone I know. I posted it to my Facebook page."

"All right, all right. I'm sorry. But forgive me for being concerned. We could get in a lot of trouble if anyone found out what we did. *A lot* of trouble, Wavonne. I just want to make sure you understand that."

"You been beatin' it into my head for four days now, Halia. I get it. You think I wanna go to jail? I know what happens to pretty, voluptuous girls like me in jail. I ain't interested in being no girlfriend to no big-assed heifer named Maxine."

Wavonne pulls into the parking lot of a small building in an industrial park. There are signs directing cars where to go to pick up phone books. Supposedly there was a training about delivering the books last night, but Wavonne was allowed to opt out since she participated last year. I'm proud of her for taking some initiative to earn some extra money, and I have to admit, somewhat surprised.

I watch as Wavonne gets out of the van, hands some paperwork to an attendant, and heads around to the back of the vehicle to open the hatch. Two men start filling the back of the van with phone books. I'm always hauling around stuff for the restaurant, so I usually have the seats folded down, and I took the back one out altogether a few years ago, which makes for plenty of room to stack phone books. As they continue to pile up, I wonder how long it's going to take Wavonne to deliver them all. It gives me some hope that maybe somewhere underneath that wig and all that makeup is a work ethic.

"Looks like your entire day off is accounted for," I say once we're back on the road. "How much are they paying you to deliver all these?"

"A hundred and fifty dollars."

"Seems like a lot of work for a hundred and fifty dollars," I say. If Wavonne would hustle and take on a few more tables she'd make about that working a shift at Sweet Tea.

"I guess."

"Okay. Well, I need you to drop me at the restaurant before you make the deliveries."

"I know. I'm working today, too. We'll head back there shortly."

"You're working today? At Sweet Tea?" I hadn't looked at the schedule, but I assumed she was off to make her deliveries. "If you're working today, when do you plan to deliver all these books?" I'm eying the paperwork one of the men who loaded the van handed her with the pages and pages of addresses awaiting their yellow pages.

"You just mind your bidness, Halia."

We travel for a few minutes while I continue to look at the list of addresses, and, when I look up, Wavonne's pulling into the recycling center in Upper Marlboro.

"What are we doing here?"

"Like I said, Halia, mind your bidness."

She stops in front of one of the paper recycling bins, gets out, and pops the back hatch. I watch her in the mirror for a moment before I get out of the van myself.

"What are you doing?!" I ask as she starts grabbing phone books out of the back of the van and begins throwing them in the recycling bin.

"What's it look like I'm doin'?"

I stand there for a moment as I watch in disbelief as she grabs phone book after phone book and tosses them in the bin.

"You didn't think I was actually goin' to trek all over PG County dumpin' phone books on people's doorsteps, did you?"

"What's going to happen when people call and complain about not getting their books?"

"Who you think is gonna complain? Who uses a damn phone book anymore? What do you do with the phone books that get left on our doorstep? You throw them on the recycling heap at the curb, that's what you do. I'm just speedin' up the process."

I don't approve of what's she doing, but she does have a point.

"You gonna help me or what?"

I sigh and take a long breath. Then, before I have a chance to answer, Wavonne steps into the van, picks up a book, and tries to hand it to me. I just look at her and leave my arms by my side.

"Don't get all high and mighty with me, Halia Watkins. Need I remind you of what I helped you with recently?"

"Fine," I say and accept the books as she hands them to me and start flinging them into the bin. We go about this for several minutes, and when we're almost finished, I notice a BMW pull up behind us. It's a shiny gold color and looks familiar. And we're not talking tan or sparkling beige—we're talking *gold*. The car is the same color and sheen of that gold foil they use to wrap chocolate coins. When the driver opens the door and steps out, I recognize Jacqueline. She doesn't see me at first and walks around to the trunk of the car, pops it open with her remote, and lifts a large cardboard box filled with papers. She hurries over to the Dumpster, and after realizing that the box will not fit through the openings on the side, she lifts it over her head and lets in fall into the Dumpster from the top. I catch myself starting to giggle. The sight of Jacqueline in her fancy clothes and four-inch heels hauling around a box at a refuse center is something to behold. It's not until she's heading back to her car that she sees Wavonne and me. I can see her hesitate for a moment, as if she's wondering if she can get away with pretending not to see us.

"Hello," I call over to her, not giving her the chance to ignore us.

"Hi, Halia," she responds, clearly embarrassed to be seen doing something that resembles manual labor. She nods at Wavonne, who's still inside the van.

"Can you believe I had to do this myself? Marcus's cleaning lady usually handles the recycling, but I guess Marcus wasn't there to let her in this morning, so she went home. I needed to get the home office tidied up for a meeting Marcus has tonight. I hope he comes back from whatever nonsense he's been up to by then."

"Still no word from him?"

"No. This isn't like him to be out of touch for so long.

And quite frankly, it's annoying me. I've got papers he needs to sign, and clients keep calling me looking for him."

"Have you thought about contacting the police?"

"If he doesn't turn up today, I may have to, but I'm not sure it's the best idea to get the police involved. The last thing Marcus needs is them poking around in his business. . . ." She lets her voice trail off as if she's said too much. "Not that Marcus has anything to hide," she adds, but the look in her eyes tells me she knows (and she knows that I know) that Marcus has plenty to hide. "He's just very private."

"Of course," I say. "I don't think *anyone* wants the police poking around in their business. I'm sure you'll hear from him soon enough anyway," I lie, thinking how Marcus isn't the only one with something to hide.

She's about to say her good-byes when she sees the remaining phone books in the back of my van.

"What are you two doing with all those phone books?" she asks.

"Nothin'," Wavonne says defensively. "Just recyclin'. Bein' green and all that jazz."

Jacqueline flashes a condescending smile. "If you say so. You two have a good day."

She gets back into her car, and I'm reminded of how much she hates it. I don't know if Marcus bought it for her or just lets her use it as sort of a company car, but I overheard her talking on the phone a while back about how tacky a gold BMW was and questioning why Marcus didn't let her pick the car out herself or at least get her something more dignified and elegant. "A gold BMW is so *PG County*," I heard her say into the phone as if she wasn't born and raised in the hood with the rest of us.

As she drives off, I start to wonder about her as I've been wondering about everyone since the night of the murder. Could she have been the one to kill Marcus? They might have been siblings, but while Marcus did seem to have a certain fondness for Jacqueline, he was a demanding boss and often dismissive with her. I'm not sure I've ever heard Jacqueline say a positive thing about Marcus, and she was probably on a fresh low from Marcus making her track down two hundred ears of corn the day he was killed. Did he make a final demand of her the night he was murdered? Did Jacqueline snap, grab a frying pan off the counter, and whack him with it in a fit of rage? She did say she was the last one with him at the restaurant, and she certainly had the strength to hit him hard and maybe even move his body on her own. She's very fit and just lifted a heavy box of paper over her head like it was it nothing.

All these thoughts are milling about in my head until Wavonne brings me back to the task at hand.

"You gonna stand there starin' off into space or you gonna help me get rid of the rest of these buggers?" She hands me another book.

I take it and throw it in the bin.

RECIPE FROM HALIA'S KITCHEN

Halia's Extra Light and Fluffy Belgian Waffles

Ingredients

2 cups all-purpose flour
3 tablespoons sugar
2 teaspoons baking powder
½ teaspoon salt
⅛ teaspoon ground nutmeg
¼ stick melted unsalted butter
½ cup sour cream
1½ cups whole milk
4 large eggs
½ teaspoon vanilla extract

- Whisk together the flour, sugar, baking powder, salt, and nutmeg in a large bowl.

- Add butter, sour cream, milk, 2 eggs, and vanilla extract to dry ingredients and mix using an electric mixer at medium speed until smooth.

- Separate whites from remaining 2 eggs. Discard yolks. Whip egg whites until stiff peaks form and fold into mixture.

- Lightly brush a preheated Belgian waffle iron with cooking oil. Pour in enough of the mix so that the batter just barely

fills the bottom of the iron. Cook according to your manu-
facturer's instructions.

Six Servings

Note: For best results use a Belgian waffle maker with a 180-
degree rotating function. Immediately rotate the waffle grids
after filling with batter.

CHAPTER 18

Wavonne and I have only been back from our little phone book jaunt for a few hours when I step out of the kitchen at Sweet Tea and see a tall man in a pair of khakis and a navy blue blazer talking with Jacqueline and Laura. From the looks on their faces, I can tell the conversation is serious.

I approach them, and Jacqueline's eyes turn toward mine. "It was him. The body they pulled from the lake—it was Marcus." She's not crying, but there is a look of anguish in her eyes.

"What? What are you talking about?" I ask, as if I have no idea.

"Marcus. The police found him over in that little lake by Wellington Acres. He's dead. After we talked I decided to call the police. I've just come from identifying the body." Again, she doesn't sound frantic or distressed. She seems more cold and spacey, like she's in shock.

I narrow my eyebrows as if I'm processing what she's saying. Before I have a chance to speak, Wavonne opens her big mouth.

"What? Marcus is dead!?" she says, raising her voice. "When? How? I don't believe it! I just don't believe it!" she adds and starts sniffling for effect. I can tell she's trying to force tears. She's doing exactly what I was afraid she'd do. She's going all *Real Housewives of Atlanta* drama queen on me and trying to pull out a show-stopping performance. Wavonne and Marcus were not close. Her acting like a grieving widow over the news of his death will just seem peculiar.

"Wavonne, baby. Let me take you in the back. You need to sit down."

"I don't need to sit down, I—"

I gently but firmly pull her by the shoulders toward the back of the restaurant before she has a chance to continue her charade.

"I'll be right back," I say to Jacqueline as I guide Wavonne to the break room, which, fortunately, is empty.

"Would you knock it off?! Why are you out there acting crazy in front of everyone? You and Marcus were little more than casual acquaintances. Why on earth would you behave like you lost your best friend? Are you trying to get both of us thrown in jail?"

"I was acting like I was upset that Marcus has been killed."

"Upset is one thing, but you were about to take it too far. We've talked about this. We don't want to do anything that will draw attention to us. We should act the way we really feel. Neither one of us was a fan of Marcus, but we didn't want to see him dead, either. Of course, we're sad for the loss of a human life, but don't overdo it, Wavonne."

"Okay. Slow your roll, Halia. We'll do it your way."

"Now you stay here while I go back out there and find out what everyone knows."

I leave the room, and barely ten seconds pass before Wavonne defies my order and appears in the main dining area. My God, she's worse than Otto, the dachshund I had growing up. Just like Otto, Wavonne can't stand the thought that she might be missing anything. I swear if I'd locked the break room door, she would have started squealing and scratching at the door just like Otto, as well.

"Keep your mouth shut," I say in a low voice after whipping my head around to look at her.

When I return to Jacqueline, I put my hand on her shoulder. I feel like I should hug her, but I'm not sure it would be a welcome gesture. Jacqueline is not a huggy type of person.

"I'm so sorry, Jacqueline. What happened?"

"I don't know," she says flatly. "He's been gone without a word for days, so I finally decided to call the police. By the time I called and reported him missing, they had already found the body and put two and two together. As far as anyone seems to know, no one has seen him since he was here for dinner on Saturday night. I didn't think to look when I was here the other day, but we checked when we drove in, and his car is still in the parking lot.

"Everything was fine when I left him here about twelve thirty. Did anything seem out of the ordinary to you Saturday night, Halia?"

The unknown man with Jacqueline turns to me as if he'd like to know the answer to that question, as well. I suspect he's with the police department even though he's not in uniform. I know a lot of the police officers in the area. They have lunch here, patrol the parking lot, and stop in here and there for coffee or sodas on the house, but I don't think I've ever met the gentleman here with Jacqueline.

"No. Everything seemed fine. As you know, we left before you did." I look at the man in the blazer. "It was late, and he was still talking business with his guests, so Wavonne and I asked him to lock up. We left shortly after midnight."

"You're the owner of this restaurant?" the man asks.

"Yes. Halia Watkins," I respond and extend my hand.

"Nice to meet you, Ms. Watkins. I'm Detective Hutchins. So who was still here with him when you left?"

I'm not sure if he's asking me or Jacqueline, so I go ahead and respond. "Gosh. Let me try to remember. He had five guests with him. They filled a six-top. Other than Jacqueline, there was a casually dressed black man, a young white couple, and Régine, his girlfriend."

"I set up the dinner for Marcus," Jacqueline says. "Charles Pritchett was the man by himself at the table. He was one of Marcus's business contacts. Marcus was working on some deals with him. The white couple is married. They're very young; Josh and Heather, but I forget their last name. I'm sure I have it in my records. Marcus and Charles were meeting with them about the mortgage program."

"The mortgage program?" Detective Hutchins asks.

"Yes. Charles is the head of a company . . . or at least the head of their operations in this area. It's called Reverie Homes. People make investments in his company, and then he uses the returns to pay off their mortgages in just a few years."

Detective Hutchins and I exchange curious looks before he asks, "Pay off their mortgages in just a few years?"

"Yes. I've only attended one of his seminars, but some people there said they had their entire mortgages paid off in seven years."

"How much do you need to invest?"

"The minimum is thirty thousand dollars."

"Thirty thousand dollars?!" I hear Wavonne shriek from behind me. "Where in hell did those people find thirty thousand dollars?"

"Some people take it out of their 401(k)s or borrow money from relatives."

"So they invest in Reverie Homes, who, in turn, takes over their mortgage payments?" I ask.

"Yes, and supposedly they pay it off really quickly."

"Supposedly?" Detective Hutchins asks.

"I don't ask questions. Marcus doesn't . . . didn't pay me to ask questions."

Neither Detective Hutchins nor I say anything, but I can tell we are both thinking the same thing: *This has scam written all over it!*

"And where does all this money come from to pay off the mortgages so quickly?"

"Allegedly, Reverie Homes invests it in ATM machines . . . you know, the ones they put in convenience stores and other places . . . and calling card kiosks, and some other things. The profits from those investments go to paying off investors' mortgages . . . or at least that's what Marcus says when he tries to get people to buy in to the program. I have the literature back at Marcus's office."

"I'd like to see that literature," Detective Hutchins responds. "So what do you mean when you say Marcus tried to get people to buy in to the program?"

"He recruited investors for Charles. Charles gave him a commission."

"So the young couple who was having dinner with Marcus and Charles . . . they were investors that Marcus recruited?" I ask.

"Yes."

"This doesn't seem at all suspect to you?"

"Suspect?"

"That someone is asking people to cough up thirty thousand dollars and then promising to pay off their mortgages in just a few years?" I inquire further.

"Of course it seems suspect. But like I said, I'm not paid to ask questions; however, I can see how some people do get enticed into the program. If you had been to one of Charles's presentations, you'd have seen, as well. The one I went to was at the Four Seasons in Georgetown. People go to an event at an expensive hotel . . . it adds credibility . . . people think the operation is legitimate. And there were so many people there who were already involved in the program, and they shared their stories. Many of them already had their houses paid off and had reinvested with new homes that they had traded up to . . . or so they said."

"Okay," Detective Hutchins says. "We've got some background on this program. I'm going to need to interview this Charles fellow and the two young people who were having dinner with him the night Marcus disappeared . . . and the girl-friend, as well. What was her name again?"

"Régine," Wavonne says before anyone else has a chance.

"Thanks. And your name is?"

"This is my cousin, Wavonne," I say.

"Nice to meet you, Wavonne. So you left with Ms Watkins Saturday night?"

Wavonne nods.

"Do you have a few minutes to talk?" he says to her, before turning to me. "And I'll need to speak with you, as well, Ms. Watkins."

"Sure. No problem. Let's go in the break room."

Wavonne leads the way with me and Detective Hutchins following. On the way down the hall, all I can think is: *Showtime.*

CHAPTER 19

"So you said nothing seemed unusual to you the night Marcus was last seen? No one at the table with him was acting strangely? Was he acting strangely?"

I hear Wavonne take a breath, and I speak before she has a chance to. "Maybe. The young couple did seem very cross with Marcus during the early part of the meal, but things seemed better by the time Wavonne and I left."

"Cross? How so?"

"That lil' white girl was all snarly with attitude," Wavonne says. "I could see it from clear 'cross the room. I bet she did it. I bet she killed him. You have to watch out for those skinny white girls. They may be tiny, but you get one of them mad, and, *ooh girl*, watch out!"

"She and her husband both seemed upset with Marcus. You could see that there was some tension between them. Darius, one of my servers, waited on them that night. I remember because he commented on how the young lady was speaking to Marcus in a hushed but terse voice."

"Really? I'll need to speak with him."

"He should be in for the evening service, or I can give you his phone number if you want to contact him before then."

"Thanks. I'll collect it from you before I leave," Detective Hutchins says. "Now, back to the night of Marcus's disappearance. Nothing else seemed out of the ordinary to you? You're sure?"

Wavonne tries to speak again, but once again, I beat her to it. "No. The other gentleman at the table, Charles I think Jacqueline said was his name . . . I hadn't met him before, but he was pleasant enough . . . and Régine has been in here numerous times with Marcus."

"And Régine? What can you tell me about her?"

"She a gold-diggin' heifer," Wavonne says.

"Wavonne—" I start to say, but Detective Hutchins lifts a finger to me.

"No. Please. Let her finish. You were saying."

"Now, I don't know if she's a murderer, but I will tell you she was in it with Marcus for one thing: his money. She's all about the Benjamins. 'Marcus, buy me this. Marcus, buy me that.' She ain't got no money of her own, and she was carryin' a Jimmy Choo bag last time she was in here. It's from last year but still musta cost a mint when he bought it for her. She's a hairdresser, and not even a good one, over at Salon Cuts in Kettering. She met Marcus when he came to pick up his old girlfriend, Jennie Becks, from gettin' her hair done. You see, my girl, Melva, told me that Jennie got a bad weave over at Madame Souls. Apparently poor Jennie never could do right by her hair. I've never met her, but Melva told me that, years ago, Jennie tried to relax it herself. Melva said she ended up looking like a buncha crows made a nest on her head, and—"

"Please, Wavonne," Detective Hutchins says. "Régine. Tell me about Régine."

"Yes. Régine. I'm sure she took one look at Marcus's fancy suit and BMW and did whatever she could to get her paws all up in that bidness. They've been together for a few months, but I think Marcus was cheatin' on her."

"Cheating on her? Why do you think that?"

"'Cause men like Marcus always cheat. And lately she wasn't spending Saturday nights with him. He said it was 'cause he had to get up early to take his momma to church, but I think he was out there gettin' it on with some other floozy."

"But you don't have any proof? You don't actually know he was cheating or with whom?"

"I don't need no proof. I know what I know. But no, I can't be sure who he was cheatin' with. Give me a few more weeks on the gossip mill at the beauty shop, and I'll get back to ya."

Detective Hutchins grins. "You do that," he says and turns his eye to me. "This Régine. You have a phone number for her?"

"I don't, but Jacqueline probably does."

"Okay. I'll check with her. Now, what else can you tell me about that night?"

"There's not much else to tell. Aside from Marcus's party, the restaurant had cleared out by eleven thirty, and they were the only ones here when Wavonne and I left."

"You left a table full of customers in your restaurant without any staff here? Who was going to close up?"

"Marcus."

"Do you normally let customers stay in the restaurant when no one else is here?"

"She do for Marcus. She owes him a shit loada money," Wavonne says, and even she realizes what a mistake divulging that information is as soon as the words leave her lips.

"What Wavonne means," I say, glaring at my cousin, "is that Marcus and I were business partners. He had an investment in the restaurant. So to answer your question, no, I don't normally let customers stay in the restaurant without any staff present, but Marcus is . . . was a business partner. Besides, I've known Marcus for years, and he has dinner meetings here all the time."

"What do you mean, he was an investor?"

"Just that. When I opened the restaurant, Marcus loaned me some money to supplement my savings and loan from the bank. I've been paying him back in monthly installments with interest ever since."

"How much money are we talking about here?"

"Well, that's getting awfully personal, Mr. Hutchins, don't you think?"

"A man has been murdered, Ms. Watkins. We need to follow up on every lead."

"Every lead? You're not accusing me of anything, I hope?"

"Just doing my job."

"It was a substantial amount, Detective Hutchins, but I've paid more than half of it back."

He looks at me as if he's sizing me up. And I don't like it. I don't like it one bit.

"When you and Wavonne left here, did you go straight home?"

"No, we stopped by the grocery store to pick up some things for my mother. From there, yes, we went straight home."

"This is true?" Detective Hutchins asks Wavonne.

Is he really asking Wavonne if what I'm saying is true?

"Ah-huh."

"Can anyone else substantiate your whereabouts?"

"I'm afraid I don't appreciate where this conversation is going, Mr. Hutchins, but I'm sure I have the receipt from the grocery store that night, and the clerk who checked us out would probably remember us. The receipt should have the time and date on it, and my mother may have heard us come in, but I'm not sure. She was probably asleep."

"Forgive the questions, Ms. Watkins. Like I said—"

Detective Hutchins is cut off by his phone ringing. "Hutchins here," he says into the phone and pauses. "Really? Okay. I'll be right there." He hangs up. "Thank you for your time, ladies. I'll be in touch if I need anything further."

"That's it? You start questioning us like we are suspects and now you're leaving?"

"I think you're off the hook. There's been a new development. Someone has been using Marcus's credit card all over town. There's bound to be some security camera footage of the assailant. I've got to run. Like I said, I'll be in touch if necessary."

CHAPTER 20

"That's odd," I say to Wavonne after Detective Hutchins leaves. "Who would be using Marcus's credit card?"

I notice Wavonne divert her eyes from me toward the floor.

"Who would be so stupid as to kill a man and then use his credit card?"

Wavonne is still looking at the floor.

"Oh, *Wavonne.* No!?"

She doesn't say anything.

"Please. Oh, *please,* tell me it's not you."

She looks at me. I can see the guilt in her eyes.

"Oh my God! That's what you were doing when you were lagging behind me after we left Marcus by the Dumpster? You said you were taking a last look at him. I can't believe it, Wavonne. You stole his wallet?!"

"I didn't *steal* anything, Halia," she finally responds. "He was dead. What was he gonna do with it?"

"Oh my God! What are we going to do? How could you do something so stupid!? Now we're both going to go to jail. And for what? What did you buy? A new Gucci bag and a pair of Manolos?"

Wavonne stays quiet. She stares at me with that "I'm just a silly child" look of hers. Like she doesn't know any better, and I shouldn't be mad at her.

"Where did you go, Wavonne? Where did you go charging stuff to Marcus's card?"

Her gaze goes to the ceiling as if she went to so many places it's going to take her some time to recall all of them. "I bought this Coach bag at Macy's . . . and I got a sweater and a pair of Juicy jeans there, too . . . oh, and a pair of heels . . . you'd love 'em, Halia . . . they're black with a bow on the toe and rhinestones along the side with—"

"I don't need the details of the shoes, Wavonne. Where else did you go?"

"I had some lunch at Applebee's and bought some skin care stuff from one of the kiosks at PG Plaza. I was gonna use it to pay for a new manicure yesterday, but I thought that might be a bad idea. You know . . . 'cause they know us at the salon."

"You thought *that* might be a bad idea. But using the credit card of a murdered man, whose body we illegally moved from the scene of the crime, in stores with security cameras and clerks who can identify you in a lineup seemed perfectly okay?"

"Well, when you put it that way . . ."

"You better hope Detective Hutchins doesn't remember that bag you have sitting on the table when he sees it on a list of the purchases charged to Marcus's card. Hand it over."

I noticed the purse yesterday, but I assumed it was a knock-off she'd bought from a street vendor or something.

"Hand it over? Why?"

"So I can get rid of it."

"Oh, *hail* no! I paid six hundred dollars for this bag."

"*You* didn't pay anything for it. A dead man's credit card

paid for it." I reach across the table, grab it, and dump out the contents. "Where's the wallet?"

Wavonne retrieves the wallet from the pile on the table and hands it to me.

"So Macy's, Applebee's, and a kiosk at PG Plaza? That's it?"

"Yes."

"Are you sure? Now is not the time to keep things from me, Wavonne."

"Yes. That's it."

"We better pray you are not on any security cameras. If you are, we are toast." I get up with the purse and the stolen wallet and walk into my office, which connects with the break room. It's really more of a storage closet with a desk and a file cabinet. In my business you don't have the luxury of grand offices. As anyone who owns a restaurant will tell you, any square footage that doesn't have a table for customers on it, is not making you any money. I run all the cards in the wallet through the shredder and toss the remains in a trash bag with the purse.

"I'm going to get rid of the evidence. If the police come back, don't answer any questions. In fact, I think it's best if you take the bus home. Don't answer the door if they come to the house. We'll need to get rid of the shoes and the jeans . . . and whatever other nonsense you bought later. This is a fine mess you've gotten us into, Wavonne."

"Me?! I was the one who wanted to call the police when we found Marcus. You're the one whose brainy idea it was to move him. You was the Lucy in this episode, Halia. I was just the Ethel."

"Which wouldn't have been a problem if you hadn't mucked up everything by stealing Marcus's wallet."

"I *told* you, I didn't *steal* it. It ain't stealin' when the owner's dead. He was—"

"Shut it, Wavonne. Just get home and don't answer the

door until we find out if they have you on any surveillance cameras."

I walk out of the break room as Wavonne gathers her things and make my way through the restaurant and out to the van. I've got to find a trash can far away to throw out Wavonne's purse, the shredded cards, and the wallet. Or maybe I should bury them . . . or burn them. As I back out of the parking space, I think about what a disaster this is, and how the whole thing will really blow up if the police are able to connect Wavonne to Marcus's credit card. I just hope the cops find out who really killed Marcus soon. But I went and made that more difficult by tampering with the crime scene. Other than the killer, Wavonne and I are the only people who know where Marcus was killed. The location may be crucial information that the cops just don't have.

When I reach a red light and stop the van, I begin to think of a way out of this predicament . . . a way to speed up the murder investigation. And then it occurs to me: *I* may have to be the one to find out who killed Marcus.

CHAPTER 21

I'm driving back to the restaurant thinking about how I just threw a six-hundred-dollar purse wrapped in a garbage liner in a Dumpster behind a 7-Eleven. I also threw out the wallet and its shredded contents in a trash can—this one a few miles away in front of the Walmart. It didn't seem like a good idea to pitch them together just in case either one is found. I'm glad to see there are no police around when I pull back into the parking lot. I won't be able to relax for a moment until I know Wavonne is not going to be arrested.

"Things okay?" Laura asks me when I step into the kitchen. I've been disappearing from the restaurant so much over the past few days, she's bound to be concerned.

"Yes. I just had to run a quick errand. Momma needed something."

"She's okay, I hope?"

"Yes, she's fine, but I've got to make a few phone calls. I'll be in my office if you need me."

When I get in my office, I close the door, but then I think about how I generally don't, and how now is not the time for me to be doing things that seem unusual, so I quickly open it again. I get seated at my desk and rest my chin on my thumb. I start to think back to the last night we saw Marcus alive and wonder if I can piece anything together that will give me some ideas as to who offed him. I think about the people at the table with him the night he was killed: the young couple that was so cross with him a few days earlier and seemed equally annoyed with him that night; his business associate, Charles, whom I know almost nothing about; Jacqueline; and Régine. I wonder if any of them have a motive for killing him. Of course, Marcus knew a slew of people, but his dinner companions seem like the most logical place to start in terms of identifying suspects. I wonder if that cockamamie mortgage program Jacqueline mentioned earlier has anything to do with his murder.

I swivel my chair around to face the computer and Google "Marcus-Rand-mortgage-program." Unfortunately, the search yields results for any Marcus Rand who has ever had a mortgage. I try "Marcus-Rand-mortgage-Maryland." Nothing useful comes up.

"What was the last name of his business associate?" I ask myself. I remember Charles being his first name, but I can't remember what Jacqueline said his last name was. I could call her, but I don't want her to know that I'm looking into this.

It's a long shot, but I type "Charles-mortgage-pay-off-quickly" into the search engine, and, bingo, the first site on the list is for Reverie Homes. The summary underneath the link to the site reads, "Recoup your investment and pay off your home IN FULL in as little as seven years." I click on the link and start perusing the site. It's a page personalized for Charles Pritchett, who apparently is "Vice President of Investor Relations" for the greater Washington, D.C., area. I see a photo of him in the top left corner, and I recognize him from the night in the restaurant. I click on the "About Charles Pritchett" button and read his bio. It's overflowing with words like "caring," "experience," "expertise," and "knowledge." It talks about how he's recruited more than two hundred home owners into the program, and how many of them are now mortgage free. I love how he uses the word "many" . . . such a relative term . . . it could mean two, or two hundred, or two thousand. Or, considering how shady this whole program appears, it may mean zero.

I continue to click around the site, which mostly confirms what Jacqueline already told us—home owners make a big investment up-front and then Reverie Homes helps them pay off their mortgage from the profits they make off their other lines of business. I'm about to close the site when I see a link that says, "Attend a Free Information Session." When I click on it, a calendar appears, and I see that Charles is hosting a forum tonight at the Gaylord Hotel at National Harbor. I'm thinking about how I just might attend that session this evening when I see Laura standing in the doorway.

"Detective Hutchins is here to see you," she says.

I feel my shoulders rise ever so slightly with tension, and tell Laura to let him know I'll be right out. I knew he'd be back, but I didn't think he'd be back so soon. As she walks away, I take a deep breath and compose myself.

"Detective Hutchins. What can I do for you?" I say when I reach the back of the dining room, where he's seated at a small table behind an almost empty glass of freshly brewed peach iced tea that Laura must have gotten for him.

"You said you left the restaurant with your cousin the night Marcus was last seen alive, correct?" he asks, bypassing any niceties.

"Yes. We left here shortly before midnight, stopped by the grocery store, and went home."

"Are you sure, Ms. Watkins?"

"Please. Call me Halia. And yes, I'm sure. Why?"

"We haven't been able to obtain any security camera footage of the person who used Marcus's credit card, but we traced one of the purchases as a handbag from the Macy's in Marlow

Heights. We found the clerk who rang up the purchase, and she remembered selling it . . . only because the woman who bought it complained that they didn't have the one she wanted in stock and then went on to criticize what a mess the store was, saying something to the effect of seeing flea markets that were better organized."

"What does any of this have to do with me?" I ask, ready to strangle Wavonne for behaving so stupidly. How could she be so foolish as to make a spectacle of herself when she was using a stolen credit card?

"The clerk's description of the woman who purchased the bag fits your cousin."

"How so?"

"The clerk said it was a twentysomething black woman with shoulder-length curly hair, flashy costume jewelry, tight clothing . . . and . . . well, an ample backside."

"A twentysomething black woman with curly hair, flashy jewelry, tight clothing, and a big behind? Are you kidding me? You just described half the hoochies in PG County."

"Maybe so, Ms. Watkins, but 'half the hoochies in PG County' didn't know Marcus Rand. Your cousin did know him, and she fits the description."

"Yes. She knew him, but not well, Mr. Hutchins. She only saw him when he came into the restaurant. I'm not sure I would even call them friends. And, frankly, Mr. Hutchins, I'm not sure I like where this conversation is going. You don't honestly think Wavonne had something to do with Marcus's murder?"

"I'm just doing my job, Ms. Watkins . . . Halia. Are you sure that was the extent of their relationship? They never dated or had a thing going?"

"A *thing* going?" I say, my irritation showing. "No. They never had a *thing* going, Mr. Hutchins." I don't like him talking about Wavonne as if she's a murderer. She may be lazy and stubborn . . . and steal credit cards off dead bodies, but she's no murderer . . . and if anyone is going to talk smack about Wavonne, it's going to be me. "Besides. Wavonne was with me all night."

"Are you positive? She couldn't have left the house quietly after you were asleep?"

"You've met Wavonne. Does she seem like the type of person who would be able to do *anything* quietly? So yes, I'm certain she didn't leave the house after we went to bed."

"I'll still need to speak to her. Do you know where she is?"

"No," I lie. "She'll be in for the dinner service at four thirty, but I need her waiting tables, not talking with you."

"I'll be back then. I'll try to keep it brief and let her get to work."

"Really, Mr. Hutchins, my cousin isn't the smartest girl in the world, and she may not be the hardest worker, but one thing I know for sure, she is not a killer."

"Let's hope you're right," Detective Hutchins says to me, nods, and turns to leave.

Once he's out the door, I scurry to my office and waste no time calling Wavonne.

"Hey," she says.

"Get in here now," I say with a sense of urgency. I'll need all the time I can get to coach Wavonne on how to answer Detective Hutchins's questions when he comes back in a few hours.

CHAPTER 22

I'm trying to act like I'm not worried, and I'm making an effort to keep my eyes off Wavonne and Detective Hutchins, who are seated in the back of the dining room. But when I do occasionally steal a glance, I see Wavonne talking way more than she should be. I told her to answer questions with simply a yes or no as often as possible and to stick to the story without adding any embellishments: *We left the restaurant around eleven forty-five. We stopped by the grocery store and have a receipt that showed we were there for almost an hour, and then we went straight home, and went to bed.*

Why are her lips moving so much if that's all she's saying? I think to myself.

I would have preferred to sit there with them, but Detective Hutchins asked to speak to her alone, and I thought it would look odd if I insisted. And yes, I did think about trying to find a lawyer to be present during the questioning, but again, I figured that would make Wavonne appear guilty. And honestly, Wavonne only needs to follow simple instructions about what to say. Even she can't screw up something so easy, can she?

I'm keeping busy checking in on tables and manning the

hosting station, when I see Detective Hutchins get up from his chair and extend his hand to Wavonne, who accepts it and gives it a quick shake.

"Everything go okay?" I ask Detective Hutchins as he heads toward the door.

"Fine. I'll be in touch if I need anything further."

"Are you sure you don't want to stay and have some dinner? Tonight's special is a butter baked chicken . . . the meat falls right off the bone."

I'm glad when he politely declines and says he has another appointment to get to.

When I see his car pull out and head toward the exit, I walk over to Wavonne, who is still seated with her phone in one hand and a glass of tea in the other as if she's a customer instead of an employee.

"So?"

Wavonne pauses from tapping the screen of her phone with her long red fingernails and looks up at me. "It went okay. He just axed me some questions about what happened the night Marcus was killed and what sorta relationship I had with him."

"*Asked* you. He just *asked* you."

"Yeah. That's what I said."

I roll my eyes and decide to save the grammar lesson for later. "What did he tell you?"

"I told him the truth. I ain't never done the dirty-dirty with Marcus."

"What did you tell him about the night Marcus disappeared?"

"Exactly what you told me to tell him. I told him we went by the grocery store on the way home, and went home, and went to bed."

"So what were you talking about all that time?"

"He asked me a lot of questions about what happened before we left the restaurant. He wanted to know if I knew anything about the people Marcus was having dinner with that night."

"What did you say?"

"I didn't know much about the couple at the table or about Marcus's friend, Charles. I told him what I knew about Régine—that she's Marcus's usual type . . . sort of hoe-baggish with big tits."

I wonder if Detective Hutchins suspects any of Marcus's dinner companions. If he knows something about them that I don't. If he knew that the murder happened here in the restaurant, he would definitely be more suspicious of them.

"You know, Wavonne, it might be nice if you'd get back to work. Darius has been covering your tables since Detective Hutchins got here."

Wavonne sighs at me, grabs her phone, and gets up from the table. As she walks away, I look at my watch and realize I've got to get moving if I'm going to make it to the Reverie Homes presentation that starts in less than an hour.

CHAPTER 23

I'm walking quickly from the parking garage to the Gaylord Hotel at National Harbor. Traffic was bad on the way over, so I'm running late. The presentation has probably already started, but if I move fast, I should only miss the first few minutes. Besides, it's not really the presentation I'm interested in. I mostly just want to grab a few minutes with Charles afterward and see what I can find out about him—how well he knew Marcus . . . how long he knew him . . . if there's anything in his eyes or his demeanor when he talks of Marcus that would lead me to believe there was some tension in their relationship.

When I get through the revolving door of the hotel, I'm taken aback by the size of the place. It's a huge building with a lobby and atrium the size of a small town. There are fountains, and trees, and even a life-sized house that serves as a gift shop. As Jacqueline said earlier, Reverie is definitely trying to send a message by holding their lecture here. People are more likely to think they are on the up-and-up and that cash is flowing when their events are held at places like this. If they had held the meeting in a Holiday Inn or a Best Western, it wouldn't inspire the same kind of confidence.

Once I've checked the daily schedule and found the room where the presentation is taking place, I scurry along a wide corridor until I find the gathering. I walk in, take a seat in the back, and see Charles in the front of the room. He has a clicker in his hand and is elaborating on a slide he has up on a large screen. He's one of those people who walks around while he presents and uses lots of hand gestures—no standing stiffly at a podium for this guy. The smile on his face is constant and, oddly, has both a charming and smarmy quality about it. He speaks loudly and with vigor. Everything about him says "salesman."

I listen as he talks about the program and clicks through his slick presentation, which makes all sorts of promises, but is short on detail and statistics. I hear about the "many, many, many" people who have quickly paid off their houses thanks to the Reverie Homes program. I hear about how an initial investment into the program will be returned fivefold through mortgage payment assistance. I hear about Mary Walker in Mount Rainer who paid off her house in just five years. I hear about Stephanie and Devon Mitchell who paid off their Greenbelt home in just seven years. What I don't hear about is how much the initial investment is or reference information for others in the program. And, while there are a few brief comments on how Reverie invests the money of people who join the program into ventures such as in-store ATMs and phone card kiosks, there's little mention about how these seemingly meager initiatives manage to earn enough profit to pay off what must be millions of dollars in home mortgages.

It seems like Charles is about to finish up his presentation when, for the first time since I walked in the door, I see the smile leave his face, and he stops speaking in midsentence. His eyes focus on the back of the room, and his expression goes from forced delight to trepidation. I and everyone else in the room turn to see what he's looking at, and there they are—the young couple who was having dinner with Charles and Marcus the night Marcus was killed. And they don't look happy.

"Have you gotten to the question-and-answer period of the evening yet?" the young lady asks in a heated tone. "Has anyone asked what the plan is when the checks from Reverie stop coming, and you're months behind on your mortgage, and the word 'foreclosure' starts getting tossed around?"

"Mrs. Williams," Charles says to the girl. He's regained his composure, and the smile, while not as bright, is back on his face. "If you'd take a seat, I'd be happy to discuss any questions you have after the presentation."

"So *now* you'll answer questions? You haven't answered a single one of my phone calls? Our main contact ends up dead in a pond, we're in debt to the tune of three hundred thousand dollars, the assistance we were promised has dried up, and you can't so much as call me back?! Have you told any of these people about that?" she asks. All the while, her meek-looking husband stands beside her, quiet as a mouse.

I see the looks on the faces of the people in the room. Mostly they are just awestruck. One woman gets up and is about to leave, but I think, although she now realizes what kind of racket is going on and must know better than to invest, she's decided she might as well stick around and watch the fireworks.

"Yes. We are experiencing some cash flow problems, Mrs. Williams. But, as we discussed at dinner a few days ago, we need you to be patient. We expect our investments to get back on track soon and produce additional profits. As soon as that happens, we will make up for any lost payments and get your mortgage back in the black. I promise."

"You promise?!" she says, her husband still silent beside her. "We are done with promises, Mr. Pritchett. We want our money back, so we can start putting it toward our mortgage and not lose our house."

"If you'll just calm down, Mrs.—"

"Calm down!? How calm would you be if you were out thirty thousand dollars and about to lose your home?"

Charles sighs and directs his attention to the audience. "Ladies and gentlemen, due to such a rude interruption, I believe we'll have to close the presentation early tonight. I assure you that the Reverie Homes program is sound, and any missed payments will be more than made up for in the near future. Please take some literature with you on the way out and call me if you have any questions."

What a quintessential salesman, I think to myself. The lid has been blown off his operation, and he's trying to salvage any clients on the off chance that one or two of them may still be naïve enough to invest with him. I'm relieved to see that not a single person takes any of his brochures as they exit.

After the audience filters out, whispering among themselves, Charles invites Mrs. Williams and her husband to sit down.

"I'm fine standing, thank you," she responds curtly, but her husband touches her on her back, gently prodding her to take a seat.

Charles grabs a chair next to them, moves it so it's facing them and takes a seat. I remain seated in the back of the room. Charles looks at me for a brief second with a "what are you still doing here?" look on his face, but says nothing. I know the polite thing would be to leave and give them some privacy, but I might pick up some important information related to Marcus's murder through whatever I'm able to overhear.

"Mr. and Mrs. Williams, I know you're anxious about the lack of payments going toward your mortgage lately, but, like any business, we occasionally experience cash flow problems. As we discussed last week, it's temporary. I promise you, the checks will resume soon, and we'll make up for any missed payments."

Charles has a natural calmness about him and a unique ability to respond to anger and hostility with a gentle demeanor that diffuses people. He's a wolf in sheep's clothing if I ever saw one, but his shtick seems to be working.

"How do I know that?" Mrs. Williams says back to him, in the most composed voice she's used all night. "How do I know you're not just buying time to skip town and leave us with no house and no money?"

"Would I be holding a presentation looking for new investors if I planned to skip town?"

Of course you would. More money to run off with, I think to myself as I pretend to be surfing the Internet on my phone.

"I need some kind of assurance, Mr. Pritchett. I . . ." she says, pausing for a moment and looking at her husband with disapproval. "*We* will not be taken for a ride. We've gotten the runaround from Marcus for months, and then he turns up dead . . . *murdered,* actually. His assistant said we would need to speak to you from now on about the program."

"Yes. I heard about Mr. Rand's unfortunate demise, but I assure you it has nothing to do with Reverie."

"When can we expect the first of many payments to start coming in again? I need a date."

"I'll need to check on that and get back to you."

"I want a date, Mr. Pritchett. I'll expect to hear from you first thing in the morning, and if I don't, I will start the process of finding a lawyer and sue you for everything you have . . . assuming you have *anything* at this point," she growls, gets up from her chair, and motions for her husband to follow her.

I see them walking toward me, and when they pass by, I get up and follow them out the door.

"Excuse me?" I call from behind, and they turn around. "Can I talk with you for a moment?"

They both look at me warily.

"You probably don't remember me. I'm Halia Watkins. I

own Sweet Tea. I believe you had dinner with Marcus at my restaurant a few days ago."

"Yes. We did. I remember you," Mrs. Williams says.

"May I ask your names again?"

"Heather. And this is my husband, Josh."

"It's nice to see you again. I'm sorry things aren't going well for you. I knew Marcus for a long time, and before he died he was trying to get me to invest with Reverie Homes, as well. I came tonight to find out some more information about the program. Honestly, I had planned to invest, but after tonight, clearly I'm reconsidering."

"I would do more than reconsider, if I were you."

"Would you two be willing to tell me a bit more about your experience? Maybe you could come back to the restaurant and have lunch . . . on me."

I figured it was better to convince them that I was only interested in investing in the program. If I told them I was really interested in what happened the night Marcus died and getting a better idea of what sort of relationship they had with him, I might scare them off . . . especially if they were, indeed, responsible for his death.

Josh is silent and looks to Heather for a response.

"I suppose we could. Believe me, you really don't want to get mixed up in all of this. It's been a nightmare."

"Any insight you have would really be appreciated. Why don't you come by Sweet Tea for lunch tomorrow? Around noon? You remember where it is?"

"Yes. We'll do our best to make it."

When they turn to leave, I make my way back to the ballroom and see Charles packing up his laptop and brochures.

"Not a great night, eh?"

"Not at all," he says back to me. "Do I know you from somewhere? You look familiar."

"We met when you had dinner with Marcus at my restaurant. Halia Watkins."

"Oh yes. Sweet Tea. Great place. I was so sorry to hear about Marcus. He was such a great fellow."

"Yes," I say. "It's all such a mystery. One minute he's enjoying my fried chicken and waffles, and, next thing you know, he turns up dead."

"Have the police figured out what happened?"

"I don't think so. At least I haven't heard anything."

"That's a shame."

"Yeah . . ." I'm trying to find a way to delicately begin questioning him, but it's just not coming to me. "Do you mind, Charles . . . if I ask you a few questions?"

"About?"

"Marcus. What the nature of your relationship was with him. How long—"

"How long did I know him? Did I like him? Did we have any quarrels? Where I went after I left the restaurant the night Marcus disappeared? Is that what you'd like to know, Ms. Watkins?"

I just look at him, unsure of what to say.

"I've already told the police everything. I left the restaurant shortly after Heather and Josh . . . probably about twelve fifteen or twelve twenty. From the restaurant, I went home. My wife can attest to my whereabouts."

"I'm sure she can."

"Is that why you came here tonight? To question me about Marcus's murder? What do you think you're going to be able to find out that the police haven't?"

"Actually no. That's not why I came here tonight. My understanding is that you and Marcus were just business partners. As far as I know, you have no clear motive for wanting him dead. I'm curious to know more about the program, and if you know of anyone . . . maybe one of the investors Marcus recruited, who would have a motive."

"I wouldn't call us partners. Marcus came to one of my presentations last year and asked a lot of good questions. He had a lot of charisma. I thought he would make a good salesman, so I talked to him about working under me to recruit new investors. He agreed."

"May I ask what the compensation structure was?"

"For each member Marcus recruited he got a commission from Reverie, and, because he worked under my guidance, I got a piece of that commission."

"How many investors did he recruit for you?"

"Two. The young rather testy couple that was just here and another client in Hyattsville."

"Well, the couple here earlier sure seemed mad enough to kill someone . . . the wife anyway. I'm not sure the husband would have the energy. Do you have the name of the client in Hyattsville?"

"I don't offhand. I can check my files and let you know, but don't you think you should leave the investigating to the police?"

"Oh. I'm not trying to trump the police. I guess I'm mostly just curious," I say before adding, "Thank you for your time, Mr. Pritchett."

He nods and returns to packing up his display table.

On the way back to my van, I think about him and whether he seems like someone who could commit murder. I didn't notice any tension or facial expressions that led me to believe he had any significant feelings (good, bad, or otherwise) about Marcus, but some people are better actors than others. Offhand, I can't think of any reason he would have wanted Marcus dead. In fact, Marcus would serve him better alive by scrounging up new clients for Charles to make a commission on. But I'm not ready to close the book on Charles.

Anything can go wrong in business dealings between people. I'll start with an Internet search on him, and see if I turn up anything of interest. But, honestly, I'm more interested in Heather and Josh, and maybe this other client in Hyattsville. Heather certainly seemed to have a lot of anger, and Josh appears to be afraid of her, which leads me to believe she might be unstable. It's plausible that she killed Marcus with a severe blow to the head, but there is no way she could have come back and moved Marcus's body. She's a petite woman, and, even though Marcus wasn't a really big man, Wavonne and I struggled to move him together. But she could have moved him with the help of her husband, who appears to do whatever she tells him to do. I hope they keep our lunch date tomorrow. I have a lot of questions for them. With any luck, they'll have a lot of answers.

RECIPE FROM HALIA'S KITCHEN

Halia's Sweet Corn Casserole

Ingredients

10 fresh corn cobs
12 ounces Muenster cheese (usually one and one half bricks)
1 teaspoon crushed red pepper ($\frac{1}{2}$ teaspoon if you don't want it too spicy)
2 eggs (beaten)
$\frac{1}{4}$ teaspoon salt
$\frac{1}{4}$ teaspoon black pepper

- Preheat oven to 400 degrees Fahrenheit. Generously grease an 8-inch glass pie pan.

- Remove corn from cobs and mince in food processor for about five seconds using the multipurpose blade.

- Pour minced corn into large bowl. Holding corn in place with large spatula, tip bowl over sink to drain any pooled moisture.

- Grate Muenster cheese in food processor using the shredding disc. (Cheese will grate more easily if you place it in the freezer for an hour prior to grating.)

- Reserve $\frac{3}{4}$ cup shredded cheese and add remaining cheese to the minced corn.

- Add crushed red pepper, eggs, salt, and pepper. Stir until well blended.

- Pour mixture into prepared pan and bake at 400 degrees for 50 minutes or until top browns.

- Cover casserole with foil, lower heat to 325 degrees, and bake for an additional 50 minutes.

- Sprinkle top of casserole with reserved cheese immediately after removing from oven.

- Let set for 20 minutes prior to serving.

Eight Servings

Note: People always ask if they can use frozen or canned corn for this recipe. My response is always the same: "Of course you can . . . if you don't want it to be any good."

CHAPTER 24

"That mean white girl and her husband are here," Wavonne says to me, poking her head through my office door.

"Did you get them seated?"

Wavonne nods.

"Tell them I'll be right out."

I close the file I'm working on and get up from my chair. When I reach the dining room I see Heather and Josh at a table near the front windows. I wave and smile as I approach.

"Thanks so much for coming," I say and pull out a chair for myself. "Have you had a chance to look over the menu? Lunch is on me."

"Thank you," Heather says with a coldness in her voice. "But that's really not necessary."

"I insist," I say while Darius appears with two iced teas for the couple.

"Is that the passion fruit tea we have on special today?" I ask as he sets the glasses on the table.

"None other." He smiles at Heather and Josh. "Are you ready to order or do you need a few more minutes?"

"This fried chicken salad sandwich sounds really good,"

Josh says to Heather. I'm not sure, but I think this might be the first time I've heard his voice.

"You'll love it. We make it with fried chicken instead of roasted chicken, so you get all the crispy breading mixed in there with some mayonnaise, sour cream, roasted pecan chips, a pinch of sugar, and a few other seasonings. It's a really popular item. We only serve it at lunch." I can always count on Darius to sell the hell out of my menu.

"Sold," Josh says with a smile. He has a friendliness about him that his wife lacks.

"On a croissant or honey wheat bread? Both are brought in fresh every day from Hot Buns Bakery down the street."

"A croissant, please."

"And for you, ma'am?" Darius asks Heather.

Heather looks up from the menu. "Do you have the corn casserole I had last time?"

"Afraid not," Darius replies. "That's an occasional special."

"We actually made it special for you," I say, trying to get Heather to warm up to me a bit before I grill her about the night Marcus was killed. "Marcus said you were a vegetarian."

"I think Marcus misunderstood. I do eat meat, but only when it comes from humane farms." She turns to Josh. "The fried chicken in that sandwich you just ordered probably came from a factory farm."

"Actually, Heather," I say, "all the chicken served here comes from a local farm near Frederick that raises them free range—they're outside most of the day. All the eggs we use come from another free range farm in Delaware."

"Told you, hooka'," I hear Wavonne say under her breath as she walks by the table.

"Really?"

"Yep. I get as many of my meats and animal products as possible from local humane farms. I like to know where the food I serve comes from. I toured a regular chicken farm . . . a 'factory farm' I guess you called it, on the eastern shore a few years ago and was horrified at what I saw. The very next day I started making calls to local farms."

Heather smiles, and I immediately sense a shift in her attitude toward me. Nothing bonds people more than a common cause or concern. "In that case, I think I'll have the chicken salad sandwich, as well . . . on a croissant, also."

"Sure. Those come with house-made potato chips. We'll have them right out to you."

"Are you going to have anything?" Josh asks me.

"I'm sure Darius will bring me a sandwich, too."

"He mentioned you bring in fresh baked bread every day?"

"We do. When I opened Sweet Tea I wanted to make everything from scratch—even the bread for my sandwiches, but bread making is very labor-intensive and time-consuming, especially when you factor in rising time for the dough. I eventually decided to compromise. I couldn't bear the thought of having institutional bread in plastic bags coming through the door, so I negotiated a deal with Hot Buns up the street. They make fresh croissants, honey wheat bread, and buns for our burgers every day. Laura, my manager, usually picks up the order on her way in each morning."

"You really have a commitment to quality," Heather says. "It's sort of refreshing."

"I try. I really do." I'm glad to hear some kind words from Heather and take them as my cue to dive in and get down to business. "So, do you two live nearby?"

"We're in Bowie."

"Nice. So you own a home there?"

"Not for long," Heather says.

"Yeah. It looks like Marcus may not have been on the up-and-up. Like I said, I was thinking about getting involved with the Reverie Homes program, but it sounds like that might not be such a good idea."

"I'd run away from the program as fast as you can, Ms. Watkins."

"Halia. Please."

"It was all a scam. Marcus took us for thousands of dollars, we've lost our savings, and now we'll likely lose our home."

Heather's demeanor has softened, but as she speaks I see something other than the usual anger in her eyes . . . sadness or maybe fear. She probably really isn't such an unpleasant person, but, more likely, someone who is scared senseless about losing her home.

"So many promises were made. We talked to people at one of the seminars who had their houses paid off . . . or at least said they did. And we met Marcus at *church*. We figured we could trust him."

"You go to the Church of Christ?" I ask with surprise. The Church of Christ, where Marcus takes his mother on Sunday, is almost exclusively black. It seems odd that a young white couple from Bowie would go there.

"No. We go to St. Pius. That's where we met Marcus."

"You met Marcus there?" I ask as it dawns on me that Marcus may have been going to churches all over town trying to find easy targets for this mortgage scheme.

"Yeah. He was there every Sunday. He was even a Eucharistic minister."

Oh, he was sly, that Marcus.

"He struck up a conversation with us at Bible study, and one thing led to another, and next thing I knew we were telling him about the house we'd just bought."

"Let me guess. He somehow managed to turn the conversation toward your mortgage payments."

"No. Not at all. He didn't mention it the first time we met,

or the second . . . or third. He never brought it up at any of
the Bible study gatherings or the few times we went out to
dinner afterward with him. He was building our trust."

"So when did he tell you about the program?"

"He didn't actually. He let us ask him about it. He invited
us over for dinner one night and just *happened* to leave some
literature about it lying around. Josh saw it on the kitchen
counter and asked about it," Heather says, narrowing her eyebrows at her husband. She seems to be implying that all of this
is his fault.

That cunning little shit, is all I can think. I look at the pair
across from me. Neither one of them can be a day over twenty-
five, and Marcus developed a friendship with them, played them
for fools, and set them up to lose their savings and their home.

"I was wary of the whole thing, much more so than Josh . . .
he's more trusting. But I agreed to attend one of the presentations, and so many people were there who spoke about investing in the program, and how they were now mortgage free.
Marcus somehow made it all make sense. We were such id-
iots."

"You said you invested thirty thousand dollars in the program?"

"*Threw away* thirty thousand dollars is more like it. At first,
the program delivered as promised and helped us pay the
mortgage down, but a few months ago the checks stopped
coming, and we can't make the payments without them. We're
facing foreclosure and financial ruin."

"So last Saturday, when you were here for dinner with
Marcus? What did he tell you then?"

"He was giving us the same song and dance as before, but
that time he brought reinforcements. Mr. Pritchett came with
him to tell us the same thing Marcus had been telling us for
months: that there had been a few setbacks with the company's

investments, but things were on the mend, and our payments would resume soon."

"That explains the tension at the table that night . . . and what a night it turned out to be. You know, that was the last night anyone saw Marcus," I say, realizing it wasn't the smoothest transition to talking about Marcus's death, but it was the best I could do.

"Yes. The police mentioned it when they questioned us."

"So they questioned you, too?" I figure mentioning that I was questioned as well will help me ease into asking them what they told the police. I can try to make it sound like I just want to compare experiences with them.

"Yes. We talked with them for over an hour."

"Really? What could they have talked to you about for so long?"

"They had a lot of questions about our relationship with Marcus. And then they actually started asking us where we went after we left the restaurant. If I didn't know better, I would think we were suspects in his killing."

I laugh awkwardly. "I felt that way, as well, when they questioned me. I think they are just talking with everyone who might have any information."

"I hope so," Heather, who's been doing all the talking at this point, says.

"So did you tell them the same thing I did—that after you left here you went home and went to bed?"

"Yes," Josh chimes in before Heather has a chance to speak. "Mr. Pritchett and Marcus's sister were still here when we left. We went home and went to bed. That's pretty much the whole story."

The way Josh uncharacteristically broke into the conversation and the "end of discussion" tone in his voice tells me that his words are so *not* "pretty much the whole story."

Heather shoots Josh a look like a mother might give a child who's spoken out of turn. "Yeah. We went home from here. It was late, and we were tired. Marcus had calmed me down some, but I was still pretty pissed off. When I got home—"

"When we got home," Josh says, interrupting Heather, "we pretty much just went to bed. And I wouldn't say we were pissed off . . . just concerned. Didn't you ask us here to talk about the Reverie Homes program?" Now Josh is the one sounding cold. He's trying to come across as firm, but you can tell it's out of character for him, and he mostly ends up sounding nervous.

"Yes, but I guess you've told me what I need to know. What was it you said? I 'should run away from the program as fast as I can?' "

"That would be my advice," Heather says.

Josh's tone has made it clear that my little question-and-answer period about the night Marcus was killed is over. He clearly does not want to talk about it, nor does he want his wife to talk about it. Now I guess the question is *why?*

When lunch arrives at the table, I decide to lay off the questions about the night Marcus died and just try to make polite conversation with them. I don't want to come on too strong, or I'll never get any useful information out of them. I ask them a few more questions about the mortgage program and tell them what I've heard about it. They tell me a little bit about their home and how much they love it and fear losing it. Otherwise, we mostly talk about general things like the weather and where we grew up, and who we like on *American Idol*. After chatting with them at length, I just can't believe that either one of them is a killer, but I do think they (or at least Josh) are keeping something from me about the night Marcus was bludgeoned on the head with one of my frying pans.

By the time lunch is over, all three of us are more relaxed. They decline dessert, but I insist they take some blueberry pie to go, so Darius boxes two slices for them. They offer to pay, but I refuse their credit card and decide to walk them out to their car.

"Thanks again for the wonderful lunch," Heather says as she puts her key into the trunk of their car, so she can put the boxed pie in there.

"You're more than welcome. I hope you'll come back," I say and, right before Heather goes to shut the trunk I get a whiff of a familiar smell . . . a very familiar smell indeed. *Why, I wonder to myself, is the scent of spiced rum mixed with dark chocolate coming from the trunk of Josh and Heather's car?*

CHAPTER 25

I swear I can still smell it—that spicy chocolate scent of Marcus's cologne. I hated it when he was alive, and I hate it even more now. The scent was still in my nose when I called Detective Hutchins as soon as I got back inside the restaurant. I asked him to come over, so I could share some important information with him related to Marcus's death.

"Hello, Halia," he says when he sees me at the host station.

"Detective Hutchins," I say. "Please, let's have a seat."

We take a seat at a two-person booth along the wall, and before I have a chance to ask, Darius shows up with two glasses of passion fruit iced tea.

"Are you hungry, Mr. Hutchins? May I offer you some lunch?"

"No. Thank you."

"Oh. Come now. You have to eat," I say, before turning to Darius. "Darius, would you bring us some cornbread and a sampler tray?"

"It's really not necessary."

"Who said it was for you?" I say with a laugh. "I have to eat, too. We'll share." I'm full from having lunch with Heather and Josh, but I want Detective Hutchins to feel comfortable and he doesn't strike me as the kind of guy who likes to eat alone.

"So what is it you wanted to talk to me about?"

I take a breath. "Okay, I know this sounds strange, but I think I know who killed Marcus." As the words come out of my mouth, I realize that I don't believe them to be true. In my heart I just don't think that Heather or Josh is a murderer. I can't see a young lady who turned down my fried chicken salad sandwich until she was assured the chickens came from a humane farm or a guy who's as timid as Josh killing a man. After a couple of hours with them, I feel in my gut that they did not do it. But then how do you explain a very distinct smell that I've only ever attributed to Marcus, coming from their trunk a few days after he was killed?

"Really?" he says with what appears to be an amused expression on his face . . . a sort of 'okay, so tell me, silly lady, who do you think the mean old killer is?' smirk.

"Well, maybe I don't *know*, but I do have some information that might be . . . *is* important."

"And that is?"

"You interviewed Heather and Josh Williams, right? The young couple that had dinner with Marcus the night he was killed."

"How do you know he was killed that night? His body didn't turn up until three days after that. *I* know he was killed that night . . . blunt force trauma to the head was the cause. But *I* have the coroner's report, which estimated the time of death. I'm curious as to how you knew that?"

I want to kick myself for making such a stupid mistake. "It just seemed like a safe assumption."

Detective Hutchins eyes me distrustfully as if he knows I've been keeping information from him all along, and there's a moment of silence between us before I speak.

"So now that you've told me he did indeed die on Saturday night, I'm telling you that on that same Saturday night he was wearing really strong cologne. It had a very distinct smell. He even told Wavonne and me that it was a custom scent he'd had developed just for him."

Detective Hutchins waits for me to get to the point.

"Heather and Josh came to the restaurant today for lunch. I walked out to their car with them. And when Heather opened the trunk, I swear I smelled Marcus's cologne."

Detective Hutchins lets out a quick laugh. "You think you know who killed Mr. Rand based on a certain fragrance coming out of someone's trunk?"

"It wasn't just any fragrance, Detective. It was *Marcus's* fragrance coming out of their trunk a few days after *Marcus,* a person they had a known conflict with, was found dead in a lake."

He scratches the side of his head and studies me for a moment as if he's trying to figure out if I'm nuts. "You really think it was a smell unique to Marcus?"

No, I dragged you all the way over here because I smelled some freakin' Jean Nate. "Yes. Yes, I do."

He seems to ponder what to do with my information for a moment and finally sighs as if I'm wasting his time. "I'll check it out, Ms. Watkins," he says, and I honestly can't tell if he really will or not. "This wouldn't be an attempt to deflect attention from your cousin, would it? We don't look kindly on people leading us on wild goose chases."

"Of course not, Detective. Wavonne has nothing to hide."

"What about you?"

"What about me?"

"Do you have anything to hide?"

"I'm an open book, Detective Hutchins," I say. *Well, except for that chapter about me dragging a corpse out of my restaurant.*

"If I may ask, what did you think would happen with the money you owed Marcus upon his demise?"

"It's not something I ever gave much thought to. But, believe me, I never thought it would just go away if Marcus died. I assume I will now be repaying the loan to one of Marcus's heirs."

"Good answer," he says, but I'm not certain he's convinced of my innocence. "Forgive my prying, but you have to admit that it's a bit"—he stumbles to find the right word—"*curious* that you owed Marcus a substantial sum of money, and your cousin fits the description of someone using his credit card, and you both happen to be each other's alibi."

"We're not each other's only alibi. Did you check with the cashier at the grocery store I mentioned? I'm certain she'd remember us. Not to mention we have a time- and date-stamped receipt showing where we were when we left the restaurant."

"Yes. The infamous receipt. You've mentioned it twice now. One might think you only went to the grocery store to set up an alibi for you and Wavonne."

"That's absurd," I say and make a mental note not to mention it again.

"Maybe so," he says and begins to rise from the table. "Thank you for the information, Ms. Watkins."

He's annoyed me with his accusations, but I don't want it to show so I decide to encourage him to stay. "No need to rush off. Won't you stay and have a bite to eat? Darius should be back with that platter any minute."

"I really must be going. I have to—"

Detective Hutchins cuts himself off as Darius sets down a platter of crispy fried crab balls, panko-coated onion rings, and mini-barbecue ribs dripping with my homemade sauce. He takes a long look at the oversized oblong plate and then looks back at me. "Okay. Maybe for a quick a bite."

CHAPTER 26

I've always hated the smell of hair salons—that toxic scent of relaxer frying up Afro like it should come with a side of bacon. But a girl's got to get her hair cut, and there's no better place to catch up on the latest gossip than the beauty shop. I usually go to Latasha at Illusions a few doors down from the restaurant. She does a nice job, and the location allows me to quickly duck out of Sweet Tea, get a trim, and be back in time for the lunch rush. But today I'm cheating on Latasha—today I'm seated in a cheap vinyl chair with metal legs in the cramped waiting area of Salon Cuts.

"Halia! So good to see you. I saw your name in the appointment book, and I wondered if it was really you," Régine says to me.

I stand up. "Hello, Régine. I need a trim, and I heard you were the best," I say, when in reality, I've heard the exact opposite from several people. I don't know who coined the phrase "Hell hath no fury like a woman scorned," but what he or she should have said is "Hell hath no fury like a black woman who got a bad weave . . . or bad relaxer, or a bad haircut." If you screw up a sister's hair, she will make sure anyone and everyone knows about it . . . while wearing a wig of course. So it's no surprise word has gotten around town that Régine is a less-than-apt stylist.

"I'm flattered. Let's take you back and get you shampooed."

I follow her back to the sinks and sit down in front of one of them, saying a silent prayer that she doesn't screw up my hair too much. I actually just got it cut a little over a week ago, but I needed an excuse to meet with Régine and pump her for information, so here I am. Detective Hutchins is supposed to be checking out Heather and Josh more thoroughly, and hopefully, he will look for some DNA samples in their trunk like they do on those crime shows. But I'm certainly not convinced that Heather and Josh are the culprits, and I had already made this appointment before I discovered the incriminating scent in their trunk. I figured I might as well keep it and find out what I can learn from, and about, Régine.

"Girl, I have clients who'd slice a finger off to have your hair," Régine says to me after she wets my hair and begins gently massaging the shampoo in.

I laugh. I do hear comments like that a lot about my naturally straight hair, and they are usually followed by words of disdain about how I waste such lovely hair by keeping it short. While it would be nice to have a long mane of flowing black hair, I just wouldn't have time to tend to it, so I keep it short and neat.

"I'm not kidding. I've been cutting hair for more than ten years, and I can think of many clients who would sell their firstborn."

"Well, certainly not you. You have lovely hair."

"Thanks."

She does have nice hair and I can tell, looking up at her from the sink, that it is, in fact, her own. Originally, I thought it might be a weave or a good wig. I see lots of wigs in my restaurant. Some of them, the human hair expensive ones, are pretty good, and others are so bad they look like they came off a hook at a Halloween costume shop.

"I guess we were both blessed with good hair. It does take some time to maintain, though."

"Yeah, that's why I keep mine short. It's so much easier to deal with," I say, beginning to wonder why neither one of us has yet broached the topic of Marcus. It's been less than a week since he was killed.

When Régine is done washing my hair, she gently pats it with a towel and asks me to follow her to her station.

"I'm so sorry about Marcus," I say as she lays a frock over me and snaps it behind my neck.

Her previously sunny demeanor changes and a more subdued expression appears on her face. She looks at my reflection in the mirror and offers a weak smile. "Thank you, Halia. It's been a difficult time. Today's my first day back since I got the news. I wanted to take some more time off from work, but in my line of business, if I don't work, I don't get paid. And if you're gone too long, your clients go elsewhere. But I'll be out again for the funeral tomorrow."

"I understand. We all have to earn a living. It was just such a shock. He was so young and charismatic."

"He was truly one of kind," she responds and looks down at the floor for a moment before starting to run a comb through my hair. "If you don't mind, I'd really rather not talk about it. I don't want to get emotional at work."

"Of course, but may I ask if you've heard anything from the police? Do they have any leads on who might be responsible?"

"They interviewed me at my apartment. They asked me if I knew of anyone who might want to hurt Marcus, and then they started questioning me as if I'm a suspect."

"I went through the same thing. I guess they have to question everyone. Surely, they don't suspect you of having any connection?"

"I don't think so. I went straight home from the restaurant Saturday night. The others were probably still there by the time I got home. I sort of went off on the police. I told them they could check the security cameras at my building if they wanted to. I had just lost my boyfriend. I was in no mood to deal with accusations."

"I hear you. I found it unnerving, as well, to be questioned . . . and they questioned Wavonne, too, but maybe we should take some comfort in the fact that they are being thorough and will bring whoever killed Marcus to justice," I say, before asking, "You didn't have any leads for them, did you? Do you know of anyone who'd want Marcus dead?"

"I don't. The police think it may have been a random robbery. After all, his wallet was missing. It may have been related to some of his business affairs, but I stayed out of Marcus's work. All that financial stuff is way over my head anyway . . . commodities, exchange traded funds, margin calls . . . it may as well be Greek."

"Was Marcus dabbling beyond his financial planning business? Jacqueline told us about a mortgage program he was involved in."

"Yes. But I didn't know much about that, either. Other than it was the topic of discussion the night I last saw Marcus."

"Heather and Josh were Marcus's clients, right?"

"Yes, and they were not happy with him that night . . . at least not at the beginning. By the time I left, Marcus and Charles had seemed to calm them down a bit. I'm not sure if they completely succeeded, but they were trying to sweet-talk Heather and Josh into thinking everything with the program was sound."

"Thinking? Were things not okay?"

"I suspect not. From what I could gather, whatever bag of goods Marcus and Charles sold them was supposed to be sending them checks to cover their mortgage, and, lately, those checks had stopped coming."

"So you said he eventually calmed them down, but when they were angry, did you think they were angry enough to . . . you know?"

"The husband didn't seem that agitated. It was really more the girl who was angry. Was she mad enough to kill someone? I doubt it, but who knows. I'm sure the police talked to them, as well." She looks at me in the mirror. "Honestly, Halia. I'd really rather not talk about it."

"Sure . . . sure. Let's change the subject."

She begins trimming my hair, and I can tell by the way she handles the scissors that this is not going to end well. Some hairdressers have a fluid, confident touch and others, like poor Régine, probably shouldn't be trusted with a pair of clippers at Petco.

"So, do you live around here?" I ask.

"Not far. I'm over at the Madison."

"Oh yeah. That's a nice building," I lie. I've been past it a few times. It's sort of run-down and in a pretty rough part of town. I ask the question about where she lives as if it were just an attempt to move on from the discussion of Marcus, but now that I'm aware of where Régine lives, I know what I need to do next. I just hope that, after Régine is done with my hair, I don't look like Don King doing it.

CHAPTER 27

I've just stepped out of the hair salon, and I'm looking at myself in the rearview mirror. And let me tell you, it ain't pretty. It may be the worst haircut I've ever gotten. My bangs generally flow in a tapered fashion toward the side of my head, but Régine cut them in a straight line across my forehead, and she seems to have left one side of my hair fuller than the other, as if she were going for a more subtle version of an eighties asymmetrical 'shroom. The look makes me think of high school and neon clothes, and the old station wagon I drove back then.

My high school is now almost exclusively black, but when I was there it was still fairly racially mixed. Despite this, the black students still mostly hung with each other and the white students did the same. I think of the black girls grooving to Salt-N-Pepa with our Jheri curls, and the white girls rocking out to Def Leppard with their bangs teased up to the ceiling. It strikes me as ironic how such an effort was made to integrate schools, and the students ended up self-segregating within the school anyway.

A few years ago, I started an annual tradition of inviting the entire senior class of my alma mater to Sweet Tea for lunch—

generally around two hundred students each year. I host them in two groups over two days when Sweet Tea is closed between our regular lunch and dinner hours. I fill them up with cornbread and spare ribs and fried chicken. Over dessert, I give a brief talk about my path to opening my own business and the work involved in running a restaurant. I encourage them to think big and ask the ones going off to college to consider coming back to Prince George's County when they graduate. I suggest they all get involved in the community or even think about opening their own businesses to provide needed services and create jobs. I just want them to know that anything is possible if you work hard enough and show them what a fellow graduate accomplished. Of course, I invite the young men, but my heart is with the girls. I want them to aim high, and while they have so many positive African American female role models these days, they're still bombarded with images of women whose greatest claim to fame is that they managed to find successful men to pay their bills or happened to land a reality show based only on their talent for behaving badly and creating drama in their lives.

I make a mental note to call Latasha and schedule an appointment to salvage my hair as best she can. I'd phone her right now, but I have another call to make. I find the number in my contacts list and put the phone to my ear.

"Charles. Hi. It's Halia Watkins from Sweet Tea. Remember? We chatted the other day at your seminar."

"Yes. What can I do for you, Halia?" He doesn't sound too happy to hear from me.

"I'm just dotting some i's and crossing some t's over here and wondering if you can help me?"

"Does this have to do with Marcus's murder, Halia? I've told the police everything I know."

"Can I just ask you a few quick questions? I promise I won't take up much of your time."

He's quiet on the other end of the phone, which I figure is better than a no.

"You were one of the last of Marcus's guests to leave the restaurant the night he disappeared, right?"

He's still silent.

"I'm not asking because I think you have anything to do with Marcus's death. I'm asking because I'd like to know what time Régine left?"

"Régine?" he asks. "I don't remember the exact time." His tone is friendlier now that I'm not asking questions about him. "But I do remember she left very shortly after you did."

"Would you say five or ten minutes after Wavonne and I left?"

"Probably fifteen minutes. She said she had a headache and was bored with our business talk."

"How long after that did you leave?"

"I thought you just had a *few* questions."

"That's my last one, I promise."

"I stayed maybe twenty minutes longer. Heather and Josh left before I did. Jacqueline was the only one with Marcus when I left."

"Thank you, Charles. You've been very helpful."

"If you have any further questions, Halia, I suggest you talk to the police."

"I will. You have a good afternoon."

I toss the phone onto the passenger seat and start the van. As I drive to Sweet Tea, I make some calculations in my head. I know it was about eleven forty-five when Wavonne and I left the restaurant on that fateful night. So if Régine left fifteen minutes after us, that put her departure at about midnight. Now I need to make the drive from Sweet Tea to the Madison, see how long it takes to get there, and determine if I can get my hands on the building's security camera footage. I don't know if Régine had a motive to kill Marcus, but Wavonne did say she thought Marcus was cheating on her. Women have certainly killed men for lesser reasons.

When I get back to the restaurant, it's almost time to open for the day. I say hi to my staff in the front of the house and make my way back to the kitchen. I had gotten Tacy started on our lunch special for the day, chicken potpies, before I left to get my hair cut. The crusts have been prepared, and he's now pouring the filling into the individual casserole dishes, laying the crusts on top, and letting it fall over the edges. He tops the whole thing with a small piece of dough in the shape of chicken (we use a cookie cutter).

"They look lovely, Tacy. Nice work," I compliment. "Isn't Wavonne supposed to be helping you?"

Before Tacy has a chance to say anything, I hear Momma's voice. "Good Lord, Halia! What happened to your hair? You're far too old to be trying those weird, trendy hairdos."

"I'm not trying a new, trendy hairdo. Is it that bad?"

"Oh my," Momma says instead of answering my question. "Stan is here with some deliveries. He just went back out to the truck. You can't let him see you like this."

Momma grabs me by the arm and drags me into the break room, where we find Wavonne seated at the table, thumbing the keys on her phone.

"You stay here until he's gone," Momma says.

"Fine, Momma. I need to talk to Wavonne anyway."

"Maybe she'll loan you one of her wigs. Lord knows, she has more than that busty girl who used to be on *The View*."

Wavonne doesn't respond as Momma goes back into the kitchen, and that's when I realize she has her headphones in. Rather than say anything, I decide to just stand there and wait for her to notice me. When she finally looks up, I expect her to start going on about how she's getting back to work right this minute, and just needed to return a quick text, but, instead, she narrows her eyebrows and lets her jaw drop.

"Halia! Why your hair all jacked up?"

"Don't you worry about my hair. I need you to run an errand with me."

"I ain't doin' nothin' 'til you tell me what alley cat your hair got in a fight with."

"I went to see Régine. I thought I—"

"Régine?! You let Régine cut your hair? Have you lost your mind?"

"I was trying to get some information out of her."

"Well, I hope you got it now that you have to walk around lookin' like a swamp rat," she says before softening her demeanor and looking at me with a concerned expression on her face. "Ooh, girl, you okay? I can loan you a wig or some of my snap-and go extensions. What do you say we go to Red Lobster and get you some crab legs? Make you feel better."

"I'll go see Latasha as soon as I get a chance. She can clean it up and even it out. Enough about my hair already. I need you go to the Madison, Régine's building, with me."

"What for?"

"I may need your . . . your powers of persuasion."

"Really? You've got me curious now, Halia. What's this about?"

"I'll explain on the way. We need to get over there and back quickly. Laura and the gang can handle the place until things really pick up at noon."

"Fine. But just so you know, my powers of persuasion may cost you time and a half."

CHAPTER 28

I look at my watch after we get in the van and buckle up. I make a mental note of the time. I know where the Madison is. I have a friend who lived there years ago. It's not a total dump, but it's an older high-rise . . . maybe twelve stories with a worn lobby and creaky, slow elevators. I figure we can get there in roughly twenty minutes, but I want to clock it to be sure.

"What's goin' down at the Madison?"

"Nothing is going down at the Madison. I just want to see how long it takes to get there from here, so we know how much time Régine had on her hands when she left the restaurant the night Marcus was killed."

"Why?"

"Régine said her building had security cameras at the entrance. She told the cops to check them if they didn't believe she was home safe and sound on the night in question. I figure if Régine left Sweet Tea about midnight, and she went straight home, she would have gotten there about twelve twenty, which means she was probably home before Charles and Jacqueline even left the restaurant. If that's the case, I can cross her off my suspect list.

"How do you know she didn't sneak back out later?"

"Another reason I want to pay the Madison a visit. There must be back or side exits. We need to know if those are monitored on camera, as well."

"Even if they are monitored, how you plan on gettin' the camera footage?"

"I thought you might help me with that."

"How so?"

"You tell me, Wavonne. If there's one thing I know about you, it's that if you want something bad enough, you'll find a way to get it."

We continue the drive, and it takes us exactly nineteen minutes to reach the Madison. As I pull into the parking lot, I begin to circle the building looking for entryways and exits. I see the main entrance covered by a torn gray awning, and there are metal doors on each end of the front side of the building that likely lead to stairwells. There are two similar doors on the rear side of the building. I have Wavonne hop out and check each of the metal doors. All four of them are locked—clearly they are for exiting the building only. If Régine wanted to enter the building through one of these doors, she'd need to leave it ajar with something, and hope no one disturbed it until she got back . . . or have an accomplice let her in. But as Wavonne is checking to see if the side doors are locked, I notice that they are monitored by cameras just like the main entrance, so Régine would have been seen on camera entering or leaving via those doors, as well.

Following our drive around the perimeter of the building, I park the car. Then Wavonne and I make our way to the main entrance. We press a buzzer, and a very bored-looking young fellow sitting at the reception desk lets us in. He's tall and lanky and probably only a year or two out of high school. His dress shirt is two sizes too big for him, and his tie has a stain on it.

Once we're in the building, I linger by the door for a moment trying think of what I'm going to say to him and attempt to come up with an excuse to get him to show me some security camera footage. I'm contemplating making up a story about looking for a lost loved one or even posing as a police detective when Wavonne unfastens a few buttons on her top and scoots ahead of me toward the clerk.

"Hi, Jeffrey," she says, reading his nameplate on the counter.

"Hello."

"Aren't you a handsome thing . . . all dapper in your dress shirt and tie," she adds, plunking her voluptuous breasts on the counter like she's setting two mugs of coffee on a table at the local diner.

Jeffrey grins and looks at Wavonne with wide eyes as I step closer to them.

"May I help you?" he asks, clearly struggling to keep his eyes off the cleavage displayed before him.

"Oh honey, a strappin' man like you, you could help me with all sortsa things."

Jeffrey lets out a nervous laugh.

"You probably work a lot of hours here, don't you?"

"Eight hours a day. Five days a week."

"You poor thing. I bet those tight executive types who own this joint don't pay you near what you're worth."

The poor kid doesn't know what to make of Wavonne and just lifts his eyebrows and shrugs his shoulders at us.

"How'd you like to make a little extra money, Jeffrey?"

"I'd love to."

"I'm Kadesha, and this here is my mother, Sinclair."

Mother?! I'm going to get her for that one.

"You see, it's all very complicated. I'd love to explain, but we're in a hurry. The bones of it, Jeffrey, is that we need to see your security camera footage from Saturday night." As she's talking, Wavonne pulls my purse off my arm, lays it on the counter, and takes out my wallet.

"Let's see. How much do we have here? Twenty, forty, sixty . . . eighty dollars," she says, counting the bills she pulled from my wallet. "That's all we have. What do you say, Jeffrey? For a quick eighty bucks, can we get a peek at the tapes?"

Jeffrey takes a quick look around and then snatches the money out of Wavonne's hand. He then gestures for us to come behind the counter and follow him into the back room.

"The cops have already viewed all the footage. This is about that guy that was found in Wellington Lake, right?"

Wavonne looks at me, unsure how to respond.

"Yes," I say. "Wav . . . Kadesha and I are doing a little investigating of our own. Trying to make sure the cops didn't miss anything. What exactly did you show the cops?"

"My boss, Mr. Maxell, worked with them, but I was here when they came. They wanted to see footage from the same night. They were looking for Ms. Alva in apartment 431. They wanted to see what time she came in to the building, and then they wanted to see hours of footage from every door to see if she left again before morning. They made copies of everything. You looking for Ms. Alva, too?"

"Yes. Régine Alva."

"Here, look," he says, sitting down in front of the computer screen and putting his hand on the mouse. "This is from that Saturday."

"There she is," Wavonne says. The film is in black and white and a bit grainy but, indeed, that is Régine coming through the front door. We get a quick look at her opening the front door and entering the lobby. She's got her phone out, and she's texting or surfing on the Internet while she's walking.

"That's the time at the bottom of the screen?"

"Yes. She came in at twelve twenty-one."

"And you said the cops already reviewed the camera footage from the exits. She never left the building that night?"

"Nope. They viewed the feed from every camera at every entrance and exit, and she wasn't seen leaving until nine a.m. the next morning."

"We ain't gonna sit here and watch hours of tape from all the exits, are we? 'Cause that's gonna cost a hell of a lot more than time and a half."

Jeffrey looks at us curiously, probably wondering why my *daughter* is expecting me to pay her.

"No. I'm sure the cops reviewed the tapes thoroughly, and we really have to get back. Thank you very much, Jeffrey," I say.

"Don't mention it," he says and puts his hand in his pocket as if he's making sure the eighty dollars is still there.

"So I guess you can cross Régine off your list, Sherlock," Wavonne says as we walk across the parking lot.

"I guess," I say, putting my key in the door of my van. "Oh, and by the way? *Your mother?!* You'll pay for that one."

Wavonne laughs.

"And Kadesha and Sinclair? Really? Someone has been watching too many *Living Single* reruns on TVONE."

"I had to come up with some names quickly. And, after all, we were there looking for information about *Régine*."

On the way back to the restaurant, Wavonne reaches for my purse, which I've set on the floor next to me.

"What are you doing?" I ask.

She digs for my wallet and pulls it out. "You know you had like two or three hundred dollars in here. I only pulled out eighty, and told Jeffrey that's all we had. So I figure I saved you more than a hundred bucks. I'm just takin' my commission for services rendered."

I divert my eyes from the road for a moment toward Wavonne. "Twenty dollars, Wavonne. You can take twenty dollars. The rest of your commission will be staying out of jail for stealing someone's wallet."

"You stop talkin' about me stealin'. He was *dead*, Halia. It ain't stealin' if he was dead."

"Let's hope we never have to find out if a jury agrees with you."

"I ain't goin' before no jury. The police will find out who offed Marcus." She gives me a long look. "If you don't beat 'em to it."

CHAPTER 29

I'm sitting next to Wavonne about twelve rows back from the front of the church. I have on a gray skirt and white blouse. I even put on some sheer black hose, but I'm still feeling underdressed. Compared to the other women around me, I look decidedly out of place. I should have known better. I try to avoid funerals as much as possible, but I've been to enough of them to know that some of the women only came today to show off their latest designer threads in black or navy blue. All around me are women in dark dresses and suits. Most of them have on hats. Some of their hats even have those ridiculous birdcage veils. They look like they cut up some fishnet panty hose and have them hanging in front of their faces.

"I wish they'd get this show on the road," Wavonne whispers to me. She's wearing a tight black dress with a wide red belt and red pumps. And she has a ridiculous red bow attached to her wig. I told her the red accents were not appropriate for a funeral, but much like many things I tell her, my words went in one ear and out the other.

It's warm in the church, which sometimes I suspect is on purpose, so these ladies have a chance to use their fans. I don't know what it is about women at funerals and their fans, but it gets a hair over sixty-eight degrees in the building, and you'd think the service was being held in a sauna by the looks of all the women fanning themselves—of course, only with fans that coordinate well with their outfits.

I look around the room and only see a few familiar faces. There's Jacqueline up front with Marcus's mother. Jacqueline is dressed . . . well, like Jacqueline always dresses . . . in a tailored dark green pantsuit. No gaudy hats for her. She probably thinks funeral hats are "so PG County." Marcus's mother appears to be about seventy. I can see a resemblance to Marcus, but she has a sweeter look about her than her son. Perhaps he got that little trace of malevolence you could always see in his eyes from his father, whom I believe died several years ago. Mrs. Rand has a tissue in her hand, but no tears are being shed at the moment. She is talking quietly with Jacqueline, who also seems to be free of any obvious emotion.

My eyes retreat from Jacqueline and her mother and start to roam the church. It's a large church, and I guess there's a decent turnout, but for someone as dynamic and "connected" as Marcus was, I would have expected a larger crowd. I only vaguely recognize a few other people, probably folks who have been in to Sweet Tea with Marcus.

A few more minutes pass and, as Wavonne removes a file from her purse and starts doing her nails (where she found a bright pink nail file, I have no idea), I notice a change in the energy in the church. People stop their whispered conversations and nudge each other to discreetly turn around. I turn my head and see Régine walking into the church alone. She's not dressed as flashy as usual, but she still wouldn't be out of place leaning against a lamppost swinging her purse around. Everyone watches as she makes her way up the center aisle and sits down a few pews back from where Jacqueline and Mrs. Rand are seated. I'm guessing there is no love lost between Régine and the Rands, or she would be seated next to them. After all, she was Marcus's girlfriend even if they only had been dating for a few months.

While Régine gets settled into the pew, I notice people looking at her and then shifting their eyes to another young woman on the other side of the aisle and then back to Régine.

"Who's that?" Wavonne asks her friend Melva, who's sitting on the other side of her.

"That's Jennie Becks, Marcus's girlfriend before Régine."

"Really?" I say, surprised I've never met Jennie. She and Marcus must not have dated very long if he never brought her to one of his dinners at Sweet Tea.

"Rumor has it she was hell-bent on becoming Mrs. Marcus Rand and moving into his mansion in Mitchellville. She was mad as hell when Régine got her claws into him."

I listen to Wavonne and Melva talk and my antennas go up. I'm picturing my suspect list in my head, and the name Jennie Becks being added to it when I see the minister walk over to Jacqueline and Mrs. Rand. He says a few words to them before motioning to the vocalist, who has climbed up on the steps in front of the altar. She breaks into a hymn that I have not heard before. She does have a lovely voice, and I see a few attendees dabbing at their eyes, careful not to smudge their makeup, as she sings. When the vocalist reaches the end of the hymn, she takes a seat, and the minister walks to the pulpit and says a few words. He keeps his address pretty generic, probably because he doesn't . . . *didn't* know Marcus very well. When he speaks about the sanctity of life and how Marcus's death "is not the end for Marcus, but a new beginning with the Lord," I can't help but wonder if I'm the only one thinking that it might not be the Lord that Marcus is having a new beginning with. For his sake . . . for all of our sakes really, I hope our Creator actually is a merciful God.

When the minister is finished speaking, he introduces Jacqueline, noting that Marcus's sister would like to say a few words. Jacqueline walks purposefully to the podium and clears her throat. "What is there to say about my brother, Marcus Rand? Some words to describe him: Charming. Smart. Attractive." She pauses for a moment between each word. "Hard worker. Fast talker. Character. Not that he *had* character. He *was* a character," she says to a few quiet laughs from the pews.

"He enjoyed life, and I can honestly say he made the most of his forty some odd years on this planet. He was constantly on the go . . . wheeling and dealing at all hours of the day and night. He enjoyed the finer things in life: custom suits, fast cars, and a lovely home that I was fortunate enough to share with him. Working so closely together and sharing a house meant we spent a lot of time with each other. He could run me ragged, but working for Marcus was never boring. Actually, nothing about my brother was boring. And I think that's what I'll miss the most about him . . . how he always kept things interesting."

Jacqueline continues with her eulogy for another ten minutes or so, and while I don't see any of the disdain I occasionally saw in her eyes when she was with Marcus, particularly when he was ordering her around, she doesn't appear to be a distraught, grieving sister, either. And though, by and large, she keeps the eulogy positive and mostly speaks of Marcus's more pleasant attributes, her speech is devoid of words like love, kindness, and generosity, which was probably a smart move on her part. She would have sounded ridiculous if she tried to paint a different picture of Marcus than we all knew to be true.

After Jacqueline returns to her seat, the minister leads the

mourners in a final prayer and the singer returns to the microphone, but this time she doesn't break into a hymn. I recognize
the familiar notes of a song I suspect Jacqueline chose. As the
words to Nat King Cole's "Unforgettable" croon from her
lips, I think about how the song is right-on. If Marcus was
nothing else, he was definitely unforgettable.

CHAPTER 30

The rest of us follow after the minister and Marcus's family exit the church. Marcus's remains were cremated, so there is no coffin and no additional ceremony at a cemetery. Instead, we all file down to the church basement, where several tables and chairs have been neatly arranged. At the far end are two long tables holding chafing dishes and platters of food. There is already a small crowd lingering to the side of these tables. They are trying to appear as if they just happen to be chatting near that particular area, but I've catered enough events to know that what they really want is to make sure they're at the front of the line when they are told that the buffet is open. Hopefully Jacqueline was smart enough to have a few folks serving the food as people go down the line. Another thing I've learned from my catering experience is that if you let people serve themselves, you essentially end up with, if I may put it delicately, pigs at the feeding trough—classless people heap huge portions on their plates. Before you know it, even though you've purchased enough food to feed fifty people, you've run out by the time guest number thirty-five gets to the front of the line.

I make my way over to the buffet—and, no, not to ensure a favorable position in line, but to check out the competition. I see place cards that say *Catering by Luette Howard*. I know Luette. She's nice enough, but she's known for her rock-bottom prices rather than the quality of her food. Honestly, I'm not even sure her business is legit. I don't think she's licensed, and I wouldn't be surprised if she runs her catering business out of her home rather than a commercial kitchen that's regularly inspected by the health department.

You get what you pay for, I think to myself as I peruse the buffet. Her fried chicken has a nice batter on it, but the pieces are small without much meat on them. I can tell just by looking that she bought a few trays of frozen macaroni and cheese and transferred the contents to her own chafing dishes after heating them up. Her mashed potatoes look okay—I'll give her that one. And maybe people probably won't notice that her gravy is from a jar. The rest of the serving tables are filled with more of the same—dishes range from acceptable to downright sad. If Jacqueline had asked, given that Marcus was an investor in Sweet Tea and a longtime acquaintance, I would have gladly catered the repast at cost, but for whatever reason, she went with Luette.

"Where you goin'?" Wavonne asks as I begin to step away from the table. "We should hang around and make sure we get a good spot in line."

"I'm going to walk around and mingle a bit. Don't get too comfortable. We need to get back to the restaurant soon."

I start to toddle around the church basement with an eye out for either Régine or Jennie Becks . . . or Jacqueline. I'd like to have a word with all of them and see if I can glean any useful information. I spot Jacqueline first. She's sitting at a table with her mother, and a few others are gathered around them offering their condolences. I approach and wait my turn to say a few words.

"Halia," Jacqueline says to me. "So sweet of you to come."

"Of course. I got to know Marcus pretty well over the years. I'll miss him."

"We all will," she says, although I'm not really sure either one of us is telling the truth.

"How are you holding up?"

"I'm hanging in there. I'm trying to look after Mother and settle Marcus's affairs."

She's very nonchalant about the whole thing. It's hard to tell if she's hiding how distraught she is, or if she just isn't that upset about her brother's death. Decorum is important to Jacqueline, so she could actually be grief-stricken by her loss but refuses to show it in public . . . or, I hate to even think it, but she might have killed Marcus and is glad he's dead.

"Can I get you anything? Would you like me to fix you a plate from the serving table?"

"Oh heavens, no. I can't have any of that food. It's all grease and starch."

I smile at her as I notice a few other people lining up behind me to have a word with her.

"I'll let you chat with the others. If there's anything I can do for you, please let me know."

Jacqueline thanks me. Then I say a quick word to Mrs. Rand and get out of the way so others can speak with them. Of course, I would have preferred to have gotten in a few questions about the night Marcus was killed, but there couldn't be a more inappropriate time for me to start asking about motives and alibis. I'll have to catch up with Jacqueline at another less conspicuous time.

The buffet is now open. As I watch a crowd gather at one end of the table, I ponder the three types of people who go to funerals: the first are the ones who truly cared about the deceased and want to celebrate their life and mourn their death; the second are the drama queens who will show up at any funeral to which they can get an invitation, so they can cry and carry on and get all sorts of attention; and the third are the ones who are in it for one thing—the free food at the repast. Many of the people I see in line I suspect are part of the afore-mentioned third group. I give the line a thorough once-over and see Jennie Becks at the tail end. If I hurry I can nab a spot right behind her. I have little interest in eating Luette Howard's cut-rate fried chicken, but it's a perfect opportunity to ask Jennie a few questions.

"Hi," I say as I step behind her.

"Hello."

"The spread looks lovely," I lie.

"Yes."

As she speaks to me she suddenly looks familiar. I feel like I've seen her somewhere before. Maybe Marcus did bring her to Sweet Tea a time or two.

"How did you know Marcus?" I ask as if I don't already know.

"We dated."

"Really? Recently?"

"We broke up a few months ago. He was cheating on me with Régine Alva." Her eyes dart toward Régine who's seated at a table with some people I don't recognize. "She works at the salon where I used to get my hair done. Marcus was wait-ing for me one day, and that's when she got her hooks into him. Part of me always knew Marcus was no good . . ." She stops herself. "Good Lord. Look at me. I should not be talking trash about Marcus at his funeral. He wasn't all bad. He could treat me right when he wanted to."

I can see the resentment in her eyes as she talks, but I can't tell if it's directed more toward Régine or Marcus . . . or maybe both of them.

"I guess we all have our good and bad characteristics," I say.

"It's terrible the way he died, and the police seem to be questioning everyone."

"It was horrible, wasn't it? I heard he was hit over the head with something . . . maybe a baseball bat or a tire iron . . . and then thrown in a lake. It gives me chills to think about it."

I was hoping my words about the police questioning everyone would prompt her to tell me if the police had interrogated her, but she doesn't seem to be biting.

When we reach the serving table I reluctantly add a few items to my plate while Jennie does the same. As we walk toward the far end of the buffet, I see a selection of drinks. I see some Coke and Sprite . . . and Sunkist, but it's when I see the bottle of cranberry juice that I remember where I've seen Jennie before. She was at Sweet Tea the night Marcus was killed. She was part of the table of young women who tried to sneak their own alcohol into my restaurant—the "cranberry drinkers." I remember they were all wearing black the night I saw them in Sweet Tea. Jennie might even have the same dress on now that she was wearing at the restaurant.

Well, isn't this an interesting turn of events? I think to myself. Jennie Becks, Marcus's wronged ex-girlfriend was at Sweet Tea the same night Marcus turned up dead. *Just a coincidence? Or was she stalking him?*

I decide not to mention that I recall seeing her from the restaurant. It will only embarrass her if she knows I remember she tried to pull a fast one on me. I'll never get her to talk to me if I make her feel ashamed. I'm about to ask some additional questions but, instead, I decide to just tell her that I enjoyed meeting her and begin to walk away. Rather than questioning Jennie, I'm well aware that there are other ways to find out just how bad the breakup between Marcus and Jennie was and exactly how bitter she was after being jilted for

Régine. Fortunately, I know just where to catch up on all the latest gossip.

"So I know Marcus broke up with Jennie for Régine, but what can you tell me about how it all transpired and how angry Jennie was after it all happened?" I say to Wavonne and Melva as I take a seat next to them.

CHAPTER 31

"The whole thing was silly and bound to happen if you axe me," Wavonne says. "Everybody and their momma knew Marcus was a playa'. What made Jennie Becks think she was gonna keep him from straying without a leash around his neck is beyond me."

"You see," Melva chimes in. "I think what really chapped Jennie's ass was that it all happened right there in front of her. She was sitting under the dryer at Salon Cuts watching with her own two eyes while Régine put the moves on her man . . . right there in the beauty shop waiting area. I'm sure Jennie wanted to hop out of her seat and intervene, but choosing between your man and your hair—that's a tough choice for a sister."

"Surely, Marcus didn't dump Jennie right then and there, did he?"

"No. Jennie thought there was just some flirting going on at the hair salon, and figured she'd think twice about ever bringing Marcus with her to Salon Cuts again. But that Régine is slick—she somehow managed to slip Marcus her number without Jennie seeing."

"So Régine and Marcus had a thing going for a while before Jennie found out about it?"

"Well, this is where it gets interesting," Melva says, rubbing her hands together. "Not only did Jennie find out that Marcus was seeing Régine. Régine found out that Marcus was still seeing Jennie after he told her he had stopped."

"Oooh, girl. This is better than *The Young and the Restless*," Wavonne says.

"Monique over at Hair Chique cuts Jennie's hair now. She gave me the four-one-one."

"I thought you went to Salon Cuts?"

"Halia, you gotta go to more than one beauty shop if you're gonna get all the good gossip," Wavonne says.

Melva nods in agreement with an "I thought everyone knew that" sort of look and continues. "For a smart man Marcus did some stupid things. He wasn't satisfied with *just* Régine or *just* Jennie—he had to have both. He and Régine did their secret thing on the side for a few weeks until Régine demanded he drop Jennie. Word is Marcus told Régine that he had given Jennie the heave-ho when he really hadn't, but then the dumb brother took Jennie out to Jasper's in Largo. If he'd paid attention when he visited Régine at the beauty shop, he'd have known that Quinn, who shampoos hair at Salon Cuts, also waits tables at Jasper's three nights a week."

"Quinn's workin' two jobs to save up for some new titties," Wavonne says. "Quinn's got a big ass, but no boobies up top. So to even things out, she looked into either gettin' the fat sucked outta her ass or some implants shoved behind her itty bitties. She opted for the implants."

"Thanks for the insight, Wavonne," I say, before turning back to Melva. "You were saying . . ."

"So Quinn sees Marcus and Jennie at Jaspers and gets on the horn to Régine. Quinn tells her that Marcus is there with his cheese stick all up in Jennie's marinara sauce. Not long after, Régine storms into the restaurant and goes full-blown Omarosa on both of them."

"Wow. This really is better than *The Young and the Restless*," I say.

"Sure is. Jennie still didn't know about Marcus and Régine at that point."

"She was about the only one in town who didn't know," Wavonne pipes in.

"After Régine's tirade at the restaurant and Jennie learning about Marcus's affair with her, Marcus didn't need to choose between the two girls anymore—Jennie made the choice for him and dumped his ass . . . probably the smartest thing she ever did."

"Hmmm. Very interesting," I say. I'm about to question Melva further when I happen to see Jennie chatting with Régine in one corner of the room. It's only the two of them and, oddly, their conversation seems to be very cordial.

Wavonne catches me staring at them. "Well, look at the two of them makin' all nice-nice."

"Kind of makes you wonder, doesn't it?" I ask.

"About what?"

"What Marcus's old girlfriend and the woman he was cheating on her with are saying to each other."

I'm really surprised when I see Jennie give Régine a hug and then start for the door.

"Let's go," I abruptly say to Wavonne and hurriedly get up from the table. I want to catch up with Jennie before she leaves, and the most discreet way to do just that would be to "happen" to leave the repast at the same time.

"Go? I've barely touched my food. I ain't goin' no place."

"You go ahead," Melva says. "I'll drop Wavonne at the restaurant."

"Thanks, Melva," I say and scurry through the church basement to catch up with Jennie.

"Leaving already?" I call behind her. She's just about to step out the door.

"Yes. I need to get back to work." She walks out the door and holds it open for me to follow.

"Did I see you chatting with Régine?"

"Yes."

"It's really none of my business, but didn't you say over by the buffet table that Marcus was cheating on you with Régine? I guess I was surprised to see you two chatting so genially."

"I'm not really into drama. It's in the past, and Marcus is dead. Régine probably did me a favor by taking him off my hands anyway."

"That's a good way to look at it," I say and wonder if Jennie is telling the truth. Has she really forgiven and forgotten, or is it all an act to hide the fact that she pummeled Marcus over the head with my frying pan? I'm about to say my good-bye when another thought occurs to me: *What if Jennie and Régine were in it together? What if they joined forces to get back at Marcus for playing both of them for fools?*

"You have a good day," Jennie says when her phone chirps, and she pulls it out to check for a text.

"You, too."

She smiles at me, and I wonder who's texting her now . . . and I wonder even more if anyone was texting her the night Marcus was killed. Régine was typing something on her phone as she walked into her building the night Marcus died. Could she and Jennie have been trading texts about a mission accomplished? Was it just a coincidence that Régine and Jennie were at the restaurant together on the evening of Marcus's death or were they communicating to each other between tables? It all raises a lot of questions. I've been good at that lately . . . raising questions . . . it's the answers I don't have yet.

CHAPTER 32

Régine and Jennie speaking so amicably to one another and seeing Jennie get a text right before we parted company in the parking lot makes me wonder even more about the two of them. As I get in my van, I think back to the footage of Régine walking into her building the night Marcus died. She was typing on her phone as she walked through the door. Clearly she was at home before Marcus was killed, but isn't it possible that she was still involved in some fashion? Of course she could have been texting anyone while she was coming into her building, or maybe she was just browsing on the Internet. I'm thinking how handy it would be if I could see the screen of her phone on the camera footage when I remember Jeffrey, the front desk clerk at Régine's building, saying that Régine was not seen exiting the building until the next morning. That meant that not only was there a camera facing people entering the building, which Wavonne and I viewed, but there must be a camera facing people exiting the building—a camera that would have been to Régine's back when she entered the Madison a week ago Saturday, and it might show what was transpiring on her phone.

It was a long shot, but I decide to make a detour back to

the Madison before returning to Sweet Tea. When I reach the apartment building, I park in a visitor space and walk toward the lobby. I press the button at the front door and am disappointed to be greeted by a female voice—I was hoping Jeffrey would be on duty again and amenable to taking a few more bucks in exchange for letting me view the security footage a second time. Not knowing anything about the woman on the other side of the intercom, I tell her that I'm interested in renting an apartment in the building. She buzzes me in, and when I reach the front desk I see a white woman of about fifty years standing behind the counter.

"Hello," she says in a gravelly voice as I approach the desk. She has the look of someone to whom life has not been terribly kind, and I detect the smell of cigarette smoke as I get closer. Her hair has a seen a few too many bottles of do-it-yourself Nice 'N Easy, and her heavy makeup has settled into the creases on her face.

"Hi."

"Hello. I'm Viola. What can I help you with? You're interested in an apartment?"

"Yes. What do you have available?"

"We've got one and two bedrooms." She hands me a piece of paper with some details about the units. I give it a quick look.

"Thanks," I say. "How is the security? You know I'm a single woman." I'm trying to veer the conversation toward the cameras and feel her out to see what I think the chances are of her letting me take a look at some of the video footage.

"It's very good. We have coverage at the front desk until seven p.m., and then a security guard makes regular rounds throughout the night. We share him with a few other buildings in the area."

"I see some cameras." I point to the one behind her that faces the entrance.

"That's camera one," she says. "It constantly monitors who comes into the building. And that's camera two," she adds, pointing to the camera behind me. "That monitors who exits the building. We also have cameras at the four side doors, which are always locked. Only staff members have keys. Residents can only exit from them."

"Good to know. Safety is very important to me."

Now that we're on the subject of the cameras, I'm trying to think of a way to ask if I can see some footage from them and relate the request to my concerns about the security of the building, but nothing that I think she'll buy is coming to mind. I briefly ponder the idea of just explaining my situation to Viola and seeing if she'll help a girl out, but I'm not getting a vibe from her that indicates she'd be receptive to violating policy. Jeffrey was young and easily manipulated—plus, when he was manning the desk, I had Wavonne and her ample bazumbas working the situation. My bazumbas are nowhere near the caliber of Wavonne's, and they wouldn't do me much good with another woman even if they were. Viola also doesn't seem like the type of person who's going to break the rules for a few bucks.

I'm about to give it up, make an excuse to Viola as to why I'm no longer interested, and head back to Sweet Tea, but then Viola leans in a bit closer, and I get another whiff of cigarette smoke, which gives me an idea.

"We have a couple of vacant units open if you want to take a look."

"That would be great, but I'll be renting with a roommate," I lie. "She should be here soon. Do you mind if I wait in the lobby until she gets here, and we can look together?"

"No. Make yourself comfortable."

The lobby isn't much to look at, but there's a reasonably comfortable-looking sofa across from the front desk. I've barely sat down on it when my phone rings.

"Hi, Momma," I say.

"Halia. I'm in line at the Giant, and I've met the nicest man . . . and he's single."

"What?"

"His name is Lorence. He's right here. Say hi."

I hear Momma put the phone up to him.

"Hello," he says.

Momma takes the phone back. "He works for a health insurance company."

"That's nice, Momma. Now leave the man alone and let him pay for his groceries."

"You'd like Halia," I hear her say to him. "She works in a restaurant."

Momma always tells men she's trying to set me up with that I "work in" a restaurant. She never tells them that I own the place. "Let them get to know you first before you tell them you run your own business," she always says. "Men can be put off by successful women."

I can't make out what he says in response, but my guess is he just wants to get away from the pushy old lady trying to set him up with her daughter.

"I'm going to give him your number, Halia," she says to me. Then I hear her speaking to Lorence. "You should call her. She's really very nice."

I'm about to protest, but then my eyes wander back over to Viola, and exactly what I've been waiting for happens.

"I have to go, Momma. Leave the man alone and work on getting your own dates."

I hang up the phone and watch as Viola gets up and leaves her post with a lighter and a pack of cigarettes in hand. Just as I suspected from the gravelly voice and ashy smell, Viola is a smoker, and we all know, sooner or later, smokers are going to take a smoke break. And thanks to the Maryland Clean Indoor Air Act, the same law that doesn't allow me to offer a smoking section in Sweet Tea, Viola has to go outside to do it. I don't smoke myself, but enough of my staff does for me to know that she'll be gone for at least five minutes, maybe more.

After I watch her walk down a long hallway to the left of the reception area and disappear out a side door, I don't waste any time scurrying behind the desk and through the door to the back office. I quickly grab the mouse next to the keyboard and start clicking. I watched Jeffrey as he was navigating the files earlier and, besides, it's pretty simple—there's one main folder for each camera and then additional subfolders by date. Fortunately, Viola was kind enough to let me know that camera two is the one I want to view. I simply click on that folder and then open the file for the night in question. I find the fast-forward button and rush the footage to 12:21 a.m. I lift my finger from the mouse to let the recording play. When I lean in close to the screen I can see Régine's back as she enters the building. I can even see her phone, but the footage is way too grainy for me see what's on the screen.

Disappointed, I close the file and exit the office. I grab a pen and a slip of paper from the desk and leave Viola a note thanking her for her time but letting her know something has come up, and I have to leave.

Annoyed that I wasn't able to garner any useful information, I head toward the main door and leave the building.

CHAPTER 33

I'm thinking about Régine and Jennie as I arrive at Sweet Tea. I can't help but wonder if they were somehow in cahoots with each other. But, then again, one would think they'd be smart enough not to be seen hugging each other at Marcus's funeral if they'd actually conspired to kill him.

When I come through the front door of the restaurant, I see that the place is packed with customers. We had exactly three chicken potpies left over from yesterday, and I see that all three of them have already made their way to some of the tables. At one table in particular I see a fork pierce the crust of one of those pies, lift out a heaping portion of filling, and follow it to the lips of one Officer Jack Spruce. I don't know Detective Hutchins well, but Jack has been coming in to the restaurant for years, and we've always been friendly. And, if Wavonne is right, and he is, in fact, a little sweet on me, maybe he'll share something with me about Marcus's case that Detective Hutchins hasn't.

"Jack. How's it going?"

"Hey there, Halia. Just fine. This pie is delicious."

"I'm so glad you're enjoying it. We made them fresh yesterday. You got one of the few we had left over." I pull out the chair across from him. "Mind if I sit down?"

"Of course not."

"Can I ask you something?"

"Shoot."

"You know an acquaintance of mine, Marcus Rand? I'm sure you're aware that he recently met with an untimely death?"

"It's been the talk of the station for days."

"Can you tell me anything about what's going on? Do the police have any leads or prime suspects?"

Jack suddenly looks uncomfortable.

"What? What is it?" I ask.

"Halia, I really can't be divulging information about active cases."

"Of course. I wouldn't want you getting into trouble, but even the tiniest bit of information would be appreciated."

He looks down at the table and then back up at me. "I don't know how to say this, Halia . . . and I probably shouldn't mention it anyway. . . ."

"Mention what?"

"There are some leads and they all . . . well, they all point to one prime suspect."

"Who?"

Jack doesn't say anything. Instead he points his eyes at Wavonne, who is taking an order at a table a few feet away.

"Wavonne? But Detective Hutchins was in here the other day and talked with her for almost an hour. I thought she had been cleared."

"Just between you and me, Halia"—Jack lowers his voice—"I don't think it will be long before they bring her in for more formal questioning. They are trying to get a Macy's clerk to agree to identify her in a lineup . . . well, not Wavonne. . . . I'm sure Wavonne is innocent. . . . I mean, whoever bought a purse from the Macy's in Marlow Heights with Marcus's credit card—that's the person they are looking to identify."

"What do you mean they are *trying* to get the Macy's clerk to agree to indentify her?"

"The young lady at Macy's doesn't want to get involved in a murder investigation and is refusing to cooperate. Can't say I blame her, even though Hutchins assured her that she won't be in any danger. He tried to get her to identify Wavonne in a photo, but she wouldn't even look at it."

God bless her! I think to myself. "How did they get a photo of Wavonne?"

"I don't know. Maybe they downloaded it from her Facebook page or something."

"I hope the clerk does agree to get involved," I lie. "Wavonne has nothing to do with Marcus's murder, and if they were to put Wavonne in a lineup, I'm sure the Macy's clerk would not recognize her because it simply was not Wavonne who used Marcus's credit card."

"I'm sure you're right, Halia."

"I wish the police would stop wasting their time on Wavonne. There are so many other people in Marcus's life they should be checking out. Jennie Becks, for instance. Do you know if they have checked out Jennie? She was Marcus's old girlfriend—"

Jack interrupts me. "Marcus's old girlfriend who he was cheating on with Régine. Yes, we're aware of her relationship with Marcus. She's been interviewed. She actually was here the night Marcus was killed."

"Yes. I know. I just saw her at Marcus's funeral and recognized her from that evening."

"She was with three of her friends all night. After they left here, they went to a bar—someplace called The Park at 14th. Apparently it's a fancy-smanchy nightclub in the city. Her friends served as her alibi, and the doorman said they are regulars at the club. He remembered letting them in ahead of several other guests waiting in line. You know how those clubs are—they always let the pretty young women in ahead of everyone else."

"So that takes Jennie off the suspect list. But what about some of Marcus's other dinner companions that night he was killed?" I ask. "You're familiar with the case, so you're aware of Heather and Josh Williams, right?"

"Yes."

"I gave Detective Hutchins a lead about them a couple of days ago? Do you know if he followed up?"

Jack smiles. "The cologne smell? Yes. Everyone had a good laugh over that one at the station."

"What do you mean?"

"I mean, I think you did Wavonne more harm than good by bringing that up to Hutchins. Now he half-thinks you're a little nutty and imagining smells . . . and half-thinks you made the whole thing up to take suspicion off Wavonne."

"What?! Imagining smells? Are—"

I'm infuriated, but Jack interrupts me again and doesn't allow me to finish the tirade I'm about to go on. "But to his credit, Halia, Detective Hutchins did follow up. He had the trunk swept for DNA samples."

"And?"

"Nada. Which isn't surprising given that Marcus shaved his head, and even less surprising considering that, at some point, the trunk liner had been removed."

"Removed?"

"Yep. Word at the station is that there was no liner or carpet or whatever you call it in the trunk."

"Please tell me the cops find that very dubious."

"Yes, I suppose, but apparently Heather and Josh said that milk had leaked from some groceries, and they had to get rid of the liner due to the sour smell."

"Sour smell, my ass! Marcus Rand was in that trunk. I'm sure of it."

Jack just looks at me, clearly unsure what to say.

"Don't tell me you think I'm imagining smells, too?"

"Of course not, but what you smelled could have been any number of things, and it's certainly not enough to lead to any arrests."

I think about what he's said and sit across from him quietly as I consider it.

"Things will be okay, Halia. Hutchins is a good cop. He'll find out who did it."

"I hope so, Jack. I appreciate you sharing what you know with me. I'll let you get back to your lunch. Pick something off the dessert menu on the house," I say and get up from the table.

It's too busy to leave right now, but when peak lunch hours are over, I'm going to pay a visit to Heather and Josh Williams. Wavonne is not going to be paraded around in a lineup for something I got her involved in. I'm not convinced Heather and Josh killed Marcus, but I am convinced they are hiding something, and I'm going to find out what it is if I have to promise them free fried chicken and waffles for the rest of their lives.

RECIPE FROM HALIA'S KITCHEN

Halia's Fried Chicken Wings

Ingredients

1 tablespoon seasoning salt (such as Morton's Season All)
2 teaspoons black pepper
½ teaspoons cayenne pepper
1 teaspoons poultry seasoning
12 whole chicken wings
1 cup all-purpose flour
1 cup cornstarch
4 tablespoons instant mashed potatoes
2 cups whole milk
4 cups Panko bread crumbs

- Fill deep fryer with enough vegetable oil for wings to be completely submerged and heat to 350 degrees Fahrenheit.

- Whisk together seasoning salt, black pepper, cayenne pepper, and poultry seasoning.

- Sprinkle seasoning mix over both sides of wings and marinate in the refrigerator for 2 hours.

- Whisk flour, cornstarch, instant mashed potatoes, and milk until blended.

- Dredge wings in the flour mixture and then into the Panko bread crumbs.

- Let coated wings set at room temperature on a wire rack for 10 minutes.

- Cook wings, a few at a time, for 7 to 10 minutes, turning occasionally.

Twelve Wings

Note: For best results, divide Panko bread crumbs into two bowls as they tend to clump after a few wings are dipped in them. Cooking times vary due to wing size. Use smaller wings for more even cooking.

CHAPTER 34

"We've got trouble," I say to Wavonne.

"Trouble? New trouble or old trouble?"

"The police are looking at you as the prime suspect."

"Me?! Oh, *hail* no!" It's after two o'clock and the restaurant has quieted down so Wavonne's words echo throughout the place.

"Would you keep your voice down?"

Wavonne lowers her voice. "Why me?"

"Because you fit the description of the person who used Marcus's credit card, which makes sense, considering you *were* the person using Marcus's credit card. Lucky for us, the salesperson who remembers you is wary about getting involved in a murder investigation and isn't cooperating."

"Remembers me? She must wait on thousands of people. Why'd she remember me?"

"Because you apparently complained to no end when she was ringing up the purse you bought."

"All I said was 'Macy's *sucks ass*.' She must hear that all the time. You've been in that store over by Iverson Mall. They don't stock half the nice things they sell over at Pentagon City or Montgomery Mall. And it's always a mess. Whenever I go in there, it looks like Porsha and Kenya just had a throwdown on top the Gucci display."

"Never mind. It doesn't matter. What's important now is getting the police off your case and moving them on to some-one who may have actually committed the crime."

"And how we gonna do that?"

"I'm leaving now to go see Heather. I couldn't find her home address, but I did a search on the Internet, and I found out where she works."

"I'm goin' with you."

"No. You stay here. We need to handle her delicately and being . . . being delicate is not your specialty, Wavonne. I think she might talk to me if I approach her in the right way."

"And she might *kill* you like she did Marcus. I'm goin' with you, Halia. That girl's gonna talk one way or the other."

Once again I explain to an increasingly concerned Laura that Wavonne and I are ducking out for an hour or so, and Wavonne and I leave Sweet Tea and make our way into the city. We're only a few miles over the border from D.C., so with no traffic, we make it to Heather's office in less than half an hour and find street parking nearby.

"Where does she work?"

"From what I could find online, she works in human re-sources for a law firm," I say to Wavonne as we enter Heather's building and look at the directory for Saunders and Kraff and Associates.

"Seventh floor."

Wavonne and I approach the elevators that eventually open to an opulent space of shiny hardwood floors, plush chairs, and a granite reception counter with fresh flowers on the far corner.

"May I help you?" asks a pretty blond receptionist.

"Yes. We're here to see Heather Williams."

"May I get your name?"

"Halia Watkins and Wavonne Hix."

She picks up her phone and dials. "Heather. I have Ms. Watkins and Ms. Hix here to see you?"

Silence.

"Halia Watkins and Wavonne Hix," the receptionist repeats into the phone.

"Tell her we're from Sweet Tea."

"They said to tell you they are from Sweet Tea," the young lady says into the phone before looking back at us. "She'll be right out."

Shortly thereafter Heather emerges from behind a dark wood-paneled door looking more mature than I remembered her, probably because of her professional dress.

"Halia. Hello," she says with a perplexed look on her face. "Is there something I can help you with?"

"Damn straight, there is," Wavonne says.

I bump Wavonne with my elbow to shut her up. "Yes. There is, Heather. Thank you. Can we talk in private?"

She hesitates for a moment. "Ah . . . yes . . . sure." She gestures for us to follow her, and the three of us walk along a softly lit hallway to her office.

"Such a nice office," I say as she closes the door behind us.

"Thanks. I really only have it because I'm a recruiter. I need a private place to conduct interviews. Otherwise, I'd be out there in one of the cubes."

I nod and there's a brief moment of silence before Heather asks, "Are you still considering investing in the Reverie Homes program?"

"No. We're here about another matter, actually."

Heather doesn't say anything so I begin. "I don't know of a good way to approach this, so I guess I'll just say it. Heather, you're a nice young woman . . . at least I hope you're a nice young woman, but I know as sure as the sky is blue that I smelled Marcus's cologne coming from the trunk of your car, and I need you to explain why."

"So you're the one who prompted the police to show up at our house and search our trunk?"

"So I am."

"Did they tell you they didn't find anything related to Marcus's death?"

"Yes. They also told me the trunk liner had been removed."

"So?" Heather asks, and I can tell she's trying to hide it, but my comment has unsettled her.

"Seems like an extraordinary coincidence that shortly after Marcus is killed, I get a whiff of his cologne from your trunk. Then, when the police arrive at your house, the piece of material that would most likely contain some DNA evidence has been removed."

"Josh had a gasoline container in the trunk . . . that he uses for the lawn mower. It tipped over. That's—"

"A gasoline container? That's funny. I heard it was a carton of milk that leaked."

Heather stumbles. "There was a carton of milk. . . . That was before the incident with the gasoline."

"You expect us to believe that?! Do we look like some kind of dumbass hood rats?"

I glare at Wavonne, and she shuts up. But I can see her simmering toward a boil. I put my hand on her leg and stroke it gently. "Take it down a notch, Wavonne. There's no need to get riled up," I say to her before turning back to Heather. "As Wavonne said, you really don't expect us to believe that, do you? And even if we did, it still does not explain why Marcus's cologne, a custom scent made just for him, was wafting out of your trunk."

Heather just stares back at us, and I can see her hands trembling just ever so much.

"You and Josh had a right to be angry with Marcus. I don't

dispute that, and one might understand . . . even a jury might understand how, in a heated moment, someone might lose it. What do they call that? Temporary insanity?"

"I'm sorry, but you two need to go. I don't have any information for you."

"We're not leaving, Heather, until you tell us what happened the night Marcus was killed."

"Do I need to call security?"

I call her bluff. "I don't think you'll do that. You'll have a lot of explaining to do when your colleagues see two women being manhandled out of your office."

Wavonne and I just sit there and stare at Heather. She looks genuinely afraid, but doesn't say anything.

"I've got all day," I say, looking at my watch.

Heather nervously shrugs her shoulders, a bead of sweat forming on her forehead. The three of us sit there in silence for a few seconds, which turns into a minute, and then two minutes. I begin to wonder if I've ever been in a more uncomfortable situation in my life. We continue to play the waiting game, and I begin to doubt that Wavonne and I will be able to outlast her. She's clearly strong-willed. I've got a restaurant to run. I can't sit here all day playing chicken with Heather Williams.

"Fine," I say and stand up. "We'll go, but we are *not* done here."

"Goin'?" Wavonne says, standing up, as well. "*Hold* up!" she adds, putting a hand in the air. "We ain't goin' nowhere." She stomps over to the other side of Heather's desk. "Look here. The police are on my ass, and I didn't do *nothin'*. We know you know somethin', and we ain't leavin' 'til you tell us what it is. I'd hate to mess up that pretty little white girl mug of yours," Wavonne says in a harsh tone before she puts her hands on the arms of Heather's chair and shoves her face right up against hers. Heather's head is pressed so hard against the high back of her chair I swear it might burst right through. Her face goes from bright red to stark white as Wavonne raises her voice even louder. "And I don't like no violence, but let me remind you in case you forgot . . . I'm from PG County, hooka', and I will *wreck* a bitch!"

"We didn't kill him! We *didn't!* Josh just moved the body. *I swear!*" Heather yelps like a scared kitten.

"Josh did *what?*" I ask, grabbing Wavonne by the elbow and pulling her away from Heather.

"He moved Marcus's body . . . dumped him in the lake. That's all. We . . . he didn't kill him."

"Then why'd he move the body?" Wavonne asks.

Heather looks down at her lap and then back up at us. "Because Josh thought I killed Marcus. I do have a temper on me, and honestly, I've gotten . . . well, I've gotten sort of violent before. But I go to an anger management program, and I'm doing better. I've done some things in the past that I'm not proud of, but I would never kill anyone. Josh and I had a fight when we got home from the restaurant . . . not really a fight . . . it was mostly me yelling at him. I've always blamed him for us getting involved in Marcus's mortgage scheme. I eventually stormed out of the house, and, when I didn't come back for a while, he got worried and went looking for me."

The color has come back into her face, and I sense she's relieved to finally be sharing this information with someone.

"He didn't know where I went, but he thought I might have gone back to your restaurant to see if Marcus was still there and scream at him the way I'd screamed at Josh. He drove back over there, but the restaurant was dark, so he figured he'd look for me at my mother's or my friend Christie's house. Once he'd passed the restaurant, instead of turning around, he said he figured he'd just loop around the back of the shopping center to the exit. That's when he came upon Marcus's body. He thought I'd killed him."

"You? You're tiny. How would you have killed Marcus?" I ask.

"I have . . . *used* to have anger issues. Poor Josh has been on the wrong side of my temper more than once. It's ridiculous . . . really it is, but I can see how, in a panicked moment, he might have thought that I . . . well, you know . . ."

"The scar on Josh's cheek?" I ask, remembering how noticeable it was when they came to Sweet Tea for lunch a couple of days ago.

Heather looks away from us. "Like I said, I've done some things I'm not proud of, but I would never *kill* someone. Josh just got all flustered and wanted to protect me. He thought he could fix the situation by getting rid of the body or at least buy some time to figure out what to do. It was a stupid thing to do. I had been at my mother's the whole time."

"Josh must be awfully strong," Wavonne says. "Halia and I were barely able to drag Marcus out of the kitchen to the back alley, and there were two of us. How'd Josh get him in the trunk and dump him in the lake all by himself?"

I frown at Wavonne as Heather raises her eyebrows. "What do you mean you were barely able to drag Marcus out of the kitchen?"

"Nothing," I say.

"Marcus was dead inside of Sweet Tea? And you guys moved the body? And you're here questioning *me*?"

"That's not important—"

"Like hell it isn't. How do I know *you* didn't kill him?"

"Fine," I say and take a breath, seething mad at Wavonne for opening her big mouth. "We did drag Marcus's body out back. We found him dead in the restaurant. Someone hit him over the head with a cast-iron frying pan. Much like your husband, I panicked and was afraid my business wouldn't survive if word got out it was a murder scene, so Wavonne and I did some body-moving of our own."

Heather looks at me thoughtfully. "Well, at least I know Josh's secret is safe with you. You blab to the police about Josh, and I'll blab to the police about you."

"Point taken." I sit back down, and motion for Wavonne to do the same. "So if you and Josh didn't kill Marcus, then who did?"

"Jacqueline," Heather says conclusively. "I'm almost certain she did it."

CHAPTER 35

"I knew that bougie ho was up to no good. How do you know Jacqueline did it?" Wavonne asks.

"Josh saw her sitting in her car when he drove into the parking lot. She drives that tacky gold BMW, right?"

"He saw her when he was driving around looking for you?"

"Yes. He said he didn't really process it until later. She was still at the restaurant when we left, so I guess it didn't seem that odd that she was still there."

"She was just sitting in her car?"

"That's what Josh said. He wasn't sure what she was doing. He was looking for me, and when he came upon the body he forgot all about her and just got to work getting rid of it. He wasn't thinking straight."

"We have to tell the police about this," I say.

"Oh no, we don't. I don't want Josh placed back at the restaurant after we left the first time. Remember, you blab, I blab."

"Fine, fine." I think for a moment. "If Jacqueline really is the culprit, we need to find a way to get the police interested in investigating her further, but I'm really not sure what we're dealing with here."

"What do you mean?"

"Jacqueline's car was not in the parking lot when Wavonne and I came back to the restaurant, and Marcus was dead when we found him. If Jacqueline did kill Marcus, she did it before Wavonne and I got there. For some reason, she came back to the scene of the crime. Why would she do that?" I ask and think about how I didn't see Marcus's car in the lot the night of the murder. I wonder if I might have missed Jacqueline's, as well, but that seems unlikely. Marcus's car is black and quite discreet at night while Jacqueline's flashy gold BMW is glaringly noticeable anytime.

"Probably to cover her tracks as best she could," Wavonne says.

"Or maybe to move the body herself or, like Wavonne said, to get rid of any evidence that would link her to the crime."

"The frying pan!" I say. "She probably came back to wipe her fingerprints off the frying pan. She could have hit Marcus over the head with it in a heated moment, ran away in a panic, and thought about the evidence she'd left behind after she got out of there."

"Makes sense. So there's a frying pan with her fingerprints on it? Where is it?" Heather asks.

"Yeah, *Halia,* where is it?" Wavonne asks with a snarky grin.

"It's not of any use to us now. When Wavonne and I were cleaning up, I absentmindedly dropped it into a sink full of soapy water."

"Really?" Heather asks, looking at me the way I often look at Wavonne when she's done something stupid.

"Yes. Really," I say, embarrassed that yet another person knows of my moment of carelessness. "I guess all I can do is call Detective Hutchins and put a bug in his ear about Jacqueline . . . remind him of her often-obvious disdain for her brother."

"Don't call him. Call your *boyfriend* instead."

"Jack is not my boyfriend," I respond, but Wavonne does have a point. I'll get a much better reception from Jack than I will from Detective Hutchins.

I pull my phone from my purse and hit Jack's number in my contacts. He gave it to me a long time ago and told me I could call him if anyone ever got out of hand at the restaurant.

"Officer Spruce."

"Jack. Hi. It's Halia from Sweet Tea."

"Hey there," Jack says, sounding excited to hear from me as Wavonne makes kissy noises with her lips. "What can I do for you?"

"I was just wondering if you had any updates on Marcus's case."

"Halia, you know I'm not supposed to share updates on ongoing investigations."

"Of course. I understand, but I just want to make sure you . . . the police . . . are considering Marcus's sister, Jacqueline. You can ask anyone. Everyone knew that she essentially hated her brother." As I'm saying this, I suddenly feel guilty for throwing Jacqueline under the bus. She's doesn't eat my food, and she's a bit of a prickly pear, but she's always been generally pleasant to me. I certainly have no ill will toward her. But if Josh really did see her back at Sweet Tea after the murder, the cops should be prodded to at least investigate her further. If she has nothing to hide, she should be fine.

"Yeah. We heard about her tenuous relationship with her brother from a few folks. I shouldn't be sharing this, but Detective Hutchins did briefly consider her a suspect. He did some investigating, and it turns out she actually co-owns the house she and Marcus lived in. Maybe Marcus thought putting her name on it, as well, would protect it in case he was ever sued."

"Sued? Say for screwing people out of their savings through a crazy mortgage scam?"

"Something like that. But once we got the lead of a, shall we say, *full-figured* woman using Marcus's stolen credit card, Hutchins backed off her. Jacqueline's lean as a string bean. She doesn't fit the description."

"That's good information to know, Jack. Thanks for keeping me in the loop."

"You're going to get me in trouble, Halia," he says with a laugh.

"Nonsense. I won't tell a soul what you shared with me. Hope you'll come by the restaurant soon."

"I will. Have a good day, Halia."

"Hope you'll come on by the restaurant soon," Wavonne says, mimicking me while batting her eyes. "I don't know why you two just don't get a room and get it over with."

I ignore Wavonne, but Heather laughs.

"So it turns out Jacqueline had more than dislike of her brother as a motive to kill Marcus. She's on the deed to the house. With Marcus dead, it's all hers. But they're not looking at her as a suspect as she doesn't fit the description of the Rubenesque woman who used his stolen credit card."

"Someone used Marcus's credit card after he was killed?"

"Apparently so," Wavonne says before I have a chance to respond.

"Thank you, Heather. You've been really helpful," I say, getting up from my chair. "I guess we'd better get going. If the cops are not going to investigate Jacqueline, then I'll just have to do it myself."

CHAPTER 36

"What's a Zumba class?" I ask Wavonne as I peck away at the computer in my office.

"Zumba? That's some Latin dancin' exercise bidness uppity heifers do at the gym. I've seen 'em on TV shakin' their behinds to Marc Anthony and Paulina Rubio. Why?"

"I found Jacqueline's fitness Web site. It says she's teaching one of these Zumba classes in a couple of hours over at the LA Fitness a few miles up the road."

"Don't tell me you're thinkin' of goin'?"

"I don't know. Seems like a good enough excuse to reach out to her and try to find out what she was doing in the parking lot so late the night Marcus was killed."

"*You?* In a Zumba class? This I gots to see."

After I wrap up a few things at the restaurant, Wavonne and I swing by the house to change clothes. Yes, I own yoga pants. I have never, nor do I intend to ever *do* yoga, but damn if they aren't comfortable as all get-out. I put them on with a big T-shirt and tennis shoes and call for Wavonne to get a move on.

A few seconds later she emerges from her room looking like she just stepped out of some Wayans's Brothers' spoof of

Flashdance. She's squeezed herself into a purple spandex leotard, cinched at the waist with a shiny black belt. She's wearing sheer panty hose and some loud neon sneakers that I'm sure cost way more than she has any business spending on shoes. She's taken off her wig and pulled her real hair back and clipped on a fake ponytail.

"Really?" is all I can bring myself to say.

"What?"

"We're not making an Olivia Newton John video from the eighties, Wavonne."

"Don't be hatin' just 'cause you ain't got no style, Halia. And who's Olivia Newton John?"

I laugh. "Hose, Wavonne? You're gonna work out in panty hose?"

"Halia, these thighs *need* hose. I get to shakin' and swayin' without hose on, I'm liable to take out a few skinny bitches. Besides, I gots to look good. There may be some handsome brothas in the class."

"I seriously doubt any men in a Latin dance exercise class are going to be interested in buying what you're selling, Wavonne." I look her up and down one more time. "No matter. Let's go."

We step out the front door just as Momma is coming in.

"Where are the two of you going looking like that? Halia, you've got to make more of an effort if you ever expect to land a man. And Wavonne, why are you dressed like you're performing at a burlesque club?" She looks us both up and down. "One of you isn't trying at all, and the other one looks like she's ready to give it away to the highest bidder."

"We're goin' to a Zumba class, Aunt Celia. We're gonna get our exercise on."

Momma laughs. "No really. Where are you going?"

"We are going to a Zumba class, Momma. Marcus's sister,

Jacqueline, is always asking us to try out one of her classes. We decided to take her up on it."

"You've left the restaurant in the middle of the day to take an exercise class? I don't buy it, Halia. What are the two of you up to?"

"Nothing. We just want to try it out."

"You're not sticking your nose where it doesn't belong, are you? I don't want them pulling your body out of Wellington Lake."

"Of course not," I lie, and I can see from Momma's expression that she knows it. "We've got to go, or we're going to miss it."

"I'm serious, Halia. You two, be careful. For all we know, Jacqueline is the one who killed Marcus."

"Don't be silly, Momma," I say, even though she may very well be right.

It takes Wavonne and me about fifteen minutes to trek across town and get to the gym. I don't remember the last time I was in a health club, and I'm uneasy walking through the front door. The place is vast and a busy beehive of activity. I see people on treadmills and elliptical trainers and working out on machines that I wouldn't even begin to know how to use. It's a younger crowd of mostly African Americans, but there a few white, Asian, and Latino people milling about, as well.

"Can I help you?" asks a cute young girl behind the counter.

"Yes. We'd like—" I'm about to ask about buying a couple of day passes when Wavonne intervenes.

"We're thinkin' of joining this gym. You know, we've heard good things about it."

"Great," the young lady says. "I'd be happy to give you a tour."

"That'd be great, but we want to join mostly for the Zumba classes. We saw online that you have one startin' in a few minutes. You think we could try out the class for free and get a tour and all that jazz after the class?"

The girl looks at Wavonne as if she's got her number, but doesn't have the energy to argue with her. "Go ahead," she says. "The studio is downstairs."

"I just saved you thirty dollars. Those day passes are fifteen bucks apiece," Wavonne says. "And you know I like to gets me a commission on any savings I get for you."

"I'll take it off your rent," I say. "Oh wait, you don't pay any . . ."

Wavonne frowns at me, and we make our way to a big studio surrounded by mirrors on three walls and enclosed with a glass fourth wall just to be sure everyone in the gym can see me making me a complete fool of myself in an exercise class.

We see Jacqueline talking to someone as we approach.

"It's all about discipline," Jacqueline says to the slightly overweight, middle-aged woman. "You have to learn how to say no and make the right choices. Is it going to be a hamburger and a milk shake? Or a healthy salad with a cold glass of lemon water?"

"You make it sound so easy," the woman says.

"It's not that hard once you get into a health regimen and make it a way of life. You need to find healthy foods you like. I make a blueberry smoothie every morning with low-fat Greek yogurt, and it's lovely. I enjoy salads and fresh vegetables. I can't remember the last time I ate anything fried. If you go to my Web site, you'll see some healthy recipes. I make them all the time, and they help me stay fit."

"I wish I had your discipline."

"Don't we all," I say, cutting into the conversation. I want to get a word in with Jacqueline before the class starts.

"Halia!" Jacqueline says with a smile. "How are you? And I see you brought Wavonne. So good to see you both."

The woman Jacqueline was speaking to smiles at both of us, then looks back at Jacqueline. "Thanks for the tips, Jacqueline. I'll check out your Web site."

"Please do. It's has all sorts of resources for healthy living."

The woman smiles and walks off to find a place in the growing crowd in the studio.

"So you two finally decided to attend one of my classes. I hope you like it."

"I'm sure we will."

"Now, just take it easy and don't push yourself too hard. You can take breaks at any time. Don't feel like you have to keep up with the regulars. If any moves are too strenuous or complicated, just take a break and march in place," she says, doing a quick marching demonstration.

Damn, do we look that out of shape? I wonder to myself as I hear her talk to us as if we haven't worked out a day in our lives and might drop dead from the stress of a couple of jumping jacks. I guess I'd be upset if it weren't pretty close to the truth.

Jacqueline looks up at the clock. "It's time to get started."

Wavonne and I find a spot in the crowd as Jacqueline slips a microphone on and presses some buttons on a console attached to the wall. Some high-energy Latin music begins to blare through the speakers while Jacqueline gets into position in front of the room. She faces the mirror rather than us, which I guess is supposed to make it easier for us to follow her moves.

"Single, single, double," she says as she waves her hands to the left and then to the right. "One, two, three, and clap." She swirls her hips three times and claps.

Well, this isn't so bad.

"Single, single, double," she says again, but this time she's lifting her legs and swinging her arms between them.

"Two bends. To the left. Two bends." Now she's doing knee bends, shimmying to the left, and doing two more knee bends.

I figure it's not a great sign that I'm already starting to get winded. I look over at Wavonne, and I can tell she's feeling it, too.

"Elbows to belly buttons, ladies and gentlemen." She's plunging her elbows toward her stomach while thrusting her hips forward. I try to follow, but I feel ridiculous while my stamina continues to wane. We barely get another ten minutes into the class before I resort to marching in place.

"Lord Jesus!" I hear Wavonne say as she continues to try to keep up, but she eventually joins in with my marching.

"What's that saying about a whore in church?" Wavonne says to me when she manages to get a breath. Even the low-key marching is doing a number on us.

"I'm sweating like one, too, Wavonne."

We manage to make it through the rest of the class. But rather than taking occasional marching breaks from Jacqueline's Zumba instructions, we take occasional breaks from marching and try to keep up with the class for few minutes at a time. I honestly thought that, given the fact that I move around all day at the restaurant, I wouldn't have found this class so taxing, but boy, was I wrong. By the time Jacqueline takes us through some closing stretches and turns the music off, I think I've lost a pound of water and poor Wavonne is a mess of sweat and smeared makeup.

"You got some scissors?" Wavonne asks me.

"No. Why?"

"'Cause I wanna chop the crotch out this leotard and take these hose off right now."

"I told you not to wear hose. Now come on. Let's go try to get a few words in with Jacqueline."

Wavonne and I take some deep breaths as we approach the front of the room.

"Thank you, Jacqueline. That was quite a workout."

"I'm glad you enjoyed it. I hope you'll come back. You'll build more and more stamina each time."

"I'm sure we will," I say, trying to shift gears. "Are you doing okay? I know it's been a rough time for you."

"I'm hangin' in there. Working . . . teaching my classes . . . staying active—that's the best thing for me right now."

"They do say exercise is a great way to relieve stress. Can we buy you something at the juice bar?"

"Thank you, but I've got another class on their way in now."

I look around and see that some people from the first class never left and other new attendees are walking in.

"You're doing this *again?*" Wavonne asks, floored that anyone would have the energy to teach two draining classes in a row.

"Yes."

"I would like to check on you," I say. "I know we don't know each other that well, but Marcus helped me get Sweet Tea off the ground, and I'm sure he'd want to know someone was looking in on you."

"That's sweet, Halia. It's really not necessary."

"Will you be home later this evening?"

"Yes. Why?"

"I have an errand to run in the neighborhood. Maybe I could stop by and say hi?"

Jacqueline smiles. "That would be fine, Halia. I should be home after five or so."

"Great."

"I've really got to get this class started, so if you'll excuse me."

"Of course," I say, and Wavonne follows me as we exit the studio and climb the stairs to the main level.

"Hold up," Wavonne says, grabbing my hand. "Wait until she turns around, or we'll get stuck takin' that damn tour."

"Now," she says, pulling me by the hand as the girl turns toward a bin of clean towels and begins to fold them. "If she turns around, don't look at her . . . and if she says anything, just keep walkin'."

I do as I'm told, and we slink past the young woman without a word.

CHAPTER 37

Welcome to Mitchellville says the sign I've just driven past. I'm on my way to what is now Jacqueline's home—the home she used to share with Marcus that apparently became all hers upon his death. Mitchellville is not what most people picture when they think of Prince George's County—stately homes and manicured lawns are not really part of the image the media has created, but Mitchellville is generally not the area of Prince George's County featured on the news when drug deals and armed robberies are reported. By anyone's definition it's a "hoity-toity" neighborhood with oversized homes, landscaped yards, and luxury cars parked in three car garages. It was named for John Mitchell, who owned a plantation in the area in the seventeen and eighteen hundreds. How ironic that a town named for a plantation owner is now one of the most affluent predominantly African American communities in the United States.

When I reach Jacqueline's house, I take in the grandeur of the place. I was here once before for a holiday party a few years ago, but that was at night. In daylight you can't help but be awed by the expansive windows, rooftop dormers, and three-car garage. One thing about Marcus: he liked to live high on the hog.

After I park the van on the street I walk up the driveway to the house and knock on the door. I'm only a little anxious at this point. In general, my nerves have been frayed since the night Marcus met his maker, so being restless has become the new normal for me.

It might not have been the best idea to come out here alone, especially if Jacqueline really did off her brother, but one of my other servers is out sick. I needed Wavonne to stay at the restaurant and help out. Besides, I'm just going to do a little questioning . . . nose around a bit and see what I can find out . . . and, just in case, my pepper spray is within easy reach in my front pocket.

"Halia. Hi," Jacqueline, dressed in sweatpants and a tight spandex top, says when she comes to the door. She has a big glass of water in her hand.

"Hi, Jacqueline. Thanks for letting me come by and say hello. We really didn't have a chance to talk at the gym."

"Sure. Please, come in. I was finishing up a workout."

She just taught two exercise classes earlier today, and she's working out again? I think to myself as I follow her into the house and see a mat and some free weights in a mostly empty room to my right.

"You're so committed. Today was the first time I've exercised in forever."

"It just becomes a way of life," she says, and I know she's not trying to sound condescending, but it sure feels that way. "And it helps with stress release . . . and, God knows, I've needed some of that lately."

"I'm sure."

"Would you like anything? A glass of tea? I was just about to whip up a salad for dinner."

I feel like saying, "Does this body look like it eats salads for dinner?" But, instead, I politely decline. "No. Thank you. So, how are you? It must be a difficult time."

"It is, but I was busy planning the funeral, and now I'm buried in paperwork, trying to clean up Marcus's business dealings. I haven't had much time to grieve. I'm not sure if that's a good thing or not."

She really doesn't look like a grieving sibling. Despite supposedly just working out, her hair is styled nicely, and her makeup is intact. She's looks well rested and almost what you might call perky.

"It's so hard to lose a loved one," I say and feel a bit ridiculous, as I'm not sure how much Jacqueline really loved Marcus. "I hope you'll come by the restaurant anytime if you need support or want to be around friends." I feel even more ridiculous now as I really consider Jacqueline more of an acquaintance than a friend, and she probably feels the same way about me. But it's hard to just jump into questioning her about why she was sitting in the parking lot of Sweet Tea when Josh came back to the restaurant.

"Marcus and I had our differences, but he was my brother. And it's just so horrible how he died. The police say he took a blow to the head before he was thrown in Wellington Lake. No one should die that way."

"Have the police told you much about the investigation?"

"Just that they have a few leads that they are following up. What about you? Have you heard anything?"

"Not really," I lie. "The police have questioned everyone at the restaurant the night we last saw Marcus alive. I don't think they got much useful information, though. I also talked with Charles Pritchett . . . you remember . . . Marcus's business associate?"

"Yes, I know Charles. Why were you talking to him?"

"I was just trying to see what I could find out. A man was seen for the last time in my restaurant. It makes a girl curious about what happened to him."

Jacqueline nods.

"Other than you, he said he was the last one to leave Sweet Tea the night Marcus died."

"Yes. He and Marcus chatted for a bit after everyone else left, and then I left about ten minutes after he did."

"After you left, did you come back here?"

"Yes. I went home and went to bed."

"So I guess you didn't wait up for Marcus?"

"Marcus was a grown man. Besides, he usually spent Saturday nights at Mother's. Why all the questions, Halia?"

I'm silent for a moment, wondering if I should play my hand and tell her I know she came back to the restaurant later that night and ask for an explanation or just see what I can find out through further questioning without telling her what I know. "Did you really come back here, Jacqueline? Straight back here?"

Jacqueline raises her eyebrows at me. "Of course I did. Where else would I go that late at night? What are you getting at, Halia?"

I remain quiet for a second or two before speaking. "Jacqueline, I know you came back to the restaurant later that night."

Jacqueline stops sipping on her glass of water, and there's a noticeable change in her demeanor. "What do you mean?"

"Just what I said. I know you came back to the restaurant the night Marcus was killed."

"Do you care to explain how you know what you think you know?" She's trying to appear calm, but I've clearly agitated her.

"Is that really necessary, Jacqueline?"

She looks at me intently, and her unease seems to be morphing into something more. I'm starting to see panic in her face, and my own heart starts to pound. *Did she really kill Marcus? Why else would she look so flustered? Am I sitting next to a murderer?* I place my hand in my pocket and grasp my pepper spray.

"Halia, you can't tell anyone. Really, you can't."

Oh my God! She really did do it. She killed him!

"Please, Halia! I don't want anyone to know."

Is she really asking me not to tell anyone that she killed her brother? "Jacqueline, how can I not tell—"

"I would just die, Halia . . . I would *just die* if anyone knew that I snuck back to the restaurant to get some of your fried chicken."

"Jacqueline, I have to tell the police that you—" I cut myself off as what she says begins to register. "Wha . . . What? Wait a minute. . . . What did you say?"

"It just looked so good . . . all juicy and crispy . . . and the others at the table were eating it and enjoying it so much . . . and I had that damn salad with grilled chicken. Do you know how *tired* I am of salads with grilled chicken?! Your fried chicken was all I could think about the whole way home."

I don't say a word. I still can't believe what I'm hearing.

"By the time I got home, my mouth was watering . . . hell, I was practically clucking like a chicken myself. Then I remembered that you told Marcus you had left a tray of fried chicken in the walk-in refrigerator. I've got copies of all of Marcus's keys, so I went back, let myself in, and got me some of that fried chicken."

Got me some of that fried chicken? Did Jacqueline, prim and proper Jacqueline, just say "*got* me some"? I know my fried chicken is good, but I didn't know it was good enough to make Jacqueline start talking like Wavonne.

"Oh Halia, it was *so* good! I grabbed a few pieces and was in and out of the restaurant in a flash. I didn't think anyone would know. I should have waited until I got home, but I couldn't help myself. I started chowing down right there in my car in the parking lot under cover of night."

"So what I'm hearing is that you went back to the restaurant to get some *chicken?*"

Jacqueline looks down at her lap, hiding the shame on her face.

"So you didn't kill Marcus?"

"Kill Marcus!?" she says, quickly lifting her head. "Have you lost your mind?"

"Quite possibly," I say. "You really just went back to Sweet Tea to get some chicken? Really?" I ask, and it occurs to me that Jacqueline's story is too ridiculous to not be true. No one could make that up.

"Isn't that how you knew I was there? You noticed the chicken missing?"

"Um . . . no." Does she think I go around inventorying pieces of fried chicken and, even if I did, I had told Marcus to wrap some for his guests, so it would have made sense that some had gone missing. "Let's just say someone saw your car in the parking lot."

"Curse that damn car Marcus bought me. It's impossible to be inconspicuous in that thing."

"Yeah, really . . . how's a girl supposed to pilfer covert fried chicken in a flashy car? You need to get yourself a Chevrolet," I say with a laugh.

Jacqueline looks at me sternly, not even cracking a smile.

"Oh, *come on,* Jacqueline. It's funny."

A slight grin comes across her face, and I can't help but start to snicker at the thought of her, probably still dressed in her designer pantsuit, holding a fried chicken wing to her mouth with perfectly manicured fingers, and gnawing the meat off the bone like a beaver collecting wood for his dam.

"It's not that funny, Halia," she says, rolling her eyes, her smile widening.

"Are you kidding? It's a riot," I say, not even trying to keep it in anymore.

Jacqueline starts laughing with me. "Oh girl, I was like a pig in shit . . . one wing after another, and when I was done I wanted more," she says, sounding less and less like the perpetually dignified woman I'm so used to. "I got a grease stain on my Lafayette jacket, and I didn't even care."

We're both laughing, and I'm enjoying a side of Jacqueline that I've never seen before.

"That was a real moment of weakness for me." She wipes her eyes. "I pride myself on discipline and healthy living, but every now and then, a girl's *gotta eat.*" She pauses for a moment. "Did you really think I killed Marcus?"

"No, no. Of course, not," I say and think about how Jacqueline must have been scurrying around my kitchen, wrangling pieces of fried chicken, completely unaware of the fact that her brother had been killed in that very spot moments earlier. "I'm just trying to figure out what happened. I guess, as a next of kin, some people might assume that you stand to inherit much of Marcus's estate. That might cause some people to wonder if—"

"Marcus's estate? Oh, now, *that's* funny, Halia. What estate?"

I look around me. "This house, for instance. Rumor has it you co-owned it with him."

"This house," Jacqueline says, looking around her the same way I just did, "will be in foreclosure any day now. Marcus tied it up in that asinine mortgage program and, just like for Josh and Heather, the payments from Reverie stopped some time ago."

"So Marcus actually thought the program was legit? He must have if he invested in it himself."

"I'm sure he knew what he was getting into. Marcus was a lot of things, but stupid was not one of them. I'm certain he knew it was a scam, but figured he'd be able to recruit enough new chumps to keep the whole thing going long enough to get this place paid off."

"Really?"

"Yes. Marcus's elaborate lifestyle was mostly a façade trailed by calls from creditors and overdrawn accounts. He was always just keeping his head above water . . . making minimum payments here and there to keep the repo man away. About the only smart investment he made, Halia, was in your restaurant. But he insisted on keeping up appearances. I guess we both did. I like nice things as much as he did. We were both living beyond our means . . . and it's finally caught up with us . . . or *me,* at this point. I'm sure I'll have to be out of here in a matter of months. Even that damn gold car will probably have to go."

"I'm sorry."

"Oh well. It will be a fresh start—a start without Marcus. I almost can't imagine it," she says, looking away from me. "He got on my nerves to no end, and it's no secret that he was a pain in my ass, but he was my big brother. He always took care of me. He gave me a job to supplement my fitness business, a place to live . . . even a car. He was slick and always scheming, but he wasn't all bad. I'll miss him. I'm a bit lost without him . . . so much to figure out."

I reach for her hand and see just a hint of tears forming in her eyes. "You'll be okay, Jacqueline. Time is the best medicine in these situations. Just take as much of it as you need to sort things out."

"Thank you, Halia." She sits up straighter and grabs a tissue from the coffee table. "I'll be fine. Like you said, it will take some time. I think I'll feel better once the police find out who actually did kill Marcus."

"I think we'll *all* feel better when that happens. I've been chatting with the others at the table that Saturday night. Régine has a rock-solid alibi, and I'm quite certain Josh and Heather are innocent. So if they didn't do it, and you didn't do it, assuming it was someone at Sweet Tea that night, Charles is the only suspect left, but he didn't have a motive."

"Oh yes, he did," Jacqueline says.

CHAPTER 38

"What do you mean? What motive?" I ask Jacqueline.

"Well . . ." Jacqueline pauses. "You know what? Before I get into it all, how about a glass of wine? I feel like I need one."

"That would be lovely."

"Red or white?"

"Either."

"Okay, let me go pick out a nice bottle before it gets repossessed with everything else."

Jacqueline gets up from the sofa and leaves the room while I remain seated and take in the vast living room—slick hardwood floors covered just so much with handmade rugs, oil paintings on the walls, recessed lighting, and a grand fireplace with a granite mantle set between floor-to-ceiling windows. Marcus could put on a show in so many ways. I guess this house was just another piece in the façade that was his life. From what Jacqueline has said, he couldn't afford any of it—not the cars, not the clothes, and certainly not this monstrosity of a house.

"You're supposed to let it breathe, but whatever," Jacqueline says as she sets two thinly lipped wineglasses on the coffee table. She sits back down on the sofa and fills the glasses with a

Domaine Maillard Pinot Noir. I recognize the bottle immediately as it's one of the more expensive bottle of red on my wine list at Sweet Tea. Most of my wines run in the neighborhood of thirty dollars a bottle, but we sell the Domaine Maillard for sixty-seven.

"So, as I was saying, Charles hired Marcus months ago. They met at one of Charles's seminars. You know Marcus . . . always trying to get something for nothing, so he went to the one of Reverie Homes presentations to see if it was legit . . . if the stories he'd heard about people paying their houses off so quickly were actually true."

"And what did he find out?"

"Marcus was no fool. He asked several questions during the seminar and then stayed behind and questioned Charles even more. The way I understand it, the more Marcus began to figure out the business model, and that they were selling nothing more than a house of cards, his questions became less about buying in to the program and more about what Charles's role was and how he was compensated."

"No one could wheel and deal quite like our Marcus."

"You've got that right. Marcus smelled an opportunity. He and Charles went out to dinner that night, and it wasn't long before Marcus was recruiting for Reverie himself. At first he was only recruiting people to come to the seminars and would get a small commission if any of the people he referred to the seminars actually signed up and made an investment. More recently he started actually signing up clients for the program himself and getting much bigger commissions."

"So how does this relate to Charles having a reason to kill Marcus? When I talked to him, he said that Marcus worked as his underling, so he got a piece of Marcus's commissions. Seems like Marcus served him better alive than dead."

"Yes. He got a piece of Marcus's commissions as long as he remained employed with Reverie. I've been rooting through

Marcus's e-mails and, from what I can tell, the Reverie program in this area has been on a downward spiral for months. The higher-ups at corporate were not happy with Charles—he wasn't bringing in enough new recruits or doing a good job at keeping the current investors reassured that the program was sound. They liked Marcus and were impressed with his moxy. Plus, he had contacts all over town through his financial planning business and all the religious and social groups he belonged to."

"Exactly how many religious groups was Marcus affiliated with?" I ask, already knowing that he had been on the prowl at two local churches at least.

"Who knows? Several. Marcus would have pretended to be a Hasidic Jew or donned a Sikh turban if he thought it would make him some money. I think Reverie liked that about him—his 'do whatever it takes' attitude. Apparently, they were grooming him to take the reins from Charles."

"So Marcus was in and Charles was out?"

"From Marcus's notes, and what I've been able to piece together from his e-mails, yes, it appears that way. What I don't know is whether or not Charles knew this. If he did, indeed, know that Reverie was planning to fire him and replace him with Marcus, and that he stood to lose huge amounts of money, then he certainly had reason to take Marcus out of the equation. Reverie is not likely to fire him now that a suitable replacement is not waiting in the wings."

"True. I guess I need to put Charles back on the suspect list."

"You? Shouldn't the police be handling this?"

"Yes, of course. I hope you'll let them know about this and encourage them to take a second look at Charles. I'm just sort of playing it out in my head, trying to make sense of it all." It was the best I could come up with. I certainly couldn't tell her that I know for a fact that the cops are heading down a dead-end path in their quest to find a woman fitting Wavonne's description.

"I will," Jacqueline says.

I take a last sip of my wine. "I guess I should get going. It really was nice to chat with you, Jacqueline."

"You, too," she says.

She follows me out of the room toward the front door.

"Please come by the restaurant anytime. I'll slip you some fried chicken to go. I'll hide it under some salad greens or something," I say with a laugh.

She smiles. "In that case, I'd better get back to my workout."

"Better you than me," I respond. I'm about to trot off to my van, but I take a moment and turn around. "And really, Jacqueline. Call me if you need anything or just want someone to talk to."

"I will, Halia. Thank you."

I can tell she appreciates the offer as she gives me a final wave and closes the door.

CHAPTER 39

"We've been over this before, Wavonne," I say. We're behind the bar, and I'm whipping up a pitcher of Sweet Tea's signature cocktail.

"I'm tellin' you, it would sell."

"I don't care. I'm not serving Kool-Aid in my restaurant."

"Just red flavored. That's all you need."

"*Red* is a flavor now?" I ask without giving her a chance to respond. "The answer is no."

"Fine. Just tryin' to help you make some mo' money, so I can get me some trickle down."

"If you want to make more money, you could take on a few extra tables and put a little more pep in your step around here."

Wavonne looks as if she's considering my recommendation for a moment, concludes it would be far too taxing, and decides to change the subject.

"So Jacqueline really said Marcus didn't have no money? He'd been frontin' all along?"

"Yep. It sounds like she might even lose the house."

"Damn shame." Wavonne shakes her head. "What else did she say? Did she give you some scoop on that Charles fella? Is that why you have him comin' over? What kinda deets do you think you're gonna get outta him?"

"I don't know. He's about my last lead at the moment. I'm hoping that if I get a few cocktails in him, he'll drop his guard and give me some useful information . . . or maybe even implicate himself."

"You really think he coulda done it?"

"I don't know what to think," I say as I catch some activity out of the corner of my eye. I turn and see Charles and a sharply dressed younger woman next to him. I called him yesterday after I left Jacqueline's, but I suspect he saw my number come up on his phone and declined to answer my multiple attempts to reach him. I eventually looked up his home phone number (yes, some people do still have landlines these days) and ended up reaching his wife. I was afraid if I left a message with her, Charles would ignore it, so I explained my situation to his wife, told her I was only interested in any information Charles could give me about the others at the table the night Marcus was killed, and invited her and Charles to come to the restaurant as my guests. She mentioned that she'd heard good things about Sweet Tea and happily committed both of them.

"Hello, Charles," I say. "How are you?"

"Good . . . good," he replies. "This is my wife, Pamela."

"So nice of you to come."

"Are you kidding? All I've heard are raves about this place. I've always wanted to try it, but we live in the city and don't think to come out to PG County for dinner . . . it's not exactly a mecca of fine dining."

"Well, I hope we'll change your mind about that tonight." I smile at her remark, even though it irritates me. Not that what she said is exactly untrue—aside from Sweet Tea and the restaurants at National Harbor, there really is little fine dining in the County, but it was her tone more than her words that put me off. "Please. Follow me, and we'll get you seated."

I lead them to a cozy booth along the wall, and they take their seats.

"Let me get you some menus. I'll be right back." I try to quickly size them up while I say this. I've met Charles a couple of times now, and much like Marcus, he is smooth but in a different way. Marcus was "Rico Suave" smooth . . . he was all muscles, and ultra-white teeth, and designer suits smooth. Charles is as fast-talking as Marcus but has more of a "nice man next door" way about him. He's probably in his fifties with a middle-age belly, wears expensive but casual clothes, and has a more honest face than Marcus. Despite the Ralph Lauren shirt and expensive watch he's wearing, he's the type of guy you'd look at and think that he probably cuts the grass of the elderly woman next door just to be neighborly, which makes him more dangerous than Marcus. We're taught to be wary of people like Marcus, but we're not as suspicious of people like Charles.

His wife is easy to figure out. She's significantly younger than Charles, and with her bitchy comment about Prince George's County being a restaurant wasteland, high-maintenance looks, and designer clothes, she's what Wavonne would call "bougie." Swindling decent people out of their savings is probably the only way Charles can afford her upkeep. She was clearly not genetically blessed but has gone to great lengths to make the most of what God has given her. From a distance I bet she appears to be a knockout, but as you look closer you can tell that her large breasts do not match her petite frame and are clearly of the silicone variety, the bulk of her hair is not her own, and the tip of her nose is just a little bit off, likely from rhinoplasty that didn't go as well as one might have hoped.

"Some menus," I say and set them down on the table. "And I took the liberty of whipping up a pitcher of our house cocktail." I set the pitcher and two glasses of ice on the table. I fill the glasses and wait for them to take a sip.

"That's very nice," Pamela says. "What's in it?"

"I'd tell you, but I've have to kill you," I joke. "It's a mix of grapefruit-flavored vodka, triple sec, Sprite, lemon juice, and a berry syrup we make ourselves. Why don't you look at the menus, and I'll send Darius over shortly to take your order. He'll take great care of you. Please enjoy a nice meal on me this evening, and we'll talk over dessert."

They nod and smile before I head toward the kitchen to check on things. It's a Tuesday, so we are busy, but it's not quite as hectic as it is on Friday and Saturday nights. When I push on the kitchen door, I hope to see a well-oiled machine in motion catering to the dinner rush, but when I walk through the threshold, I see Wavonne grasping one of the stainless steel counters. She's bent over, gyrating her hips back and forth.

"Work it," I hear Darius say from behind her as Tacy and the rest of the kitchen staff look on.

"What are you doing, Wavonne?" I ask, and everyone freezes as if the school principal just barged into the detention room.

"Tacy axed me what it meant to twerk. I was just givin' him a demo."

"Give Tacy twerking demos on your own time, Wavonne. We have a dining room full of customers."

"Oh, come on, Halia, twerk with me," she says and bends over again and starts bumping the side of her hip into mine. "Come on, Halia. Get your twerk on, girl!"

Some song by honorary brother Robin Thicke is playing on whoever's iPod is docked in the kitchen speaker. Generally, you can barely hear it with all the kitchen commotion going on, but things are suddenly quiet with all eyes on me. I see my staff watching me, waiting for me to reprimand Wavonne. And you know what? I decide to surprise them.

"Turn it up, Tacy," I say. He does as he's asked and, let me tell you, I get my groove *on!* I do love to dance and never get

the chance to do it anymore. Women my age are hardly welcome in the clubs downtown, and I wouldn't have the time or
energy to go even if we were. But in my twenties, I'd hit Zanz-
ibar on the Waterfront in Southwest D.C. with my girlfriends
and shake my moneymaker with the best of them. As the
music cranks up, I start swinging my hips and moving my
shoulders. Wavonne gets in front of me and gives new meaning to the words "jiggly parts." I'm laughing and dancing and
snapping my fingers . . . feeling the most relaxed I have in
weeks. Our dancing is contagious, and it's not long before the
whole kitchen has abandoned their burners and fryers and
dirty dishes, and we're all jamming to the tune. Even Tacy,
who clearly has no rhythm, is giving it a shot. He looks like
he's having a bad reaction to some medication, but you've got
to give the guy credit for trying. It's a fun time, and I'm glad I
have a chance to prove to my staff that I'm not a complete
stick in the mud, but as the song ends, I motion for Tacy to
turn it back down and steady my feet.

"Okay, ladies and gentleman . . . and *Wavonne,*" I say.
"Back to work. We've got a restaurant to run."

The gang returns to their duties, and I touch Darius on the
arm on his way out to the dining room. "Take good care of
the couple at table sixteen. Let me know when they order
dessert."

"Sure," he says. "That's the same guy who was here the
night Marcus went missing, isn't it?"

"Is it?"

Darius smiles. "Okay. If you want to play it that way.
You're the boss." He scoots out the kitchen door.

I spend the next hour and change between the kitchen, the
dining room, and the host station, making sure everything is
running smoothly, saying hi to regulars and some new customers, running checks for hurried servers . . . whatever needs
to be done. When Darius finally lets me know that Charles

and Pamela have ordered dessert, I head to the kitchen to fill
the order myself. Shortly after, I emerge from the kitchen with
two slices of three-layer caramel cake.

As I walk by a table Wavonne is waiting on, I overhear one
of the customers ask about the desserts I have in my hands.

"My aunt Celia made that fresh this morning. It's her
caramel cake. We also have these big assed cookies that Aunt
Celia made, too. We serve 'em with—"

I backtrack to Wavonne's table. "Wavonne, would you
please not refer to our desserts as 'big-assed,' " I say to her before I turn to the four-top with three ladies seated at it. "We
have some hearty-sized cookies for dessert. Three chocolate-
chunk cookies served warm with vanilla ice cream, hot fudge,
and fresh-made whipped cream. Wavonne will be happy to tell
you about the rest of our selections tonight." I smile at the
women and, before heading over to Charles and Pamela's table,
I give a Wavonne a look that will hopefully remind her to
choose her words more carefully when speaking with customers.

"Two slices of caramel cake. Made in-house today." I place
the plates on the table and take a seat next to Pamela. "Thanks
again for agreeing to talk with me tonight. I know the police
are doing their thing, but the last place anyone saw Marcus was
here in my restaurant. It just makes me uneasy, and I'd really
like to do anything I can to help figure out what happened."

Darius had followed behind me and is just now finishing
pouring us each a cup of coffee.

"That makes perfect sense, Halia," Charles says. "And I
wish I could help you, but I've told you and the police all I
know." He takes a bite of the cake. "Wow. This is really good."
There is a more friendly tone in Charles's voice than when I've
spoken with him recently—must be the power of Momma's
caramel cake.

"Can you go over the events with me one more time after Wavonne and I left the restaurant?"

"I've heard him recount it to the police so many times, *I* can go over the events the night Marcus disappeared," Pamela interjects. "And I wasn't even there."

"Have at it," Charles says.

"You and Wanda left—"

"Wavonne," I correct her.

"Her name is *Wavonne?*" Pamela asks in a "what the hell kind of name is that" tone, which makes me dislike her even more. "So you and *Wavonne* left about eleven forty-five. Marcus's girlfriend left a few minutes later. The rest of the party stayed while Marcus and Charles discussed the Reverie Program with their clients . . . I can't remember their names. . . ."

"That would be Heather and Josh Williams," I say. "My understanding was they left roughly a half hour or so after I did, followed by Charles. Then Jacqueline left and Marcus was here alone."

"That's pretty much covers it. After Régine and the Williamses left, I stayed and talked with Marcus for a few more minutes. We had hoped another client would join us that night, but she wasn't able to make it, so we needed to make plans to have a meeting with her and assure her that the Reverie program was sound. Her checks had been interrupted much like they had been for Heather and Josh."

"Yes, the Reverie Program," I say, and, from Pamela's reaction, my feelings about the program must have shown on my face or come through in my voice.

"Don't say it like that. It's a sound program. We have invested ourselves."

I wanted to say that I *bet* they have. Much like Marcus, they figured they could keep swindling investors into the program long enough to get their house paid off and make a lot of money on commissions in the process. But the Reverie program is not my concern. Finding out who killed Marcus is.

"Who is the other client? This is the first I've heard of him or her . . . or them."

"Audrey Whitlock."

"So her payments had stopped coming, as well? Have the police talked to her?"

"I'm sure they have, but believe me, Mrs. Whitlock did not kill Marcus."

"How can you be sure?"

"Because she's in her eighties and can barely leave her house."

I want to ask Charles how . . . *how* he can sleep at night when, during the day, he's duping eighty-year-old women out of their homes, but I stick to the business at hand.

"I knew she was calling Marcus regularly about her concerns. We just wanted to reassure her that the checks would resume soon."

"Have they?" I ask, even though I know the answer.

"We're having some cash flow issues, Halia. We're trying to stabilize the program with some new investors, but that's been hard these days, especially when people like Heather and Josh show up at our presentations and scare off new recruits."

"Where does Mrs. Whitlock live?"

"She has a little house in Hyattsville. I can get you the exact address if you'd like, but I'm telling you, it's a dead end."

I want to lay into him . . . him and that wife of his who are living the high life off the homes of senior citizens, but it will be much easier for him to give me Mrs. Whitlock's address than for me to have to hunt it down online, so I decide to play nice. "I would appreciate that, Charles," I say. "So getting back to that fateful night, after you left Sweet Tea, did you go straight home?"

"Yes. I've told you that already, Halia."

"And I can confirm it," Pamela interjects. "He was home by twelve forty-five. I remember it very clearly. I was sitting in bed watching TV. I was wearing my pink silk nightshirt. I had curlers in my hair. I can even tell you what Charles was wearing when he came in—khaki pants, a green polo shirt, and his brown loafers. He told me he had a very nice meal here . . . fried chicken and waffles and pineapple upside-down cake for dessert."

Pamela's lengthy description makes me uneasy. All that detail was certainly not necessary, and isn't that what people do when they're lying? Invent a bunch of detail?

"What was on when he came home?" I ask.

"On?"

"On TV. You said you were watching TV when he came in." Surely if she remembered the color of her nightshirt and what Charles was wearing, she'd remember what she was watching when he came in the bedroom.

"Um," she stumbles, likely realizing that whatever program she mentions should be regularly scheduled to run on Saturday nights at twelve forty-five. Granted, in a time of TiVo and DVRs, that might not be true, but the question seems to throw her. "I . . . I don't remember offhand . . . maybe *The Tonight Show* . . . no, it was Saturday . . . you know, I'm really not sure. Why?"

"Just curious. The only time I have to watch television is late at night before bed. I was wondering if we liked any of the same shows."

I'm sure she knows that was not my reason for asking the question as much as I do . . . and as much as Charles does for that matter. There's a hint of tension between the three of us now as they both clearly know I'm trying to determine Charles's whereabouts after he left the restaurant that unfortunate Saturday night. And the more I look at the two of them, the more it makes me think of Heather and Josh . . . and Mrs. Whitlock . . . and all the other people they have swindled out of their savings and homes. I really don't care to be in their company anymore, and I figure the evening has been about as fruitful as it's going to be in terms of me drawing out useful information. I know from Jacqueline that Charles had motive to kill Marcus, and it now seems that he might not have gone straight home after he left Marcus and Jacqueline at the restaurant. Either his wife has a very detailed memory when comes to everything *other* than what she watches on television, or she's lying to cover for him.

"I'll let you get to those desserts. You have my number, Charles. If you can get me Mrs. Whitlock's contact information as soon as possible, I'd really appreciate it." I get up from the table and look at them. I note the Rolex on Charles's wrist and the David Yurman necklace nestled in Pamela's cleavage—spoils obtained off the backs of people who trusted them with their money and their homes. "And thanks so much for agreeing to talk with me. Enjoy the cake." I refrain from adding, "I hope you choke on it."

RECIPE FROM HALIA'S KITCHEN

Celia's Banana Pudding

Vanilla Wafer Cake Ingredients

½ cup softened butter
1 cup sugar
2 eggs
3 teaspoons vanilla extract
2 tablespoons honey
1⅓ cups all-purpose flour
¾ teaspoon baking powder
¼ teaspoon salt

- Preheat oven to 350 degrees Fahrenheit. Grease bottom and lower sides of a 13in x 9in x 2in glass pan.

- In large bowl, cream together butter, sugar, eggs, vanilla, and honey using an electric mixer at medium speed.

- Mix flour, baking powder, and salt. Add to wet mixture.

- Stir until well combined.

- Spread into prepared pan.

- Bake for 20–25 minutes or until golden brown.

- Cool.

Pudding Ingredients

1 cup sugar
⅛ teaspoon salt
2 tablespoons cornstarch + 2 teaspoons
3½ cups milk
4 eggs (beaten)
1½ teaspoons vanilla extract
½ stick butter
4 medium bananas

- Mix sugar, salt, and cornstarch.

- Begin heating milk and eggs in a double boiler over medium high heat. Slowly add mix of dry ingredients. Whisk constantly while adding dry ingredients and until pudding thickens (about 7 minutes).

- Remove from heat and stir in vanilla and butter.

- Strain pudding through a fine mesh sieve/strainer.

- Let pudding cool to room temperature.

- Spread cooled pudding over vanilla wafer cake.

- Place a layer of sliced bananas on top of pudding.

Meringue Ingredients

5 egg whites
¼ teaspoon cream of tartar
3 tablespoons sugar

- Preheat oven to 425 degrees Fahrenheit.

- Beat egg whites, cream of tartar, and sugar using an electric mixer at high speed until stiff peaks form.

- Spread over pudding.

- Bake for five minutes or until delicately browned.

- Cool final dish at room temperature for 30 minutes. Then chill in the refrigerator for 1 hour prior to serving.

Eight Servings

CHAPTER 40

"I don't know why I agreed to do this. We shouldn't be getting involved in something like this, Halia."

"It's no big deal, Momma," I respond. We're on our way to Mrs. Whitlock's house. I thought it might help if I brought Momma along. I don't know much about this woman and have no idea if she'll even let me in when I show up on her doorstep. I thought I might have a better chance of her opening up to me and telling me about her relationship with Marcus if Momma came along. If I can't relate to her and get her talking, I'm hoping Momma can—one old lady to another.

"This is work for the police."

"I told you the police already talked to Mrs. Whitlock and Jack . . . you know, Jack Spruce . . . he's in the restaurant all the time . . . he said she was very guarded and didn't give them any useful information. I simply offered to chat with her myself and see if she might be less anxious around someone who isn't in a police uniform. I thought having you with me might make her feel more comfortable."

Okay, so only some of what I said is true. Jack told me nothing about the police speaking with Mrs. Whitlock, and he has no idea I'm planning on meeting with her, but I needed to tell Momma something to get her on board. I certainly can't tell her that Wavonne is a prime suspect in Marcus's killing, and that I'm trying to figure out who the murderer really is before Wavonne ends up in jail. It would worry her to death.

"Why would I make her more comfortable? Because I'm old, too?"

"Pretty much."

Momma glares at me.

"Oh, come on, Momma. I'm just kidding. But you do have old lady friends all over town. Don't you drive a whole gaggle of them to church every Sunday? I just thought you might help keep the conversation going."

My van smells of fried chicken as Momma and I pull into the driveway of Mrs. Whitlock's house. It's a typical Hyattsville home—a small one-story brick rambler probably built in the forties or fifties. The lawn is mowed, but you can tell it's done by a cheap service rather than a caring home owner. The shrubs are a little overgrown and the areas up close to the house have not been edged.

I tried calling Mrs. Whitlock, but she didn't answer the phone, and there was no machine or voice mail. When we get out of the car, I can see her looking at me and Momma through one of the front windows. I walk over to the other side of van, open the sliding side door, and grab a small tray of fried chicken, a container of coleslaw, and another of macaroni and cheese.

When we reach the door, I decide to knock rather than ring the doorbell. Somehow it seems less intrusive. She doesn't come to the door, so I tap on it again.

"No thank you," I hear her call from the other side of the door.

"Mrs. Whitlock. My name is Halia Watkins. I'm a friend

of Marcus Rand's. You know . . . from the Reverie Homes program?"

I hear her unbolt the door, and she opens it just enough for us to see her face. I'm not a tall woman, but even I tower over her. I don't think she clears five feet. Her hair is a mix of black and gray, and the years show on her face. She stands slightly hunched over in a loose-fitting floral print dress.

"Hi, Mrs. Whitlock," I say. "I was wondering if we could talk to you for a few minutes about Marcus and the Reverie Program."

"I've already spoken to the police. I've told them everything I know about Mr. Rand." She begins to shut the door.

"Wait . . . wait," Momma says and takes the tray of fried chicken out of my hand. "My name is Celia Watkins. Halia here is my daughter. She owns Sweet Tea, the soul food restaurant at the King Town Center a few miles from here. Maybe you've heard of it?"

Mrs. Whitlock doesn't say anything, but she does look at the tray in Momma's hand with curiosity.

Momma peels back the foil on the fried chicken to show it to Mrs. Whitlock and let some of the scent waft to her nose. "We brought a few goodies with us . . . some fried chicken and coleslaw . . . and macaroni and cheese."

Mrs. Whitlock lifts her eyes from the chicken toward me and Momma, and then looks back at the food again. "What is it you want to know?"

"As you've heard, Mr. Rand met an untimely death over a week ago." I try to think of what to add next. I don't want to focus on Marcus's murder and scare her into closing the door in my face. I'm stumbling for words when Momma pipes up.

"I'll be honest with you, Mrs. Whitlock. The last place anyone saw Mr. Rand was at my daughter's restaurant, and they seem to suspect that my niece has something to do with his death. I assure you, she's innocent. Halia here is doing a little investigating on her own, and we're just wondering if you might have any information that could help us."

I look at Momma, surprised that she knew what was going on all along. You can't keep *anything* from that woman.

"What? You think I don't know what goes on just because I'm getting on in years? Just like when you were a girl—you thought you could get one by me. I've got eyes in the back of my head and the hearing of a bat, Halia. And don't you forget it."

Mrs. Whitlock opens the door a bit wider as Momma reprimands me like I'm a child. I guess she figures a bickering mother and daughter can only be so dangerous. "What did you say your names were again?"

"Halia Watkins and this is my mother, Celia."

"You own a restaurant, you say?"

"Yes. Sweet Tea."

"I think I've heard of that. I don't really eat out. I'm on a tight budget."

"You'll have to come as my guest sometime," I say. "And you can sample some of my cooking right now."

She eyes us for a moment longer, her head bent upward and twisted a bit to the left. Then she opens the door all the way and gestures for us to come in. We step past her, and she closes the door behind us.

"Please. Have a seat."

Momma sets the food on the coffee table, and we sit down on a well-kept, but dated sofa and take in the surroundings. The inside of Mrs. Whitlock's home is exactly as you would expect—it's very "grandma's house." There's old wallpaper on the walls, wood floors that could use refinishing, two high-back chairs across from the sofa, and a CRT television in the

corner . . . you know, the ones Goodwill and the Salvation
Army won't take anymore as even poor people want flat screens.

We look at her family photos and bric-a-brac displayed on
the table next to us as she makes her way to one of the chairs.
She moves slowly, but without assistance from the walker I see
by the window—she must only use that when she leaves the
house.

She gradually lowers herself in a chair across from us.

"Thank you again for inviting us in."

"You're welcome. What is it you think I can help you
with?"

"We wanted to talk to you about Marcus—"

Momma cuts me off. "No need to get into that just yet.
Why don't we have some of this lovely food?"

"Let me get some plates," Mrs. Whitlock says.

"Why don't you let me do that?" I ask, getting up from the
sofa. I can see the kitchen to my right and head in that direction. "You just tell me where to look for plates and silverware."

"I'll give you a hand," Momma says and follows me.

"Dishes are in the cabinet to the left of the sink, and the
silverware is in the top drawer by the oven."

"What were you thinking? Just diving in to asking her
about Marcus? If you're going to stick your nose in where it
doesn't belong and get us caught up in this mess, at least do it
right," Momma whispers to me as I reach for the plates, and
she gets some knives and forks from the drawer.

My first instinct is to protest and defend myself. I guess because that's what I'm so used to doing with Momma, but
when I take a moment to think about it, I realize she's right.
The cops didn't get any useful information from Mrs. Whitlock, and if we start questioning her immediately, we probably
won't, either.

"You're right. We should—"

"What? What did you just say?"

"I said you're right, Momma."

"Well, write this day down in the record books, Saint Peter. Mahalia Watkins just told her momma she was right."

"Right about what?" Mrs. Whitlock asks when we come in the living room. Momma was so flustered by my words she forgot to speak in a whisper.

"She was right about us digging into this food," I say, set the plates on the coffee table, and lift the foil from the tray of fried chicken. "What can I get for you, Mrs. Whitlock? White or dark meat?"

"I think I'd like a breast."

I lift a breast from the tray and spoon some coleslaw and macaroni and cheese on the plate and hand it to her.

"Thank you, dear," she says. "I have a pitcher of iced tea in the refrigerator, and some glasses are in the cabinet above the dishwasher."

"I'll be right back," I say and return to the kitchen. By the time I get back in the living room with three glasses of ice and a pitcher of iced tea, Momma and Mrs. Whitlock are talking like old friends. I might have been wrong about questioning Mrs. Whitlock too soon, but I was right about bringing Momma along.

"Halia's been cooking since she was a little girl," Momma says as I pour three glasses of tea and fix a plate of food for myself.

"Is that right?"

"Yes. I used to help my grandmother prepare big Sunday dinners."

"Sunday dinners after church," Mrs. Whitlock says. "Now, there's a tradition worth keeping. Families don't stick together like they used to . . . or go to church like they used to. When

I was a girl, church was a big deal. They didn't let us into the fine restaurants back in the day, not that we could afford them if they did. So church was the only place for us to get all gussied up for. If you bought a new dress or a new hat, you just couldn't wait for Sunday to roll around so you had somewhere to wear it. My mother loved hats. She had some the size of a large pizza. I still have some of them upstairs in the closet. I even pull out one or two of them and wear them to church myself every now and then."

"Where do you go to church?" Momma asks.

"First Christian Methodist."

"Is it close by?"

"No, but volunteers pick up old people like me and take us to service. They have volunteers for everything—they teach Sunday school, and clean the church . . . some even came to spruce up my house months ago. That's how I met that Marcus fellow."

"Really?"

"He came here . . . oh . . . almost a year ago with a group of other volunteers from the church. They did some cleanup in my yard . . . painted the trim . . . things like that. I invited the group in for some refreshments. That Marcus fellow, he was very chatty . . . seemed so nice. He even stayed after the others left and helped me wash dishes and put them away. I guess, at some point during the evening, I mentioned I had a lot of medical bills. You know, Medicare only covers so much. Well, then this Marcus fellow starts telling me about this program . . . this mortgage program. My house . . . you see, my house has been paid off for years. My husband, God rest his soul, and I barely paid thirty thousand dollars for it back in seventy-one."

I nod and think about how that amount barely covers the cost of my van outside.

"But I've been sick, and I've had four surgeries . . . a hip replacement and both knees . . . and a disc . . . a disc in my back. And the medical bills . . . oh Lord . . . the medical bills. They just kept coming in and coming in. And this house is nearly as old as I am. Just like me, it requires a lot of upkeep and repairs. The furnace went a few months ago. You can't re-place furnaces on Social Security."

I swallow hard as I listen to her. Her story must be the story of so many elderly people.

"So, Marcus . . . you see, Marcus told me about his pro-gram. He said I could take a new mortgage out on the house. Then I could use some of the money to pay off my bills and the rest to invest in the program that was supposed to help me make the mortgage payments and pay the bank back in no time."

"The Reverie Homes program."

"Yes . . . yes, that's what it was called. Marcus picked me up and took me to a seminar about it. It was at some fancy hotel in the city. People there said how the program had worked so well for them . . . and that Marcus . . . he seemed like such a nice young man . . . a churchgoing man."

"So you took out a mortgage and bought into the pro-gram."

"Yes."

"But it didn't help you with the mortgage payments?"

"It did. At first. I got checks just as I was promised for the first few months, but then they stopped coming, and I started getting letters and phone calls from the mortgage company. I don't even answer the phone anymore."

"When was the last time you made a payment?"

"It's been months. I'm not sure how much longer it will be

before they foreclose on me. I've been in this house for forty years. I raised my kids in this house. My husband died in the bedroom upstairs." She says this in a way typical of women of her generation. She doesn't cry, but you know she wants to. She's been raised to be strong, and strong she will be.

"I wish there was something we could do." I look at her— a proud women in her golden years wondering how much longer she is going to be able to keep a roof over her head. I begin to think that if Marcus weren't dead, I might have killed him myself. I also think about Charles, the ringleader of this charade, and how he and his wife are living the high life while Mrs. Whitlock may end up homeless. If Charles is willing to hustle old ladies for the sake of the almighty dollar, then it's not such a stretch to think that he might have knocked off Marcus if he thought Marcus was a threat to his income.

"Thank you, but I'm not sure what anyone can do at this point. And I'm not really sure there is much else I can tell you that would be of any help to your investigation."

"That's okay. We won't bother you with any more questions," I say.

We chat some more and enjoy the food before I get up from the sofa. "Can we help you clean up?"

"You're leaving already? Stay and have a slice of pie. I have some in the refrigerator."

"Yeah. Stay and have a slice of pie," Momma says, and gestures for me to sit down. "She's always in such a hurry."

"Of course," I say. "Let me get the pie."

"It's lemon meringue. It's on the bottom shelf. It's from the grocery store, so I'm sure it's not as good as the pies you make at your restaurant, but it's not bad."

"Actually, Momma makes the pies at Sweet Tea." I head toward the kitchen again and keep an ear out for their conversation as I slice the pie and put it on plates. I thought Momma

might ask some more questions about Marcus, but no such
luck.

"Can you believe she's over forty and still doesn't have
a man?"

"No? A girl who can cook like she does?"

"I know, right. That church you mentioned . . . you don't
know of any single men there for her, do you?"

CHAPTER 41

"Sweet Tea. How may I help you?" I say into the phone. I've only been back from Mrs. Whitlock's for a few minutes and was reviewing our reservations for the evening when the phone rang.

"Hello. I was there last night with my husband, and I think he left his jacket on the back of the chair."

"I'm happy to check for you." I walk with the portable phone toward the break room. We have a locker in there that we use for a makeshift lost and found. "What does it look like?"

"It's a gray fleece jacket. It's not much to look at, but my husband likes it."

"Yes, it's here. We'll hold it for you. May I ask your name?"

"Pamela. Pamela Pritchett."

"Oh yes. Hi, Pamela. It's Halia," I say. "I'm so glad you came to the restaurant. I hope you had a nice evening." I try to hide my disdain for the woman.

"We did. Thank you."

"You know," I say, an idea coming to me. "I have an appointment downtown later today. Didn't you say you lived in D.C.? I might be able to drop the jacket off if you'd like."

"We're on Capitol Hill. Not far from Eastern Market. Will you be in this neighborhood?"

"I won't be far from there," I lie, but then I don't have an appointment in the city at all so what does it matter? I just think I might be able to have a more productive conversation with Pamela in her own home away from the noise and prying ears at Sweet Tea. "I'd be happy to swing by. It will save you a trip."

Pamela proceeds to give me the address, and I hang up the phone and grab my purse. We just started our midday closure. If I leave now, I might be able to be back before we reopen for dinner at five.

As I leave the break room, for no real reason other than curiosity, I unzip one of the pockets of Charles's jacket and feel around inside. I don't find anything in the first pocket, but when I reach in the second, I feel something and pull it out. It's a glossy book of matches with the words ODYSSEY LOUNGE printed on the cover in raised letters. When I flip the package over, I see an address in Cheverly printed on the back, but there's no phone number.

I pull my one foot that was out of the break room door back inside, drop the jacket and my purse on the table, and walk over to my desk and sit down. I type Odyssey-Lounge-Cheverly into Google. I get some results in other areas of the country, but nothing comes up in Cheverly. Since I'll pass through Cheverly on my way to Capitol Hill, I decide to swing by this Odyssey Lounge before heading to the Pritchetts' house to return the jacket.

I poke my head in the kitchen and tell Laura I'll be back in a couple of hours and make my way out to my van. Traffic is light on the Southeast Freeway, so it doesn't take me long to reach the exit for Cheverly. With the help of my navigation system, I make a few turns after I get off the highway and find that the address on the back of the matchbook belongs to a run-down auto repair shop in a pretty sketchy-looking neighborhood. The sign on the building looks like it used to say Radcliff's Garage, but the *d* and one of the *f*s are missing.

I look at the address on the book of matches again just to make sure I have the right place, and it appears that I do. I'd consider popping inside and asking someone if they had any information, but this repair shop looks like it's long been out of business. There's not a single car in the parking lot, so I decide to drive on.

I get back on the highway toward the city, and it's not long before I am maneuvering through the quaint tree-lined streets of the Capitol Hill neighborhood of D.C. When I pull up in front of the Pritchetts' house, I see a sizable three-story brick row house—not huge by suburban standards, but considering it's in a highly sought-after D.C. neighborhood near the Capitol Building, it could be, depending on the condition of the inside, worth well over a million dollars.

"Hello. This is so nice of you," Pamela says. She must have seen me pull up because she's already opened the door, and I'm not even up the front steps yet.

"No problem. I was in the neighborhood anyway." I hand her the jacket.

"Thanks again," she says. "I really appreciate you saving me a trip to come pick it up. But I do hope to come back to Sweet Tea sometime soon. We really enjoyed the food."

"I hope so, too."

She smiles at me and starts to back into the house as if she's trying to wrap things up and send me on my way—well, I'm having none of that.

"Such a nice home. I'd love to see the inside." I'd generally never be so forward, but I didn't drive all the way to Capitol Hill to drop off a jacket. I'm here seeking information, and I'm not leaving until I get some.

"Um . . ." She stumbles for a moment. "Please . . . come

in." She steps farther back inside and opens the door nice and wide.

"Don't mind if I do." I walk through the door she's holding open onto sparkling marble floors lit from above by a mammoth crystal chandelier hanging from the high ceiling—yes, well over a million dollars.

"I only have a few moments, but why don't we take a seat in the parlor."

I follow her to the adjoining room and realize that "parlor" is just a fancy word for living room.

"Please. Have a seat." She's polite, but I sense that she's not thrilled about having to associate with someone she probably considers to be the help.

"Would you like something to drink? I can ask Roberta to prepare some tea."

"No. Thank you," I say. "Honestly, Pamela, I just wanted a few moments of your time, so we could chat."

Pamela audibly sighs. "Is this about Marcus Rand? I've told you everything I know."

"Have you? Really?"

"Yes," she says firmly. "Now I really do have some things that require my attention. If there's nothing else . . . I do appreciate you dropping off the jacket."

I don't know what to say, and I have no idea if this Odyssey Lounge has anything to do with Marcus but, on a whim, I decide to throw it out there and see what happens. "I know all about the Odyssey Lounge, Pamela."

Her eyes widen and her mouth drops open. "That's my husband's endeavor. I have nothing to do with it."

"It doesn't surprise me. You seem too classy to be involved in something like that." I have no idea what I'm talking about, but it seems prudent to play off her reaction.

"Of course I am," she says, lifting her head slightly higher. "I wish he'd never gotten involved in such a thing—nearly

naked women dancing around for men in abandoned buildings turned into makeshift nightclubs. It's disgusting."

I try not to show my surprise as she reveals what the
Odyssey Lounge is. It shouldn't surprise me. Charles was already involved in one sleazy business—why not two?

"Are you planning to tell anyone about this?"

"I'm not sure," I respond. "Perhaps if you tell me the truth
about what you know about Marcus's death, I won't need to."

"Charles has told you . . . I've told you . . . my husband
had *nothing* to do with Marcus's murder."

"Maybe not, but I suspect he did not come straight home
after leaving Sweet Tea the night Marcus was killed. Perhaps
he went to the Radcliff's Garage to check on things at his go-
go club."

Pamela diverts her eyes from me.

"Did you not tell the police because the club is illegal?" I ask.

"It's not exactly illegal. Charles manages to keep the club
going through some sort of loophole in the county ordi-
nances, but the police and civic groups are still always looking
for ways to shut it down. Charles manages to stay one step
ahead of them, though. For now, it's the Odyssey Lounge at
Radcliff's Garage in Cheverly. In a few weeks the name will
change, and it may move to an abandoned strip mall in District
Heights or a shuttered restaurant in Hillcrest."

"If it's lawful, then why did you lie about where Charles was?"

"Halia, I'm a woman of certain standing in the community. We tell everyone that Charles works in finance. What
would the neighbors think if they knew my husband was running a barely legal strip bar that moves from location to location like a traveling circus? If the ladies at the country club
found out about it, I'd just die. How could I ever look any one
of them in the eye again?"

"Um . . . I don't know," I say, unsure how to respond. I'm almost sad for her. She has this beautiful home, fabulous clothes,

and apparently someone named Roberta to do her bidding,
but it all has been obtained through businesses that may or
may not be operating within the law. I want to ask her if it's
worth it—if all the wealth and privilege is worth the look of
shame I see on her face, but, instead, I decide I'd rather just relieve myself of her company.

"So you won't tell anyone?"

"Who would I tell? We don't exactly run in the same cir-
cles, Pamela."

"No. I guess not."

Clearly neither one of us has any idea of what to say to one
another at this point so I break the growing silence between
us. "I think you've told me what I needed to know. I guess I'll
be on my way. You really do have a lovely home."

"Thank you. And thanks again for dropping the jacket by."

"No problem." I make my way quickly to the front door
and can't exit the house fast enough. The longer I stayed and
the more I talked with Pamela, the more the negative energy
either emitting from her or the house (or both of them) began
to overwhelm me. As I get in the van, I think about how it's
tempting to feel jealous of people like Charles and Pamela
with their grand home, designer clothes, and fancy cars, but
spending time with them makes me pity rather than envy
them. I might not be rich, but at least I earn an honest living
and don't live in fear of my friends and neighbors finding out
about any shady businesses I'm running.

CHAPTER 42

I'm feeling melancholy on my way back to Sweet Tea. It's been a long week and a half since Marcus was killed. The shame on Pamela's face when she spoke of the Odyssey Lounge makes me sad, and hearing Mrs. Whitlock's story earlier today about how she stands to lose her house is really weighing on me. I'm not far from the restaurant when I decide I'm not up to going back just yet. I need a few minutes to regroup and process everything I've learned over the past few days. I see a Starbucks on the other side of the highway and decide to make a detour, get a latte or Frappuccino, and sit and think for a few minutes.

I pull into the turn lane at the next stoplight and make my way over to the coffeehouse. Once inside, I order a tall mocha Frappuccino and take a seat at a small table in one corner by the window. I sip my drink and watch the traffic go by . . . so many people going so many places. I ponder the events of the last few days and how my amateur sleuthing has gotten me nowhere. Well, maybe not *nowhere*. At least I feel fairly confident about who *didn't* kill Marcus. I just still have no idea who *did* kill him. Maybe I've been going down the wrong path all along. Maybe none of the people having dinner with Marcus the night he was killed had anything to do with his death. Perhaps he was killed by someone who was not there at all. His murder might have had nothing to do with the mortgage program. Only God knows what other sort of mayhem Marcus was involved in both personally and professionally.

I'm feeling like I've failed, and that I've wasted huge amounts of time for little, if any, real return when I see a familiar face in line at the counter. My first instinct is to try to pretend I don't notice her. I'm just not in the mood to have polite conversation. But before I have a chance to look away, Régine's eyes meet mine, and neither one of us really has the option of acting like we don't see each other.

I force a smile and get up from my chair.

"Hey, Régine. So nice to see you. How are you?"

"I'm okay," she says. I notice that she's not alone. She's with another woman with short hair who's about the same height as her. I look at the other woman, waiting for Régine to introduce us. There's an awkward pause before she finally says, "This is my friend Cherise."

"Halia," I say and extend my hand.

As Cherise's grasp meets mine, I have this feeling that I've seen her somewhere. I can't place where, but she definitely looks familiar to me. "Have we met before?"

"No," she says with a smile. "I don't think so."

"I feel like I recognize you from somewhere."

She laughs. "Maybe I have one of those faces."

"Maybe," I respond before turning back to Régine. "How are you doing, Régine? I know it's been a rough time for you."

"I'm holding up okay. I'm trying to get out with friends some . . . take my mind off things." She gestures toward Cherise.

"Good. I'm glad. Being around people is probably the best thing."

At this point we've made it to the front of the line. Régine orders coffees for both of them and hands her credit card over to the barista.

"Come by the restaurant anytime. There're always plenty of people there."

"Halia owns Sweet Tea, you know the restaurant over by the—"

"I know where Sweet Tea is, Régine. I've been there a number of times," Cherise says as the barista gives Régine the credit card slip to sign. She takes the receipt from the clerk, grabs a pen from the counter, and signs the little slip of paper. Then I follow them as they walk over to the cream and sugar station.

As I watch Cherise grab a packet of sugar, dump its contents into her cup, and stir it around with a little wooden stick, I have what Oprah would call an "aha" moment. Suddenly, there's a domino effect going on in my mind—one piece of the puzzle has started to make sense of the other pieces of the puzzle . . . the pieces of the puzzle I've been collecting for over a week. Suddenly, I can feel adrenaline pulsing through my veins.

"If you've been to Sweet Tea, that must be where I've seen you before," I lie.

"It's always delicious. I hope to go back soon."

"How about this evening?" I say to Cherise and then look at Régine. "I'd be happy to host you and Cherise as my guests tonight. It's the least I can do. You've been through so much. Come by with Cherise and have a nice meal."

"Thank you, Halia, but I'm not sure—"

I put my hand up. "I won't take no for an answer. Let's say seven thirty?"

"If you insist," she says.

"Then it's settled. We'll see you both at Sweet Tea tonight. It really was good to see you."

I force a smile and turn to leave. As I walk out, I'm excited and nervous . . . and even a little afraid. After all the questioning and snooping around and, now, following a chance encounter at Starbucks, I'm ninety-nine point nine percent certain I know who killed Marcus.

CHAPTER 43

"I don't want to go into details over the phone. I'd really rather discuss it in person," I say. I'm on the phone with Detective Hutchins, trying to convince him to come by the restaurant tonight. I left a message for him earlier, but he's just getting back to me now, and it's nearly seven thirty already.

"Ms. Watkins, I can't drop everything and head over to Sweet Tea because you have a hunch or think you've found a new clue. This isn't an episode of *Scooby-Doo*." I've asked him to call me Halia, but I've noticed he reverts to calling me Ms. Watkins when he's annoyed with me or thinks I'm wasting his time.

"Very funny, Detective. I assure you it will be well worth your time. We have my spare ribs on special tonight . . . rubbed in my own seasoning, then cooked low and slow . . . the meat falls right off the bone."

I only hear silence on the other end of the phone.

"Did I mention we also have an orange Creamsicle cake tonight?"

He breaks his silence. "What time?"

"In about a half hour?"

"Fine. I'll stop by on the way home."

"You may want to bring some backup, Detective," I say before I hear a *click* on the other end of the phone. I'm not sure if he didn't hear me, or if he got every word and just didn't bother responding to what he probably deems as my hysterical antics before he disconnected.

When I hang up the phone, I fill two pitchers with iced tea and take them to a table in the back of the restaurant.

"Wavonne, can you get some glasses for the table? Four please." I set the two pitchers of tea on a table: one with unsweetened tea and one with sweetened tea.

"Four?" Wavonne asks. "You said you were expecting Régine and her friend . . . and Detective Hutchins. Countin' you and me, won't we need five glasses . . . and a bigger table?"

"Wavonne, I think Detective Hutchins and I can handle this on our own."

"You can set a place for me now, Halia, or I can pull up a chair and squeeze in when they get here. It's your choice."

I let out a sigh. "Well, then help me move this table over." I don't have the time or energy to argue with Wavonne, and God knows the girl's going to do what's she's going to do regardless.

"So what's goin' on, Halia? Why are we hostin' the detective and Régine? I know you got somethin' up your sleeve."

"You'll find out when they get here, Wavonne."

"Why can't you tell me now?"

"Because some things need to be handled with kid gloves . . . some things need to be done carefully. And let's face it, Wavonne, tact is not your strong suit."

"You must think Régine knows somethin' . . . either that or you think she did it. And who's this friend of hers?"

"All in due time."

I walk away from Wavonne toward the kitchen before she can question me further. I doubt any of my invited guests will be in the mood for dinner after our discussion this evening, but we have a restaurant full of other customers to feed, so I make a check on tonight's special, my slow-cooked spare ribs. Laura is pulling them out of the oven as I come through the kitchen door, and the air is fragrant with the sweet smell of tender pork. I buy it from a local farm in Hanover, Maryland, that breeds Hereford pigs with Black pigs (yes, there are different breeds of pigs . . . who knew?).

Before we cook the ribs, we rub them with a mix of brown sugar, paprika . . . some garlic, salt, and black pepper, and a hint of cayenne pepper to give them a little kick. Then we cook them on low heat for hours. The result is ribs so tender they make you want to slap your momma. Before we serve them, they get a quick brush of my apple cider vinegar-based barbecue sauce followed by a light coating of my sweet brown sugar sauce. This gives them a tangy sweet flavor that might just make you want to slap your momma a second time.

"They look pretty good, don't they?" Laura asks.

"Pretty good? They look delicious. I'm sure they'll go fast."

"Hopefully your guests will enjoy them."

"Honestly, I'm not sure they'll be eating. We'll see."

"Really? What do you have planned?" As Laura asks this, I see Wavonne make her way into the kitchen and saunter over toward us, clearly hoping to overhear our conversation and see if she can get any details about how the evening may unfold.

"I'm still trying to figure that out myself, Laura. I'd rather not go into details."

"I'm assuming this has something to do with Marcus?"

"I'll neither confirm nor deny," I say with a smile.

"Okay. I won't press, but are you okay? You seem anxious."

"I'm just trying to figure out how to play my hand tonight. I think I've figured out what I want to say, but now I'm thinking a visual aid would be helpful."

"Visual aid?" Laura asks.

"Yes. A wig. If I could just get my hands on a wig before they all get here, that would be perfect."

"Halia, this is PG County. There's a wig store on every corner," Wavonne interjects.

"There's not enough time for that."

"Well . . . you could go with a more readily obtainable resource," Laura says and points her eyes toward the top of Wavonne's head. My gaze follows, and when Wavonne notices two sets of eyes staring at her bangs, it only takes a moment for her to register what Laura and I are thinking.

"Oh, *hail* no," she says. "You ain't takin' my wig!"

I look at her with eager eyes.

"Don't look at me that way, Halia. This is *gen-u-whine* synthetic hair. I paid forty-nine dollars and ninety-nine cents for this at Lolita's Lavish Locks." She starts backing away from me as I approach her.

"Come on, Wavonne. I assure you it's for a good cause. I'll get it back to you as good as new."

"The answer is *no.*"

"Hand it over, Wavonne." I'm starting to lose patience. "Don't make me snatch it off your head."

I continue to approach her, and she puts her hands on her head and presses down on the wig, backing away from me more quickly now.

"No. You can't make me." I guess she realizes I mean business because she darts out of the kitchen to the dining room with me following her.

"No, no, no, no!" she yells, running through a restaurant full of customers with her head down and her hands on her wig.

"You get back here, Wavonne!" I call behind her. I'm not proud of this, but I chase after her with my customers looking on. Both of us are "healthy" girls, if you know what I mean, and between the two of us running through Sweet Tea . . . well, let's just say bowls of Jell-O have jiggled less.

Wavonne bolts toward the ladies' room and runs inside.

When I reach the restroom door, I catch my breath and try the handle. She's locked the door. I'm about to call out to her, but I remind myself to keep my voice down. It's bad enough that I just chased a waitress clutching her wig for dear life through my own restaurant. I certainly don't need to be scream-ing to said waitress through the bathroom door.

I knock softly. "Wavonne, honey, open the door," I say in a low voice.

"No!"

"Wavonne, I think you know what's at stake here." I'm just loud enough for only her to hear me. "You're the cops' num-ber-one suspect in this whole dog and pony show. Going wig-less for an hour or two seems a small price to pay if it helps clear your name."

I hear only silence from the other side of the door before she speaks. "You really think you can get the police off my ass?"

"Yes . . . yes, I do."

"Really?"

"Yes, Wavonne, really. I'm sure of it."

Once again, she's quiet on the other side of the door.

"Let me borrow the wig, Wavonne, and I'll buy you a new, better one."

"A *new* one?"

"Yes."

"With European hair?"

"Yes, Wavonne. With European hair."

Silence yet again for a moment or two before the door opens just wide enough for Wavonne to stick her arm out, wig in hand, from the other side of the door.

CHAPTER 44

"Hello," I say as Régine and Cherise step inside the restaurant. "I have a table all set for you." I motion for them to follow me. They are all smiles until we reach the table, and they see Detective Hutchins already seated.

"I think you've met Detective Hutchins," I say to Régine as he stands to greet them.

"Yes. We . . . we *talked* after Marcus's death. This is my friend Cherise." Régine is plainly rattled by seeing Detective Hutchins. "I didn't realize you would be here," she adds, first looking at Detective Hutchins then at me for an explanation.

Rather than explain Detective Hutchins's presence, I ask the girls to take a seat. As they sit down, I slide into a chair across from them, next to Detective Hutchins. "Can I pour you a glass of tea?" I ask. "We have unsweetened and sweetened."

"Either is fine," Cherise says as they both eye me and the detective curiously.

I pour glasses of tea all around, and while I'm topping off my own glass, Wavonne appears at the table wearing one of my napkins as a scarf. "What up, ya'll?" she says to Régine and

Cherise and sits down next to them. "You don't mind if I join you, do you?"

The girls don't answer Wavonne's question. Instead Régine asks, "This wasn't a simple dinner invitation to enjoy your cuisine, was it?"

"No." I take a deep breath. "I wanted you to come here to tell me and Detective Hutchins what really happened the night Marcus was killed."

"I'm not sure what you mean, Halia."

"I think you do, Régine."

Both Régine and Cherise remain silent so I decide to try to get things rolling. "You know, Régine, all along some things about you just didn't add up."

"Once again, Halia, I'm not sure what you mean."

"She means she thinks you're a phony baloney," Wavonne pipes in.

"I mean," I say, eyeing Wavonne with a look that says *Leave the talking to me,* "that the more I investigated you, the more I thought something . . . *several* things about you were not quite . . . shall we say, *authentic.*"

"Like what?"

"Where to begin?" I ask and pause for a moment. "You told me that you've been a hairdresser for more than ten years, but what you did to my hair last week says otherwise."

"You ain't lyin'," Wavonne declares. "I've seen sistahs on hot ghetto mess with better dos."

Everyone at the table does what I often do when it comes to Wavonne—we ignore her.

"And your name, *Régine.* It didn't occur to me until Wavonne and I borrowed names from *Living Single* ourselves during a certain delicate situation last week when—"

"What didn't occur to you?" Detective Hutchins interrupts.

"It's common knowledge that new parents are notorious

for naming their kids after popular television characters, and Régine didn't become a popular name for babies until *Living Single* premiered in 1993. In fact, it was fairly uncommon before then," I say to Detective Hutchins before turning back to Régine. "Now, you're holding up pretty well, but I'm quite certain you were born well before 1993. So, while it's possible that Régine is your real name, it's not likely."

"That proves nothing."

"It sure doesn't. But that's not all. I noticed your Jimmy Choo bag sitting on the counter at your station the day you were cutting my hair and remembered what Wavonne told Detective Hutchins about it when he first questioned us and asked what we knew about you."

Régine looks at the bag next to her and instinctively grabs the handles.

"You can thank Wavonne for noticing that it's from last year. *Last year*—meaning Marcus couldn't have bought it for you. You had only been dating Marcus for a few months before he died. You didn't even know Marcus last year. So, if he didn't buy it for you, someone else did . . . or maybe you bought it yourself. But where would an incompetent hairdresser get the money for a two-thousand-dollar purse? That didn't make sense either unless it was from, say, a former life when you weren't a hairdresser—perhaps you bought it back when you were gainfully employed in a more lucrative profession . . . say, a hedge fund manager?"

With my last comment, there is a discernible change in the expression on Régine's face. I see a look in her eyes that says, *How the hell did you know that?*

"Yeah, I didn't figure that one out until later. When you were cutting my hair, you said Marcus's work was over your head. But, at the same time, you were spouting off words like *commodities, exchange traded funds,* and *margin calls*—not words used very often by hairdressers . . . or by anyone for that matter . . . *anyone* not schooled in the workings of the financial investment world, that is.

"You see, Régine, things about you were just not making sense. Two plus two did not equal four. But you had a rock-solid alibi—you were filmed coming into your apartment building before Marcus was killed, and you didn't leave until long after he was dead, so I let my suspicions about you go. Until recently, nothing I learned about you proved you killed Marcus anyway.

"Maybe I'm a little slow on the uptake, but I was having trouble putting it all together until . . . *until* I ran into you and Cherise at Starbucks. When I was chatting with the two of you, I suddenly remembered where I saw Cherise before, and it wasn't at Sweet Tea. Actually, I remembered where I saw both of you, *together,* before."

"And where was that?" Cherise asks.

"In the family photos on display at the home of a Mrs. Audrey Whitlock in Hyattsville. You," I say in Régine's direction, "didn't have the heavy makeup or the flashy clothes on, but it was you . . . you and Cherise posing with your mother, the woman Marcus scammed out of her home of forty years. A home that maybe you could have helped her keep, Régine, if the world of high finance hadn't collapsed, but no such luck after your layoff."

Régine's eyes continue to widen, and her jaw drops.

"Don't look so surprised," I say. "I probably would have figured out you're sisters anyway. The resemblance is uncanny. And it just took a few Internet searches to uncover your real identity once I concluded your last name is really Whitlock. It wasn't long before I found your real first name, *Denise*." I pause. "Denise Whitlock, a former big shot at a hedge fund firm who was laid off last year."

"None of that proves anything," Régine, who is unmistakably shaken, responds.

"No, it doesn't. But this does." I lift Wavonne's wig from the seat next to me.

"What's that?" Cherise asks.

"Funny you should ask, Cherise. Would you mind putting it on for me?"

Perplexed, Cherise stares blankly at me for a moment before responding. "Yes. I would mind."

I'm not sure what to do. I can't very well force a wig on her head.

Cherise continues to look at me. All is quiet and no one moves until Wavonne speaks. "I gave up my wig, and I'm sittin' here with my nappy hair hidden under a dinner napkin, so, mind or *no mind,* you're puttin' that damn wig on your head."

Wavonne grabs the wig from my hand, gets up from the table, and gruffly places it on Cherise's head. As Heather learned earlier in the week, Wavonne can be intimidating when she wants to be. Cherise knows better than to resist.

"Now, look at that," I say to Cherise. "With that wig on, you and Régine almost look like twins. Yep, with that wig on you could have easily passed for Régine on grainy security camera footage as you walked into her building at twelve twenty-one a.m. the night Marcus was killed."

"This is ridiculous," Cherise says, pulling the wig from her head before getting up from the table. Régine is about to join her when Detective Hutchins rises himself. "I suggest you two ladies return to your seats," he says sternly.

"It's okay, Cherise," Régine says to her, gesturing for Cherise to sit back down. "None of this means anything. You looking like me with a wig on proves *nothing.* No jury in the world is going to reach a verdict that all black women look alike."

"Maybe so," I say. "So what if Marcus scammed your elderly mother out of her home. So what if Cherise looks remarkably similar to you in the right wig . . . at least similar

enough to pass for you on low-quality black-and-white security camera video. Those things alone don't prove anything."

"Those things *alone?*" Detective Hutchins asks.

"You said it yourself," Régine says before I can respond to
Detective Hutchins's question. "Even if it was Cherise, and
I'm not saying it was, who appears on the video, no one will
be able to tell for sure that it wasn't me—particularly not anyone on a jury. So I guess we're done here."

"That would be true, Régine, or should I call you Denise?"
I ask, even though I don't expect or get an answer. "If it wasn't
for one small hiccup in your plan."

"Hiccup?" Wavonne asks.

"When *you* were entering *your* apartment building," I say
to Régine, doing the air quotes thing with my fingers as I say
the words *you* and *your.* "Perhaps *you,* and by *you* I mean
Cherise, were texting or just surfing the Internet on your
phone for the weather for all we know. My guess is you
planned to have Cherise doing something on her phone as she
walked in, so she had an excuse to keep her head down, making it even harder to discern that it wasn't actually you."

"What does that have to do with anything?"

I don't answer her question. Instead I ask, "Would you
do something for me? That tea I poured you earlier—it's
unsweetened. How about you add some sweetener to it." I
hand her a little pink packet.

Régine eyes me cautiously. "I prefer the yellow," she says
with attitude, declines my offer, and grabs another packet from
the ceramic container on the table. She rips it open, pours the
contents in her glass, and stirs the tea with her spoon.

"Funny how, just like when I saw you sign your credit card
slip at Starbucks earlier today, you used your left hand to stir
your tea, but when *you* were walking into your apartment
building the night Marcus was killed . . . and I didn't notice
this until I viewed the security footage a second time, you

were typing on your phone with your right hand, the same hand Cherise used at Starbucks to stir her coffee."

"Oooh, *girl,* put a fork in you, 'cause you *is done!*" Wavonne says from across the table.

Régine's eyes go blank and her face freezes up. The rest of us are silent as sweat begins to form on her brow. She looks intently at me and then down at the table. Then her gaze seems to go off past all of us toward . . . toward nothing in particular.

"We never intended to kill him," she says, still not looking at any of us.

"Denise, no!" Cherise says.

"No. We are not the bad guys here, Cherise!" Régine says, raising her voice. "We never planned to kill him. We only wanted to get enough money out of him to keep our mother in her house. I did a little research on him and figured out what sort of girl he was attracted to. It wasn't hard to transition myself into his type. All I needed were some tight flashy clothes, too much makeup, and a good push-up bra. I became Régine Alves and quickly formulated a plan to meet Marcus. I dated that monster for months, and all I managed to get out of him was some clothes and cheap jewelry that were barely worth a few hundred bucks."

"Not enough to pay off a mortgage," I say.

"Certainly not. We needed to think bigger. We needed access to bank accounts and brokerage funds . . . and we needed to search his house and see if there was anything of real value to take . . . *real* jewelry or stashes of cash. I tried to do it while he was asleep on a few occasions, but he would notice me get out of bed, and that sister of his is often up half the night milling about."

"So you and Cherise decided to do your search the night you were here with Marcus and the others?"

"Marcus and I didn't normally spend Saturday nights together, so I knew I could duck out early and have some time to search the house before he or Jacqueline got home. I knew Marcus would be the last to leave, and Jacqueline would stay at least as long as business was being discussed."

"You have a key to Marcus's place?"

"No. I unlocked the basement door when I was there the night before, and I've watched Marcus disarm the alarm. I know the code."

"Why not just send Cherise to the house while you were here with Marcus?"

"If I happened to get caught . . . if Marcus or Jacqueline came home while I was still there, I could have made something up to explain it—that I was there to surprise Marcus or something. Cherise would have just been a burglar to them. Besides, I knew the layout of the house and could be in and out quickly. But, if I did find anything to steal, I needed Cherise to pose as me on the security cameras at my building, so I wouldn't be a robbery suspect.

"Like I said, all we wanted to do was get access to his accounts and see if he had any stashes of cash or expensive jewelry . . . anything that would help our mother keep her home."

"And you found?"

"What she found was that Marcus was one broke-assed mother—"

"Shut it, Wavonne!" I say before Régine continues.

"Wavonne's right. There was nothing to take. All I found were statements about overdrawn accounts and past due bills. From what I could tell, he was on the verge of losing his own house, which would have served him right. I was furious! All the planning and time it took to assume a new identity and enmesh myself into Marcus's life was for nothing. *Nothing!* In a frenzy I drove back to the restaurant. I might not have been able to get any money out of Marcus, but I was going to give him a piece of my mind."

There is an overall sense of relief emoting from Régine. It's as if she's being freed by telling her story. There's a way about her as she speaks that shows she really doesn't think she did anything wrong.

"I got back here and found Marcus in the kitchen by himself. Everyone else had gone. He said he was going to pack up some of your fried chicken to take to his mother. I just looked at him with rage as he talked about how things went well over dinner and how he thought he and Charles had calmed Heather and Josh down for the time being. Then he noticed I was unsettled and asked what was wrong. All I could say was, 'You rat bastard. Do you have any idea who I am?' He just looked at me like I was crazy. 'Do you?!' I screamed at him."

"What did he say?"

"He asked me what I was talking about. That's when I asked, 'Does the name Audrey Whitlock ring any bells?' Do you know what he said when I asked him that?"

No one answers, and while we sit quietly and wait for her to tell us, I see Detective Hutchins discreetly press some buttons on his cell phone.

"He said, 'Audrey Whitlock? That silly old bag out in Hyattsville?' That's what he said about my mother. He called her an *old bag* as if she were nothing. *Nothing!* He wasn't even looking at me when he said it. He was bending over to get a takeout container. I was livid. The woman who raised me and my sister, nursed my father on his deathbed, and sometimes worked two jobs to make ends meet was nothing but an old bag to him. As he began to straighten himself up, I grabbed the first thing I could find, a cast-iron frying pan sitting on the counter. I completely lost it and walloped him over the head with it. Before I realized what I'd done, he'd dropped like a sack of flour. From there it's all a blur. I vaguely remember dropping the frying pan, running back to my car, and calling

Cherise in a panic. Honestly, I didn't know if he was dead or alive."

"But you were covered if he was dead because you had already arranged for Cherise to pose as you and ensure that your whereabouts were accounted for." As I say this, I see two uniformed policemen come through the front door of Sweet Tea. Régine and Cherise have their backs to the door and do not see them. *Well, I'll be,* I think to myself. *Detective Hutchins took me seriously when I told him to bring backup.*

Régine nods. "I drove around for a long time, and Cherise and I talked. We decided I'd try to get some sleep in the car, and Cherise would leave the building posing as me the next morning as planned."

"What about the frying pan?" Wavonne asks. "Weren't you afraid it had your fingerprints on it?"

"I was wearing gloves while I searched Marcus's house. I was in such a state. I never thought to take them off before I got here."

"If you ask me, he deserved it . . . evil snake," Cherise says. "Régine did the world a favor."

"That may be," Detective Hutchins pipes in. "But you'll have to sell that to a jury. I'm placing both of you under arrest. We have two squad cars outside—one in the front and one in the back. We can make this easy or hard. It's up to the two of you." He stands up and gestures for the women to follow. The girls do as they're instructed, and he motions for them to turn around and gently but firmly reaches for Régine's hands and places them in cuffs behind her back. The restaurant falls silent and everyone stares as he does the same with Cherise. He then directs the two uniformed officers to read them their rights and walk them out to the cruiser.

"Oooh, child, that is a hot mess," Wavonne says as we watch Régine and Cherise be escorted out of Sweet Tea.

"It sure is, Wavonne."

"We should have known it was Régine. Anyone who jacks up a hairdo like she did yours surely had to be up to no good."

I don't respond as I'm not really paying attention to Wavonne. I'm too upset over the whole situation, and it breaks my heart to see the two girls who cared so much about their mother . . . who could have had bright futures . . . be led off to a police car.

"You okay, Halia?" Wavonne asks.

"I'll be fine."

"Are you sure? You don't look good. What do you say we go to Red Lobster for some crab legs, make you feel better?"

RECIPE FROM HALIA'S KITCHEN

Halia's House Cocktail

Ingredients

1 12-ounce package frozen unsweetened mixed berries
¼ cup sugar
½ cup water
1 cup fresh lemon juice
1½ liters Sprite
1½ cups grapefruit-flavored vodka (more, if Wavonne is coming to your party)
¾ cup triple sec
1 orange (sliced)

- Combine berries, sugar, and water in saucepan. Cook on medium heat.

- When sugar dissolves, bring liquid to a boil for three minutes, stirring continuously.

- Strain mixture and discard solids.

- Combine berry syrup with lemon juice, Sprite, vodka, and triple sec in large pitcher.

- Serve over ice in tall glasses.

- Garnish with an orange slice.

Eight Servings

EPILOGUE

It's been almost a week since Denise and Cherise were arrested at Sweet Tea, and my entire being is decidedly more relaxed than it was this time last week as I sit at a table in the
dining room proofreading our list of specials for the day It
took a few days for me to finally drop my guard and start to
feel like myself again now that I know Wavonne is no longer a
murder suspect, but things are finally starting to get back to
normal. I feel like I can return to focusing on running Sweet
Tea rather than trying to track down a killer.

I look at the clock and see that it's ten thirty. We'll be
opening in a half hour, so I figure I'd better get this list of specials on the copier. I'm about to get up from my chair when I
see Laura approach.

"Have you seen the morning paper?" she says as she hands
today's edition to me before going back into the kitchen.

I scan the front page and see a headline in the lower left
corner: "Local Man Charged in $18 Million Mortgage Fraud
Scheme."

I call over to Wavonne, who is filling ketchup bottles a few
tables over. "Wavonne, listen to this." I begin reciting from the
article: "Charles Pritchett, age fifty-six, of Washington, D.C,

along with other Reverie Home leaders, was arrested today for participation in a mortgage fraud scheme that promised to pay off the mortgages of home owners, many of them local D.C. area residents. According to evidence that led to the arrest of Mr. Pritchett, he and his colleagues convinced several area residents to participate in what was called the Reverie Homes Program. In exchange for a minimum thirty-thousand-dollar initial investment, Mr. Pritchett agreed to make the investors' future monthly mortgage payments and pay off their mortgages within seven years. Reverie encouraged home owners to refinance existing mortgages on their homes and use any equity to fund their initial investment in the program.

"Investors were told that their initial payment would be used to fund investments in in-store ATMs, phone card kiosks, DVD rental machines, and other automated business ventures. They were led to believe these ventures generated enough revenue to provide generous mortgage payment assistance. To instill confidence in the Reverie Homes Program, executive management spent thousands of dollars conducting seminars at luxury hotels such as the Gaylord National Resort & Convention Center at National Harbor in Oxon Hill, Maryland.

"According to records obtained by this newspaper, Mr. Pritchett and other Reverie executives never advised participating home owners that the company's ATMs, phone card kiosks, and DVD rental machines generated no significant income. Instead Reverie Home leaders used money from the program's later investors to fund the mortgages of the program's earlier investors. Records also show that home owner investments were used to fund the personal indulgences of Reverie executives, including salaries of up to three hundred thousand dollars per year, luxury company cars, and even an all-expenses-paid trip to the Super Bowl.

"The program lured more than six hundred participants (forty-three in the Washington, D.C., metro area), who invested a total of more than eighteen million dollars. When Reverie began to have trouble recruiting enough new investors to cover the payments of current program participants, Pritchett and his coconspirators stopped making the promised mortgage payments, and the affected home owners were left to fend for themselves. Mr. Pritchett—"

"Does it say anything about Marcus?" Wavonne asks, interrupting me.

I scan the rest of the article and see no mention of him. "It doesn't look like it," I say, relieved. The more Marcus Rand and his murder stay out of the press, the better. The day after Denise and Cherise were escorted from the premises, we did receive calls from the newspaper and local television stations for comment. Some of my patrons must have given them a tip about two young ladies being led away from Sweet Tea in handcuffs. Of course, I declined to comment and instructed my entire staff to do the same.

The next day there was a brief story about Denise and Cherise's arrest on the local TV news, and there was a little snippet about it in the newspaper. Fortunately, my restaurant wasn't specifically named in either, but I'm guessing that as the juicy details of Marcus's murder begin to emerge, perhaps when the case goes to trial, interest, and therefore news coverage, will increase. One way or another, it seems as though the fact that Marcus was murdered in my restaurant is going to become public knowledge, which makes me wonder if Wavonne and I going to such lengths to get Marcus's dead body out of Sweet Tea was worth it. But when I think of the circus Sweet Tea would have been become if the police had been alerted to Marcus's body on my kitchen floor, I wonder a bit less. For all I know, my restaurant might have been shut down for days. What kind of notice do you post on the door in that case? *Closed due to a murder in the kitchen?* Sweet Tea would have been the epicenter of the tragedy, and rather than a news crew filming at Wellington Lake, they would have been filming in front of my restaurant. The idea of Sweet Tea being featured on the news with yellow police tape across the front door or the chalk outline of a dead body on my kitchen floor accompanying a newspaper article sends chills down my spine. At least now, when and if word gets out, there's some distance . . . some time between the event and the press. Either way, I'm just thankful it's over.

I set the newspaper down, and as I get up from the table, I see Jack Spruce at the front door. I walk over and let him in.

"Good morning, Jack. Looking for a cup of coffee?"

"You read my mind," he says and walks with me toward the coffee station.

"I haven't seen you in a while," I say as I pour him a cup.

"I've been on vacation. I just got back yesterday and heard the news about Régine . . . or Denise and her sister."

"Yes, we definitely had some excitement around here while you were gone. Honestly, I'm just glad the whole thing is resolved. Do you have any more news about the girls?"

"They're still being held at a local facility. They've been arraigned. Cherise was granted bail and may be able to leave the detention center if she comes up with the money. Denise was deemed as a flight risk as her charges are much more serious, and she has not been granted bail. She will have to stay in jail until her trial, and who knows when that will be."

"Maybe I shouldn't," I say to Jack, "but I can't help but feel a little sorry for the girls. They were only trying to keep their mother in her home, and the whole thing got out of control so quickly."

"Denise will probably plead temporary insanity. When a jury gets the details of the situation, she might stand a chance of an innocent verdict. Pounding someone over the head with a cast-iron frying pan hardly sounds like premeditated murder. I guess only time will tell."

"I guess so."

"And you know, Halia, while I think Detective Hutchins has pretty much closed the case, word is that Denise swears up and down that she hit Marcus over the head with a pan in the kitchen of this very restaurant, then left and never came back. At this point there doesn't seem to be any reason for her to lie, so we still have no idea how Marcus's body got from here to Wellington Lake."

"That's interesting, but I do recall Régine saying that everything that happened after she popped Marcus was a blur. Perhaps she really doesn't remember what happened or blocked the memory of her disturbing Marcus's body. Who knows."

"It's plausible, I guess," Jack says. "And true or not, it might be the best reason we have to explain how Marcus got from here to Wellington Lake."

Jack looks at me while he sips his coffee as if he's checking for my reaction to everything he's shared with me. At this point, I've gotten pretty good at hiding my angst and keeping a poker face. In a relaxed manner I just respond with, "When Denise was here last week, she said she left the scene of the crime so quickly that she didn't even know if Marcus was alive or dead. For all we know, he got up and walked away and somehow ended up in the lake. So many things could have happened."

"True. I guess the reality of the situation is that we may never know." Jack takes a sip from his mug. "I guess I should get going. Thanks for the coffee, Halia. I'm sure I'll see you again soon."

"You're quite welcome."

I walk Jack to the door and go ahead and leave it unlocked after he exits since it's almost eleven o'clock anyway. As I walk toward the kitchen, I'm thankful that finding out how Marcus's body got from my kitchen floor to Wellington Lake doesn't seem to be a priority for the police. I'm even more grateful that the whole messy situation seems to have come to a close.

"Hey there, Tacy," I say as I walk through the kitchen door. "What do you say we get these waffle irons fired up? We're going to have a lot of hungry customers in here in just a few minutes."

I grab an apron from a hook on the wall and slip it over my head. *Yes, an apron is a much better fit than the detective hat I've been wearing recently,* I think to myself as I tie the apron around my waist. And with that, I get back to doing what I do best and join Tacy in mixing up the waffle batter.

"I'm sure you have more important things to do, Miss Watkins. I can handle making the waffles."

"You know what, Tacy?" I respond. "For some reason, right now at this moment, there is nothing I'd rather be doing."